THE CRITIC

A NOVEL

STEEL CITY MYSTERIES

LL KIRCHNER

For every woman who's ever been dismissed, ignored, gaslit: you were never the problem.

PROLOGUE | TED

Seen from above, I don't look as fat as I think I am. Like I was taught to think I am. "Shamu," they called me, long after I stopped visiting the pool. Could I help it if my Italian grandma lived with us? Her idea of love was an after-school snack of Sunday gravy. Assholes.

"Sir, can you hear me?"

Or maybe it's him, the exquisitely proportioned gentleman hovering overhead. His gaze drills down to where my lean soul lives. Where I, like him, have forearms thick as dictionaries, cum gutters, and a Minotaur-like backside.

If only I could touch him back, but I am succumbing.

This cannot be, the end of me
    I must... I must...

Ach, bother. People think writing musicals is so easy. All piano playing and riffing, like Ishtar. If that movie taught us anything, it's how difficult it is to write a hit.

"Did he just laugh?"

This from another, albeit significantly less attractive female first responder. She is setting up a stretcher and—

Good gods, no!

A viscous milky liquid bubbles at the left corner of my mouth before snaking down my neck. So much for me and Dr. Fabio. There's nothing noble or enchanting about frothing at the mouth.

This is not how this is supposed to go, not this moment, this day, or anything. I should be in Manhattan. Should've gone directly from college. Sure, I might yet be off-Broadway—we can't all be Gershwin —but not off-off. Surely not a decade in. They say those who can, do. Those who can't, teach. What about the critics? Have we all been thwarted by forces beyond our control?

This is my parents' fault. Not how most claim in therapy, though a case could be made. No. I mean directly their fault. I have no brothers or sisters, aunts or uncles. I'm all alone to carry the burden.

But I may yet see my name in lights. Ben is here. Everything should be converging.

Unless... No, no! This feeling is unfamiliar. I fear I'm too far gone. The room is fading, swallowed in a bright white light. I've lost sight of Dr. Adonis. Of me.

No, this is not going according to plan.

1

JESSICA

I can't see it, but I know it's there, the axe, dangling over my neck. Poised to drop—I'm about to be fired.

There's no other reason Ethan Silver would call me up at the last minute and invite me to lunch. My old editor at *City News*, Kris Novak?

Beer at Hambones? Sure. Lunch at the Oyster House? As if.

I am but a freelancer. Freelancers don't get the schmooze treatment, even if they've been a regular columnist for years, like me. Which is how I know how wrong this rendezvous is.

After his call I'd spent the morning writhing at my terminal —such an apt name for my place at Zimmerman—trying to convince myself the sinking feeling I had was the aftereffect of my bridge dream. That my new editor, Ethan, simply wanted to meet me. All the while I kept trying, and failing, to come up with some pitches for our meeting.

On the short walk from Zimmerman to the Oyster House, I finally give up. My mind is a blank, so I try focusing on the weather. The sun has briefly escaped the clouds, turning the rainy October morning into an ironically lovely afternoon. As if the whole city has been scrubbed clean of things unwanted.

"It's nothing against you, Jess," the new guy says, the minute the waitress leaves with our orders, "but I'm bringing Ted over to do our theater column."

We're seated inside near a window overlooking Market Square, and the sky has gone dark. I'm trying to focus on Ethan but can't stop staring at the Heinz bottles lined up on all the tables like little red sentries. I remember joking about making them squeezable so you could get the ketchup already, and then Carson went and pitched the idea to Heinz and turned it into a whole campaign. *His* campaign.

So it's a beat before I react.

"Ted? As in Ted *Harvey*, the theater critic for *Pittsburgh Voice*?"

Ethan nods.

I'm stunned. This is a real coup. *Pittsburgh Voice* is considered the final word on all things cool. *City News* is more like the daytime TV version. And, in much the same way as I am with Carson's, I can't help but be a little in awe of Ethan's maneuvering. He's only been in town a few weeks.

I need to at least pretend otherwise.

"*Our* theater column? As in *my* theater column? You're firing me?" The indignation isn't feigned entirely, though I won't miss critiquing theater. It's the byline I can't bear to lose. My oxygen. The only thing that lets me keep a job where the wage is livable even though the work is soul-crushing.

The waitress swings by for a dump-and-run, dropping the appetizer Ethan ordered on our table. I don't blame her for trying to get away from the dish as quickly as possible. Ethan obviously isn't aware, but *nobody* orders the oysters. Unless they want to call in sick.

"Weeelll," he says, drawing out the word. Unlike Kris Novak, my former editor and longtime champion at the paper, I suspect this new guy—with his complex geometrical-framed glasses and ironic bowling shirt emblazoned with the name "Andy" over the left breast pocket—sees Pittsburgh as a temporary stop.

"Technically, you're not an employee," Ethan continues. "And of course I wouldn't fire you, you're a solid writer. I'll keep you in the stable."

Right about now, I'm especially pleased I haven't warned him about the mollusks. Today is the paper's deadline day.

But Ethan isn't done. "My plan is to email the upcoming editorial calendars out to my stable for first dibs." He reaches for an oyster shell. "May the best pitch win. Absolutely."

I'm tempted to neigh, the patronizing prick. He wants me to pitch him? On the regular? As in, make the waking nightmare that was this past morning—trying and failing to come up with a story idea he won't be able to resist—part of my life? That's nothing like having a weekly column. Much as I downplay my day job, it *is* demanding. I don't have the downtime to crank out fresh story ideas, let alone deal with the rejections I sense this dude loves to dole out.

The smile is still plastered on my face as I watch him slurp down the brine and meat.

"That sounds like a great idea." I stop. Take a purposeful sip of water to see how Ethan will react to my change of tone.

Putting down his shell, he leans forward ever so slightly. I've got his attention.

"I see this as an opportunity."

Freelance writing isn't my end game. I'm not sure what is. Not because I see my day job as selling out. You have to be making real money to sell out. But there does come a point where saying, "When I grow up..." morphs from relatable to pathetic. I've got exactly one more birthday before that expiration date, the big three-oh.

I take a deep breath and match his posture, time to make

some shit up. "I've been wanting to expand my repertoire at the paper."

The waitress arrives with our meals. Dipping one of my chips into the garlic aioli meant for Ethan's fish, I steal a glance at my watch. Already twenty to one. I have to start throwing some ideas out there or this thing is tanking. Plus, I need to get back to Zimmerman. I can't lose my *job* job.

"I can tell you're a foodie," I say, having endured his lament about the lack of moules frites. His nod is him halfway to agreeing. "What do you think of interviews with local luminaries where I ask about their favorite recipes? We could call it something catchy. Like, *Celebrity Dish.* What do you think?"

I try to read his face. Can he tell that this idea is essentially about me trying to meet the town's most influential people, set myself up for *when I grow up*? "It could really beef up advertising."

"Pun intended," Ethan deadpans.

I laugh despite myself. I don't want to like this guy.

"Maybe we could include one as part of our upcoming holiday food issue," he says.

Not what I meant.

"I was thinking of it as more of a regular feature."

You owe me, I want to scream.

But he doesn't. Not really.

Ethan dabs at the sauce with his cod. "I'm not sure there are enough local celebrities."

"Sure there are." I smile, lifting a shoulder in his direction. "You're a celebrity. What's in your fridge right now?"

Am I flirting with this snake?

"Wanna come see?" he asks.

Is it working?

He looks a bit like Lyle Lovett but has that same inexplicable charisma. I bet he puts out for favors. "That depends. Do you want to be featured in my new column?"

Ethan shakes his head. "Ehn. What else you got?"

Dammit. Time to switch up the flattery. "Okay, I think you'll love this one since you're clearly into clothes. *Style Phile.* This one would be all about fashion trend spotting. As a bonus for advertisers, we could also feature where to buy the looks."

Ethan puts down his knife and fork and considers a moment. "I like it. But again, I see that more as a supplement insert. Something seasonal, maybe. But not a regular column. Fashion-forward isn't how I'd describe Pittsburgh."

"You don't think much of your new hometown, do you?" Crap. I did not mean to say that out loud.

"No, not at all." He sits back. "I love it here."

He's a terrible actor. Why is Ethan here at all?

"Jess, I've been running an alt weekly since I got out of grad school. I know how much material you need to run something every week. Plus it doesn't feel right for the demo."

He's talking demographics? Jesus, this is feeling more like a staff meeting at Zimmerman than an alt-newsweekly column pitch. I need to change course. "How did you end up moving here? From where? Iowa?"

"*Prairie Call* does have a... different reputation," he begins. "If I had to define it, I'd say we're more like *Pittsburgh Voice.* The difference is, Pittsburgh's a top-twenty major metropolitan area. Iowa City doesn't even make the top fifty." He stabs another piece of fish. "And I don't know if you know this, but alt newsweekly editorial positions don't come along all that often."

All true, but he missed something. Pittsburgh's population has been in steady decline since the last census.

"How about a dating column?" I blurt without thinking. I hate men, and love, and especially dating.

"I like this one." Ethan nods and touches my arm. "But will you have enough time, though? With your job?"

Time? Is he thinking I plan to write up my own nonexistent dates? My idea is for an advice column, like dating etiquette. "I'm not going on the dates, Ethan. Christ." I pull my arm away. "I'll flesh out the idea and—"

Before he can respond, he starts chirping, *da dee da daa, da dee da daa, da dee daa daa daaa.* He doesn't move.

"That's you," I say.

Ethan bristles, starts digging into his man bag.

Kris Novak did not have a man bag, let alone a cell phone. I watch with revulsion as Ethan retrieves the little black box, absent-mindedly picks at the price sticker still on it. *Did he pick up a floor model?* That tag's going to leave behind gray residue and paper. It's not so easy to erase evidence of what something cost you.

He points at me with the thing. "I'm writing a piece. Advertiser supplied it for a story."

Novak wouldn't have accepted filthy lucre either.

"You know, actually"—he pauses for another series of chirps —"Novak recommended Ted Harvey."

Is he reading my mind?

If he is, he should be shutting off that damn phone. But no. Right in the middle of our conversation, he turns his chair in the opposite direction and takes the call. Why turn around? Discretion? *That ship sailed when you took the call.* And what is he doing writing a puff piece? Kris wrote new stories. Though, come to think of it, I'm not so sure how I feel about Kris right now either.

One thing is clear, this guy is into gonzo journalism. He'd never go for it, but he's given me an idea for an actual etiquette column:

Q: Dear Rules Lady, What are the rules for cell phones? We can carry them anywhere, but does that mean we should be using them everywhere? Sincerely, Mixed Signals

A: Dear Mixed Signals, It is a truth universally acknowledged that any man in possession of a mobile phone must be in want of a way to show off said device. No doubt, these are modern times. Our lives are more portable. We may carry boomboxes on our shoulders and telephones in our pockets, but should we? It's long been possible to carry dental floss and nail clippers, but—

"So sorry, I have to run," Ethan says, sounding less than apologetic. If anything, he seems excited. "I'll get the next one."

Is he not even buying lunch? *Crap.* "Is everything okay?" I ask.

Ethan doesn't reply, but summons the waitress with his credit card. *Thank God.* Mine is maxed. I've got to stop calling the psychic hotline.

On the bright side, he expects we'll have lunch again. Maybe to discuss my column idea. Or is this more flirting? Damn if I don't want to dial Ms. Cleo right now.

Moving at a brisker pace than I'd thought her capable, our waitress appears and snatches the card. Ethan turns his full attention on me, a feeling more spotlight than sunbeam. "It's Ted," he says, leaning closer. "The police are at our office right now."

"You mean Ted Harvey? Your new theater critic? Are you joking?"

Ethan looks around as if I'm the one being gauche. "Shh."

Now he's shushing me? After he had the gall to answer his telephone while we were having lunch together. *Rich.*

He nods.

"What happened?" I lower my voice despite myself. I have to hear this.

"I couldn't say, but I've got to go back to the office. Apparently the place is crawling with investigators, and we've still got a paper to get out."

Investigators? Did this happen *at* the paper? How long has Ted been on board? So what if I didn't want to keep writing theater criticism? I'm offended that this transition is not breaking news. Shouldn't I have been the first to know? At least the second.

It's like my mother loves to say, I lost all interest in my dolls until she donated them. Why am I so predictable?

I grab my purse and a handful of fries. "I'm coming with you." The story of the year has dropped in my lap. Maybe this can be my new beat: Steel City Crime.

Ethan scans me up and down. "I wouldn't do that if I were you."

"Do what?"

"Come with."

"It's fine, I'll tell the office I got sick on the oysters. They'll understand, happens all the time at this place. It's like our satellite conference room. We—"

"No, it's not that. It's..."

"What do you mean?"

"It's... Well... You're a suspect."

"A suspect? In what?"

Ethan gathers his coat and bag, ignoring me now.

Part of me wants to laugh at the absurdity. Another part is calculating. My eyes drift to the Heinz bottles. This time I don't disappear. If I'm some sort of suspect, I need to know a lot more. I might hate my job, but if it has taught me anything, it's that damage control works.

"I'm coming with you." I stand, shrugging into my coat. "Unless you want to be my accomplice. C'mon."

LYDIA

Light rain splashes the glass-paneled box as Lydia Cole drops a quarter into the pay phone slot. She can hear her wiper blades from the street, that hideous scraping sound. This is what she gets for racing out the door. The Bureau services fleet cars free, but they're slow as molasses. Normally Alice handled all things car. She would've replaced the blades so Lydia didn't lose half a day to the chore, but not after this morning's fight about the police scanner.

She would try not to gloat about being right, but Alice would have to see it. Yes, it was ugly and obtrusive on the kitchen counter, but if Lydia hadn't heard the scanner lead, she wouldn't be sitting on a potentially career-making case right now.

Her fingers tremble slightly as she dials Powell. For a second she's back in Chicago. That goddamn Christmas party from four years ago. Someone asking, loud enough for everyone to hear, wasn't Cole a *carpet muncher*? She felt the change in the room, knew it was a bad thing. But it wasn't until she got home later that night and Alice told her what those words meant that she knew how bad. The next morning her advanced training rotation was canceled.

The Bureau had changed since then. A little. But still it's not like she can march into *City News*, flashing her badge and asking questions, without her supervisor's approval. She'll downplay the bioterrorism, convince him it's local. After talking to the people over at *Pittsburgh Voice*, the other alternative newsweekly in town, she's sure she's right about that.

Look, Ted was a critic. He made enemies for a living. That was the job.

Lydia checks her notes. Thanks to her friend at the station, she knew *City News* was Harvey's new employer. She had to be the only person in the Bureau even aware Pittsburgh had not one, but *two* alternative newsweeklies.

The music editor was the one who made that particular comment.

They all seemed to agree—she'd played a "concerned neighbor"—Ted taking the new job rubbed a lot of people the wrong way. As she listened to their complaints, she knew the case had to be personal. Not a nationally focused nutjob with a manifesto. Sheer luck whoever did this sent their death wish through the U.S. mail, otherwise she'd have nothing. Alice would be right again.

She shoots a column of air through her mouth, psyching herself up. Powell doesn't want D.C. to come in and take over this situation any more than she does. So long as she plays her cards right, he won't take this case seriously enough to do anything but give it to her.

"Fortune favors the bold," Pops would say.

She dials the last number.

"Are you out of your mind?" Powell asks after Lydia describes the scenario—local theater critic, lots of enemies, suspected ricin poisoning from a baked good sent via U.S. mail.

"After Oklahoma City, the Sarin gas attack, and the

Unabomber's manifesto," Powell continues, "you think Quantico won't be all over this?"

"Eddie, the guy is a local theater critic who had a talent for pissing people off. I can prove that." The rain intensifies. "All we have to do is get in front of it before they can mobilize. Make it ours."

There's a long silence on the other end. Lydia takes that as a good sign. Means he's considering her plea. Finally he lets out a great sigh.

"All right. Get over to *City News*. I'll send Klavon over."

Lydia's jubilation barely has time to breathe before Powell finishes his sentence. *Klavon*? He wasn't trying to beat her to Washington, the man seemed content to stay in Pittsburgh as a Special Agent for the rest of his life. That almost made it worse. Ross Klavon wouldn't try to usurp her case, but he was an objectively handsome man. People would automatically defer to him. She'd been hoping for Michelle Chen.

"But sir—"

The dial tone cuts her off. *Fine.*

It's more than fine, really. She's elated. At last, her own case. She slides back into her car and is immediately brought back to earth by the shriek of metal scratching across glass.

3

JESSICA

"You know I was joking," I call to the back of Ethan's head, "about you being an accomplice."

He turns and opens his mouth, producing an exasperated grunt before resuming his pace, his dark-brown curls bobbing farther and farther ahead.

The flirting is definitively over. He's trying to lose me.

I pick up the pace to keep up, but it's a struggle on Smithfield's water-logged sidewalks. Up ahead, Ethan is dodging the puddles with ease. How? The only place I know of where it rains as much as Pittsburgh is Seattle.

Oh, who am I kidding? Mom's been saying for years how I should work out more. Which would mean, work out. All more noise from her until moments like this, when I can see her point. Not that I'd ever tell her that. She called again this morning with her signature *don't panic* opener. Long before she could get to the part about Seth's engagement, I'd begun strategizing his ransom because my brother was obviously being held at gunpoint. "Not everything is an emergency," she'd pointed out. My therapist would agree. I'm working on it.

Then she brought up how Dad never liked his fiancée. Like

that little tidbit would make me feel better about my inability to land a second date. I was in no mood for it. But Dad's been gone five years.

I hung up on her, felt terrible. Forgot about it the moment I turned back to my cursor. Till now.

I give up the chase. It's been a while, but I know where the offices are. The day has turned chilly since I'd arrived at the Oyster House. The sun that had briefly appeared over Market Square is gone, and the wet sidewalk reflects broken pieces of gray sky. I zip my jacket.

As I near Fourth the street opens up enough to put me face-to-face with the Smithfield Street Bridge, its distinctive yellow arches rising against Mount Washington. Seeing the bridge over the Monongahela from this distance wouldn't usually bother me. But today?

The bridge's arched entry beckons like an open mouth.

With everything that's been going on with Carson and the sense that something's been off at *City News*, I shouldn't be surprised. After three nights in a row of the bridge dream—waking in a panic, watching the ceiling for hours—my eyes are like sandpaper. I try counting the rivets on the bridge but can't keep track. I try the box breathing they taught me, but can't hold the exhale, can't get enough oxygen.

I keep moving. Ethan's too far ahead to keep my attention away from the bridge so I look at something else. Fix my eyes on the ground and cut over to Cherry Way at the next break in the block.

By the time I reach the door, Ethan has long since buzzed into the lobby, which leaves me waiting for the next rando to come along and let me in. What happened to him in Iowa to inspire such a speedy gait?

My first thought in the elevator is a common one. Thank God I didn't end up afraid of elevators. Then the smell hits, microwave lunches, burnt coffee, and... Is someone baking brownies?

Sofia would have a comment.

She'd announced this morning, with complete confidence, that my middle-of-the-night brownie binge was a condition. Even had a name for it, sleep-baking. Very dangerous, apparently. "I just wrote about this for SmithKline. Did a sleeping pill brochure." I'd laughed and moved on, but this is why I've never told her the extent of my anxieties. If I listened to every diagnosis, I'd still be in a locked ward. Except PTSD. Between the things I avoid, the memories that show up uninvited, and the occasional urge to do something reckless, that one I buy.

I know all of that.

The doors open, and I push the thoughts down.

"Hi, can I help you?" the receptionist asks.

When did Shitty News hire a receptionist? "Hi, I'm here with —?" I shoot a furtive glance at the knot of people gathering in the massive office behind her. I knew they'd been hiring staff, but this many? Compared to the last time I'd seen it, the place is unrecognizable. How long ago was that? Since before Ethan.

"Ethan?" I finally spurt out. Not convincing. "Oh, there he is, that scallywag. Never mind." *Scallywag?*

I don't wait but speed past her. The paper had moved beyond a cramped single office some time ago, but I hadn't realized it had taken over the whole floor. Gone is the mismatched furniture and dingy paint, replaced by crimson and black accents that match the logo they recently rolled out. Glass walls surround the perimeter with a sea of open desks in the middle. How does anyone get any work done?

Staff is streaming toward the corner office, and at last I see a few faces I recognize, as well as the uniformed officers visible among them.

A woman in a pantsuit stands at the center of it, square

jawed, zero frills. Like a TV detective. She's slight but still the fixed point everything else is organized around.

It occurs to me, this is an active crime scene. I don't know if I should be thrilled or worried. Or jealous. *Did Ted get a corner office?*

I'm definitely going to ask Ethan for more money. Between what I spend on parking and drinks and grabbing a bite before shows, I generally wind up in the hole for every piece I write.

Someone says something into the lady detective's ear. She looks my way, pushes off the desk, and comes straight at me.

Unsettling, but I don't stop moving. Extend my arm. "I'm Jessica Greer? The—" I stop myself. I was about to say, the theater critic, but I'm not. Not anymore. I go with the next best thing. "The person you're looking for?"

Why am I ending all my sentences in a question mark like some deranged Valley Girl?

She looks at my hand but doesn't take it.

"Ms. Greer," she says.

Much as I like that she called me Ms. and not Mrs.—or worse, ma'am—I'm weirded out by her certitude.

"I'm Lydia Cole. Special Agent. FBI."

FBI? What the...

Forget thrilled. And worried doesn't begin to cover it. I go right to terrified.

4

DINA

Dina Kowalski returns to her desk at *City News*, folding her coat into her shoe drawer, angling to keep the newsroom in view. The office is still in chaos. Photographers. Fingerprint kits. Police salmoning between the desks. Once they'd determined Ted's deadly delivery had come through the U.S. mail, things escalated quickly. No one had even noticed she'd stepped out.

And now Jessica Greer is here?

The person she'd called was Ethan. She'd known the two of them were having lunch, of course, she'd put it on his calendar for him. But for Jessica to show up and walk straight at that agent with her hand sticking out.

Is the woman losing it? It wouldn't be a first if what they say is true, but even so, it's an unusual choice considering how the questioning is going.

From what Dina has overheard—and she'd designed this space for maximum overhearing—the police began forming a narrative quickly. Ted Harvey was poisoned the same day he nabbed the job. His theater reviews are toxic, but that's nothing new. The difference is the woman he replaced, Jessica Greer, by all accounts somewhat unstable.

Before the police finish talking to staff, this woman shows up in her best GAP business casual, flashing FBI credentials. Now said unstable former employee is introducing herself.

Dina wonders, briefly, if Ms. Greer is regretting the slept-in hairstyle she favors. She doesn't understand the appeal of looking like you've rolled out of bed and somehow found yourself out in public. Certainly not a look that projects credibility. Serves her right for blowing past like Dina was the receptionist. Never mind she's been at *City News* almost as long as Jessica. Ever since she'd refused the job Kris Novak offered. Laughed in his face.

No matter. Dina has plenty to attend to. And nobody in this office has her skills. She pulls her Rolodex closer, flicking through cards as she considers the options, all the while keeping watch.

Behind her, in the publisher's corner office, staff is whispering about Jessica Greer. So attuned is she to their sounds, Dina doesn't have to turn her head to know who's speaking.

She looks good. Of course the head of classifieds would say that. Geoff is such a tool.

I didn't know about the funny farm. Leave it to "news" to bring up that angle.

When a collective gasp goes up, Dina can't help but snap up her head.

In plain view of the entire staff, Agent Cole is ushering Greer toward the conference room. Dina's eyes go wide. It's deadline day. There's an all-hands meeting in that room at 4:00 PM. Does it not occur to anyone that someone is responsible for these things? Makes the schedules. Of course it doesn't.

You think she did it? She overhears Rita asking.

Dina would have to give the arts editor a pass. Not much of a nose for news on that one. Jessica Greer could murder a brownie, but she can't imagine the woman has the patience to bake up a batch, let alone concoct a poisonous treat.

Interesting Ted knew he'd been poisoned, but no one has brought that up yet. We all heard the nine-one-one call.

Before Dina can form another opinion, Agent Cole returns to the all-staff meeting in the publisher's office. The woman is self-possessed all right, Dina will give her that, but it's not so much natural as hard-won. Confidence she must've learned as a lesbian from whatever hick town spit her out.

At this rate, Dina will need to push the final editorial meeting. She'll have to join them in MacCormac's office eventually as well, but for now the phone buys her more time to observe.

Hospital first, she decides, pulling her Rolodex closer. Then Ben.

By the time she reaches the nurse's station on Ted's floor, rain is hitting the windows again in earnest. After she's identified herself for the third time, Dina fires off her questions.

"What can you tell me about Mr. Harvey's condition? His next of kin hasn't been notified yet, and I—"

"We admitted Mr. Harvey about two hours ago with suspected poisoning." The nurse goes quiet. In the background, someone calls for a gurney. "He's not out of the woods by any means. He's having difficulty breathing. They've got him on oxygen, but his family should get here right away."

Dina makes a note. "Do the doctors know what kind of poisoning?"

"Nothing confirmed, but his organs are failing. He's going in and out of consciousness. The next thirty-six hours are crucial."

"Has he been able to speak with anyone yet?"

She waits a beat. "Is this really his workplace calling? Or some scumbag reporter?"

Dina bristles. Why is it that reporters—and in her experience, fact-checkers—are vilified for simply doing their job?

"Ma'am, he works at a newspaper, where we're all very concerned for him. Ted Harvey's emergency contact information isn't up to date in our files." All true, technically. "And I need to notify the next of kin before they see this on the news."

"Look, I hear what you're saying. But if you're calling about next of kin, the police are here asking the same questions. You should coordinate with them."

"Of course. Thank you. Just one more—"

But she's gone. Dina hangs up and makes a notation: Semi-conscious. Oxygen. Poisoning not confirmed. She holds the phone close to her chest as one of the officers approaches her desk.

"Ma'am, Agent Cole is gathering everyone in Mr. MacCormac's office right now—" He nods toward the corner.

"Oh, I see." Dina makes an effort to smile sweetly. Tilts her head toward her phone. "I'll be right along. Soon as I notify Ted's next of kin." She lets urgency creep into her voice. "They can't learn about this on the news."

The officer nods, uncertain, but moves on. Dina turns her chair slightly, shielding the Rolodex from view as she flips to Ted Harvey's card.

Other than Ted, the only contact listed is Ben Jones. His San Francisco number is written there in Dina's neat hand. But she happens to know Ben Jones isn't in San Francisco. He should be at Ted's house by now. Ted had mentioned he was coming into town for a conference. Dina suspects it's why Ted wanted to move up his start date.

She allows a smile as she plucks *HARVEY, Ted* free. The man lived alone. No one else would have thought to call his home number.

It rings four times. She's about to hang up and check for airport delays when a man answers, slightly breathless. "Hello?"

"Is this Ben Jones?"

"Yes? Who's calling?"

"Mr. Jones, my name is Dina Kowalski. We've never met, but I work with Ted Harvey at *City News* in Pittsburgh." She lets the information settle. "You're listed as his next-of-kin and, well, I'm afraid I have some difficult news."

He doesn't say anything for a beat. "What kind of news?"

"Sir, Mr. Harvey has been hospitalized. He received a consumable gift at our office this morning, and we think they may have been poisoned. He's at Allegheny General."

"Poisoned. Jesus Christ."

Dina stops, pen hovering. Either he already knew or Ben Jones is the calmest man she's ever spoken to. Is he wondering how she knew where to reach him? Of course she has access to everyone's calendar, but still, Dina should have thought about that.

Ben Jones clears his throat. "Is he going to be okay?"

Finally, something more on script. "The hospital says he's conscious. But it's serious. They won't know if he's out of the woods for thirty-six hours."

Silence.

"Would you like his room number?"

Another throat clearing. "I... I'm only in town for a conference. I'm on a panel this afternoon."

"I see." She waits.

"I'm staying at Ted's place, but we aren't... We broke up last year."

"You don't have to explain anything to me, but the FBI is here, at the office. They'll probably want to speak with you."

"The FBI?" Now he sounds genuinely alarmed.

"The package was sent through the U.S. mail. Federal crime." She keeps her voice helpful, informative.

Ben whistles. "Ted had a way of making enemies. But someone who'd poison him? He's a theater critic. That's crazy. Who would poison a theater critic at an alt-weekly in Pittsburgh?"

Dina sits up slightly. This is her chance to win him over. "Right? Kurt Cobain's been dead for two years, and we've spent more column inches writing about his cardigans than on Frank Gehry's achievement at the Bilbao."

A surprised laugh. "God, so true. You get what I mean."

"You'd think they'd target the editor at least." She makes her tone conspiratorial, singsong. "But if you tell anyone I said that, I'll have to kill you."

"Your secret's safe." He sounds looser now, almost friendly. "Look, I really should—"

"Of course. One more thing." She glances at Ethan's empty office. "Since you'll probably be talking to the FBI anyway, I mean, I'm joking, but also, the new editor? Ethan Silver?"

"What about him?"

Hunching over her handset, she drops her voice to a whisper. "He was forced out of his last paper. Some scandal involving mail fraud?"

"Wait, Silver was involved in a mail crime? Before he hired Ted?"

She sits back, voice back to normal. "Nothing was ever proven. Several people resigned. But yes, interesting timing." She straightens a stack of papers on her desk. "I thought you should know. The FBI will probably dig it up."

"That's... yeah. Thanks for the heads-up."

Outside, the rain has turned to proper sleet, drumming against the glass. She looks over her shoulder toward the publisher's office, Agent Cole is talking and pointing. She needs to slip in there, and—she checks her watch—Ben needs to be on his way if he's going to make it to his conference on time.

"Can I ask you something?" Ben's voice drops. "What are they saying? The FBI. Do you know who they're looking at?"

"The FBI has only just arrived, but people are saying..." She trails off deliberately. She lives for this, to be at the nexus of information people want.

"Saying what?"

"The woman whose column Ted was taking over. Jessica Greer? She didn't know he was being hired. Found out today over lunch with our new editor."

"Oh wow." Ben sounds like he's moving, maybe pacing. "What an asshole."

"I'm sorry?"

"Ethan Silver. The editor. He should have told her. That's just—" He stops himself. "Never mind. I should go. If anyone asks, give them my cell number."

Dina adds it to her file as he rattles it off.

"Okay. Thanks for calling."

"Mr. Jones?" She lets the urgency in her voice come across. "It must be so difficult, being in town the same time this happened. Horrific coincidence."

"Yeah." The word comes out flat. "Coincidence."

"I hope the conference goes well, at least."

"What? Oh. Yeah, it's fine. Frank Gehry's speaking tomorrow, actually."

Actually, she did know that. But she could let him underestimate her too. "Take care, Mr. Jones. I hope for your sake Ted recovers quickly."

She hangs up before he can respond, then makes a quick note. Time to join the meeting in progress. After a mirror check.

Sliding open her drawer, she sees Kris Novak's piece—*The*

Man Who Survived the CIA—right where it's always been. After a quick fluff of her bob, she slips the compact into her tote along with the article.

She'd gone above and beyond for that piece—confirming the symptoms, the critical thirty-six-hour window, survival odds, and every possible vector for ricin poisoning. She didn't typically do that much of the reporting as the fact-checker, but once she'd started pulling the thread on Ted, the subject had taken on a life of its own. Who knew the story would lead to a book deal for Kris? Not that she'd expected him to leave the paper, but she should've. What man could multitask?

Reporter's pad in hand, she's back to concerned colleague. Helpful employee. Ready for MacCormac's office. Ready to record every word.

WITNESS STATEMENTS — FBI CASE NO. 95-PGH-0047

CITY NEWS OFFICES

James MacCormac, Publisher

This is a terrible tragedy. We're all a little bit in shock. I came up in a time, you know, when people thought alt-newsweeklies could change the world. Now I run a business. I know better. But hey, adapt or die, right?

No, I don't mean—

What I'm saying is, we've made changes. To better align with Pittsburgh. The cultural sector's getting a lot of attention, but the people paying for it? They're conservative. They want coverage that reads like *Talk of the Town* but is about Pittsburgh.

Bringing Ted on board, just a business decision.

Ethan Silver, Editor-in-Chief

Did Jessica Greer seem upset? Not, no. More like she was ready to meet with me. Had some new column. We'd not met before then. I've seen a couple of her columns come across my desk, but we haven't really worked together.

That said, we're looking to elevate our coverage in general. Ted was part of that. Is, I mean. I only met him at his interview last week, and he beat me into the office that day. On deadline days I like to work from home till midday, they're always late nights.

That said, bringing Ted over wasn't strictly my idea. I've only been here a month.

Kris Novak. It was his idea. You should talk to him. From what I hear, he and Jessica were tight. He'd know more about her than I do.

Gail Hayes, Admin/Receptionist

Ted had already eaten the brownie by the time I saw the note. Went around asking everyone who had sent it. He said it wasn't signed?

"Congratulations on your new job," it said. *City News* stationery, yes.

Patricia Dugan, Human Resources

Jessica Greer has been a contributor since 1993. Still on the roster, far as I know. No formal record complaints. HR doesn't typically get involved beyond that with freelancers.

Ted's hire was not a surprise, no. But he did insist on starting prior to the date we'd anticipated.

Ray Donnelly, News Editor

Oh please, the arts page doesn't sell ads unless someone's dead or naked, and even then it's iffy. You want my opinion? Everybody hates a critic. But murder? That would take someone a little unhinged. I hear Greer has that background.

For sure she could've had *City News* stationery.

Rita Holt, Arts Editor

We're always expanding our coverage. Making the theater position full-time worked because we combined a couple of part-time roles into one. That role should report to me, not the editor.

Yeah, no, I didn't tell her but… Come on. She had to know. Pittsburgh is small, but the theater community? It's like *Flowers in the Attic*. Everybody knew. Plus I heard she had a few pitches lined up when she met with Ethan.

Dina Kowalski, Editorial Admin

I'm actually the fact-checker. Verify names, dates, that sort of thing. So I don't know much but did want to talk to you because, has anybody wondered how he knew he'd been poisoned? Which—how would you know that?

Well, that's what I heard.

I don't really know Jessica. Like I said, I verify facts. Not opinions.

5

JESSICA

Agent Cole shuts the conference room door with a chilling finality, leaving me alone with that weird new-carpet smell. The paper must've done this renovation recently. Reminds me of Zimmerman when I first started there. They were remodeling the reception area, and that chemical stink infiltrated the lobby for a month. Different sterile environment, same stomach drop. I knew things were changing at the paper, but this feels dramatic.

Is this why Novak left? I feel like I've landed in the principal's office, the difference being that—from where I'm sitting—the whole school can watch. Thanks to their weird open floorplan, I can see all the desks, all the way into the corner office, right to a clean view of the staff gathered there. Every last one is looking my way, pretending they're not. But even the office walls are made of glass. No one on either side has anywhere to hide.

Now she's made it to MacCormac's office and she's addressing the staff, her chestnut bob catching the overhead fluorescents in an incongruously flattering way. She's spent more on her hair than her outfit, that's for sure. The woman is small, but she takes up a lot of space. Everyone is straining to hear her, all heads tilt forward slightly. She has the kind of authority that can command a room, and I have to admire that. Even if I'm on her shitlist.

Ethan emerges from somewhere, possibly the men's room. He's smoothing his hair, which, I note, does not need smoothing. He's changed his shirt also. When did he have time to change his shirt? He must keep a spare handy. Of course he does.

The distinct aroma of CK One wafts by, mixing with the industrial nylon pile. He must've really doused himself for the smell to penetrate. For a split second I think he's headed my way—perhaps to apologize?—but he pivots toward Cole. There's something in his hand, a piece of paper. He's unhurried but purposeful, heading for Cole. I'm shocked. He is clearly about to interrupt her.

Whatever he says works. Cole tips her head, reaches for the paper in his hand. He's saying something, and I roll closer to the glass, irrational, since the room is fairly soundproof. I want to know what he's telling her. Did they talk before I arrived? He's the one who said I was a suspect. How did that get started? It's so ridiculous. He better not have mentioned my accomplice crack. Why did I say that? I wish I could read lips.

It's fine, I'm sure. They're probably flirting.

He'd sleep with her, I have no doubt. Ethan doesn't strike me as particularly choosy. A little like Carson in that regard. Agent Cole, on the other hand, she seems more inclined to sleep with me. Not that she'd given any indication she was interested, but she came across as someone who hadn't wasted much time on men.

I desperately want to call my work wife, Sofia. She's going to lose her mind when I tell her about this. Probably not as much as when I told her about Carson.

Sof had wisely skipped the golf outing—*it's work, if they're not paying me to go, why would I go?*—and I was relaying all the gory details. The break room was empty, there we were, sitting across from each other, me with a cup of office sludge and her, finishing off a Big Gulp, her enormous earrings bobbing as we dissected the whole thing. How I'd drunk way too much. How we'd spent the day on the links, one long seduction. Until finally, in the clubhouse near the end, I'd leaned over and kissed him.

And he'd kissed back.

She'd been proud I didn't take him home, especially considering the announcement about Carson's promotion. Not that I had much of a choice. My mom's birthday party was the next day. I didn't remind her either.

"Then he didn't call you all day Sunday? Just let you find out this morning?"

"He's not a monster, Sof. He could've just found out this morning."

"Bullshit," she said, tossing her plastic cup in a perfect arc into the waste bin.

"How do you do that without even looking?"

"Three brothers." She let out a burp.

We laughed like we were fifteen.

"The only thing my brother ever tried to impose on me was musical theater."

"And you're sure he's not gay?" Sof had asked.

I cross my arms and roll back to the conference table, drop my head onto its surface. I'd laughed then, but my mom was right to warn me this morning. It felt depressing that my brother, who was studying to be a doctor, had managed to find a fiancée.

From the corner of my eye, I catch Ethan laughing at something Cole says. He genuinely laughs. I don't know whether to feel sick or envious. Or both. I add it to my file on him.

The mental file I'm keeping on a man I met four hours ago.

I look around the conference room. There's a dry-erase board on one wall with the remnants of something—a budget breakdown, maybe—erased but not quite gone. There's a phone on the table that I have not touched and will not touch because I've watched enough true crime to know that is exactly the kind of thing that gets noted down in a legal pad by someone like Agent Cole. There's also, I realize, a vending machine visible through the glass partition, and I am suddenly and aggressively aware that I never ate my lunch.

Ethan has moved away from Cole, back toward what I assume is his desk. He doesn't look toward the conference room. That could mean anything.

Cole addresses the receptionist I'd blown past earlier. *Oops.* That won't look good if she mentions it. She's such an odd thing. A body like *Xena: Warrior Princess* that she hides under quirky embroidered sweaters and twee skirts. But the platinum hair and Doc Martens suggest there's another side to her personality. It looks like she's trying to hand Cole a notepad. Cole does not take the notepad. Like she didn't take my hand.

There you go, Greer, I tell myself in my best pep talk voice. Cole's rude to everyone.

I wonder how they're going to get the paper out today. The whole newsroom has the held-breath quality of a waiting room. Everyone clotted up in the corner, not working. It's going to be a late night. They say the show must go on, but I've been to plenty of plays that started late. The review of the show, though? That deadline's sacrosanct.

Weirdly, I'm not scared. I should be. An FBI agent put me in a glass box while a man I find irritating chats her up like I'm a suspect. I might've signed my own death warrant at my day job thanks to the golf day. My brother is getting married, and my mother is catastrophizing, though she called it something else.

And there's a hole in my memory from last night that involves a Duncan Hines box.

I steady myself on the table. There's nothing to worry about. Not for me. There's no way I did whatever it is that's been done. Basically, I'm sleep-deprived.

Ever since the Carson incident I've been waking up every night from the bridge dream. Which is weird since the dreams started when I found my father. I close my eyes and make a mental note to mention this to my therapist, knowing in advance it's going to be another rough night.

This is all fine. I'm fine. I'll talk to them. Explain I barely knew Ted Harvey. That I had no strong feelings about the column. I can control this story. I've spun scarier narratives. Like the time I helped convince Champa Brakes it was good for their business to tell their customers about a brake defect before the federal safety board did.

Beverly Jo is going to absolutely die when she hears about this.

There's movement from the corner office. Staff is streaming out, back to their desks. Cole is heading straight for me.

A tall, thin Black man is behind her, notepad already open. I like that too, a woman who comes with a note taker.

I straighten in my chair, smooth my skirt and place my hands flat on the table. Calm. Composed. Like someone who has nothing to hide.

Or is this too obvious?

Before I can recall a single *Cagney and Lacey* interrogation episode, the door is opening, accompanied by the hiss of a pressurized seal releasing.

Here we go.

6

JESSICA

Lydia Cole and her colleague, Ross Klavon, introduce themselves as Special Agents.

Special Agents? Since when is the Bureau a "first-responder" agency? *Law & Order* didn't prepare me for this.

"You're *FBI*?" I ask. "What's going on? What happened to Ted?"

Klavon is seated at the head of the table, catty-corner to me, while Cole circumnavigates.

"We'll be asking the questions," Cole barks, playing "Bad Cop" with a gusto to rival any man with a Napoleon complex.

What's left of my warm feeling evaporates. We're in a glass box. The entire office is watching, and I'm hoping there's a special place in hell for whoever designed the open concept office. I miss the sweet mauve cocoon of my cubicle.

"Do I need a lawyer?" I ask.

"Do you?" Cole replies.

"Okay, okay," Agent Klavon says. His dark eyes are kind and set off by white flecks in his close-cropped afro. Obviously the good cop. "Ms. Greer, nobody's accusing you of anything here, but we understand Ted Harvey took your job. That does make you a person of interest."

I've read enough true crime I should know the difference between a suspect and a person of interest, but I don't. My face must ask for me.

"That just means we want to ask you some questions," Klavon says.

"And don't go anywhere," Cole adds. "You're not planning any trips, are you?"

I'm tempted to say, "I am now." But despite what my brother calls my 'diarrhea mouth,' even I know that antagonizing FBI agents is not a smart move. "No, ma'am."

"Good." She nods, her chestnut bob swaying. Up close I see this is clearly not the hair color of someone on a government salary. Either she has some alternate income, or something to prove. Like me, truth be told.

"Guys, I'm happy to talk to you," I say. "I haven't done anything. Certainly didn't murder Ted. I only knew—"

Cole stops dead. "Where did you get the idea this was a murder investigation?"

"Ethan Silver." *Did he say murder?* "We were at lunch when he got called to come back. He said I was a suspect. Doesn't that mean there's been a murder?"

Klavon scribbles something into his legal pad. "Mr. Harvey was poisoned, taken out of here on a stretcher," he says. "He's still alive but experiencing hallucinations, seizures, kidney and spleen failure. We won't know if he's in the clear for another thirty-six hours."

Ted was poisoned?

Every instinct screams *shut up*. But another voice—the one that keeps me at least marginally employed—says I need to control the narrative. I open my mouth.

"You think I poisoned Ted Harvey over this job? I barely knew him. I didn't..." Then it strikes me—those symptoms, that timeline, the FBI presence. "Wait... thirty-six hours?" Seizures, kidney and spleen failure. She'd read about this somewhere. "Was it ricin?"

Cole smacks her hand on the conference table. "Ricin? Who said anything about ricin?"

Is she joking?

"Everybody knows about ricin," I say, glaring at Cole. "Like the Minnesota Patriots? Hello?"

Cole and Klavon exchange looks, and I hear my mistake.

"I mean, *City News* ran a piece on domestic terror crimes. *The Bomber Next Door* was the title, I think. Didn't you read it? They talked about it on the Morning Zoo because it came out right before the Unabomber's manifesto. Anyway, that's when—"

I stop short. I learned all about ricin from my editor. The last one. The nice one. He'd written that article. Novak had been so proud of it, she'd framed a copy for him. Did I incriminate my friend? I need to walk that back. Ted was either singled out or in the wrong place at the wrong time. Whose desk *did* he take? Plenty of people must have grudges against Ted.

"Have you talked to anyone in the theater community yet? He was friends with the head of Pittsburgh Public, Mary Beth Purcel is her name—"

"And how do you know Ms. Purcel?" Cole stops, fists gripping the back of a chair.

"Because I wrote about theater?"

The questions come rapid-fire after that, and I have the distinct impression I was not on their radar until I showed up. Klavon resumes his furious note-taking while Cole gazes on coolly, her eyes so dark they look almost black.

I assure her I only learned about the job today. It was a blow but... No, I don't have a background in chemistry. And I learned ricin comes from the easily obtainable castor beans from that article. I'm answering honestly and I think well, but the more I talk, the worse Cole's expression gets.

Despite the icy stare, I feel like I could catch fire.

"Agent Cole," I blurt out, "you have to believe I didn't do this?"

Why does everything I say sound like a question?

Cole doesn't blink. "What makes you say that?"

"Because—" I'm talking too fast, force myself to slow down. "If I wanted to hurt Ted Harvey—which I didn't, but if I did—I wouldn't have used poison."

Klavon's pen stops moving.

"Oh no?" Cole asks, voice neutral though something flickers in her eyes. "What would you do?"

My words tumble out. "Well obviously your best bet is to make it look like an accident. At least make sure the body disappears. You'd want to drive somewhere isolated. Like one of those old steel mill access roads along the Mon—nobody goes there anymore—take 'em to one of those abandoned loading docks by the water."

"Then what?" Klavon asks. Cole hasn't moved.

"Then you point to something outside the car. Get them to get out of the car and have a look, then you floor it. Back up. Hit him again to make sure." I'm animated. Not even close to done. "Any of those docks would work. They have concrete ramps running right into the water. You'd just have to roll him down. After you weighed down the body, there's rebar and old chain everywhere, current would do the rest."

Why am I still talking?

"By the time anyone finds the victim—if they ever do—the body's in Ohio and it looks like he got mugged and dumped. No murder weapon, no physical evidence. Nothing linking you to the scene."

The words have scarcely left my mouth when I hear my own voice echoing back—*you'd just have to roll him down.* For a split second it doesn't sound like something I came up with on the spot. It sounds... familiar?

But no. That's ludicrous. Has to be.

Now Cole leans forward slightly. "You've thought about this."

The room, I suddenly notice, has gone silent. Both agents staring at me. "No, I—" My mouth is suddenly dry. I swallow, try again. "I think—"

Nothing is coming. Not a single coherent thought. Only the sound of my own voice a second ago, looping back.

I force a laugh. Too loud in the small room.

"Wasn't that an episode of *Rockford Files*?"

Neither of them reacts.

I keep talking, because quiet feels worse. "You know, the docks, the—" I make a vague circling motion with my hand, like I can sketch my way out of this. "He was always—there was always, like, a car, and—"

Jesus, stop talking.

"I don't—think about this stuff. Not like that. I just—watch a lot of TV."

This is what got me in trouble before, speaking aloud whatever popped into my brain until everyone, myself included, was convinced I was dangerous. 'Intrusive thoughts are normal,' they'd said. 'Thinking something isn't the same as acting on it,' they'd said. What did *they* know? What if I made those brownies for Ted and don't remember?

"I mean," I stammer on, "Hypothetically. If someone wanted to, which I obviously didn't. I'm just saying ricin seems unnecessarily complicated and traceable." But I'm failing to convince myself.

Hypothetically?

I hear it as they must hear it—neat, clinical, like I'm work-shopping variations. Look from Cole to Klavon and back. The air in the room feels thick, like I'm breathing through wool. Cole's face has shifted from professional curiosity to something colder, more final. Klavon is looking at me like I've confessed. *Oh shit.*

"We tend to find," Cole says quietly, "crimes match person-alities."

All moisture leaves my mouth. I'd come to prove my inno-cence and instead managed to explain what I would have done differently. It doesn't matter that what I described has nothing to do with poisoning. What matters is that I sound like someone who's given real, unnecessarily complicated thought to killing people and getting away with it.

"Did you ever work out of this office?" Cole asks. "At one of the temporary desks?"

"Did I, what? Use a desk here? No."

"Never?" Klavon asks. "In all three years you've been coming in?"

Where are they going with this? I shake my head. "I haven't been in here since before all this." I wave my hand around. "They just renovated the place."

Cole motions to Klavon. "Give us a minute," he says.

They walk out, leaving me alone with my thoughts.

"Oh shit oh shit oh shit," is the extent of my thoughts.

Feel your feelings, Jess, they'd said.

Moments like this all I *feel* is what a bad idea that is. I *feel* like a failure. I *feel* like they think I'm a murderer.

Not *might* be, or, *could* be. In their eyes, I did this. And I can see it, how the story makes sense. Motive, access, and a clearly volatile freelancer, handing over a murder manual all wrapped up in a bow.

I'd come here to prove my innocence by seizing hold of the narrative. Instead, thanks to my true crime fixation, all I've done is talk myself into looking like a psychopath. If this is the story they're building, I need to keep digging. Figure out what's in it. And how to change it. Like Carson always says, *The truth doesn't matter if no one believes you.*

7
____

LYDIA

Lydia and Klavon head for the kitchen, the most private space on the floor. The walls are actual walls, not glass. Even in a glass house the employee break room must have camouflage.

"What the hell was that?" Klavon says once they've crossed the threshold.

Lydia taps her index finger to her lips and motions toward the entry. There's no door. Out of habit, she walks to the fridge. A cake sits inside. "Happy Birthday Tom," it reads in blue icing. Someone's celebration, forgotten, like the lunch she'd left on the counter at home. She wishes Ted Harvey had left behind some of his brownie, but figures if nobody thought to move this cake, it's probably a dead end.

She points at it. "Anybody check this?"

"On it," Klavon says, scrawling into his notebook before looking up. "Seriously though. That was some serious strange."

Cole closes the fridge. "I'm still recovering. Who leads by introducing herself as a suspect?"

"She is now." Klavon shakes his head. "Where'd she even get that idea?"

Cole looks out into the office. It's a head-on view of Jessica Greer—white woman, single, twenty-eight years old. Same age Lydia made Special Agent, back when she still believed competence mattered more than politics. Greer's head drops onto her forearms. Has she figured out how she sounded?

"We don't have enough to arrest her, though."

"Really? She comes up with the poison from some symptoms then goes into Kaczynski? That shit is totally unrelated."

"I hope so," Cole says. The visibility appeals, but if this case drags on for seventeen years like the Unabomber's, she'll be readying for retirement before it ends. What good would it do her then? "Except that both attackers used the mail."

"Okay. But... Even if you do buy her story that she learned about ricin from the old editor—Novak, was it?—there was that whole step-by-step guide to disposing of a body in the Monongahela. That's not something you come up with on the spot," Klavon says.

Cole crosses her arms. "The weird thing though, we didn't ask her to come in. So she's either..." Lydia trails off. Either what? She's guilty? Monumentally stupid? Both? Why swan in and hand over a murder manual? "Any halfway decent attorney walks her out."

Klavon tosses his notepad on the counter. "You sure about that? We don't even have definitives on the ricin, just the self-reporting. And Pittsburgh PD is already convinced."

The evidence does fit, no doubt about that. Greer has a grievance. She'd know the office routine. And ricin slipped from her tongue like it was common knowledge. That's not coincidence, that's a profile. But Cole wants this win too badly to lose it to a premature arrest.

"You know same as me how tricky alibi is in a mail crime. So no. We need to look at and eliminate competing theories. I want this airtight before we move."

"Okay, but..." Klavon reaches for his notebook, jots down a few words. "Jessica Greer sure knows a lot about ricin."

"Knowing isn't the same as doing." She watches her partner. If he hears her quoting Powell, he doesn't say. If he's thinking what she is, that the profile is almost too perfect, well, neither one of them is saying that. She sets it aside.

"It's closer to guilty than not."

Lydia holds his gaze for a moment. Reminds herself she is the lead here. She'd actually gotten her way. Not because of the intel she'd picked up at *Pittsburgh Voice*, but because she'd convinced her supervisor the case was trivial. Powell would "oversee" the task force, meaning he'd leave her enough rope to hang herself if the case goes sideways.

"What we need is evidence. Physical evidence that connects her to the crime."

"A warrant?"

Lydia shakes her head. "We need more. The freelance job she may or may not have known was ending before today at a place that still technically employs her doesn't cut it."

Klavon squints, which means he's framing his reply. He's not with her. This could turn into a bigger problem.

"Lyd, this is bioterrorism." Klavon pushes his thin frame off the counter. "Post-Oklahoma City? Judges are signing warrants faster. We should at least try. Before there's another hit."

Lydia glances toward the conference room again, where Greer is shoving a candy bar down her gullet. Now? Is that stress-eating or the nonchalance of a sociopath?

"*If* there's going to be another hit. This feels local to me. Personal. We need to look at all the angles here. Harvey's theater connections. Find out what's the deal with the ex. Talk to that editor who was writing about ricin."

"Kris Novak?" Klavon asks. "You want me to track him down?"

Lydia considers the offer, but only briefly. She wants to work that interview, pay him a visit. Truth is, she wants to avoid Alice. Conceding Lydia's point on the police scanner wouldn't make up for all the extra hours this case is going to demand.

"I'll take Novak. You start paper for that warrant. Ask Chen to dig up intel on local theater groups." She twirls her index finger to indicate the room. "Enlist the officers here to collect statements from everyone in this office. We can regroup before the press conference."

"You sure you don't want me to talk to Novak? Free you up some?"

He knows she's sidelining him. Today was Harvey's first day at the paper. He's unlikely to turn up much at *City News*.

"I appreciate that, Ross, but we're going to have to be strategic if we want to keep this for our office and wrap it quickly." She smiles. "Besides, you'll be much better at sweet-talking the judge."

Klavon smiles through pursed lips. "You're not wrong there."

As they exit the kitchen, Lydia reconsiders Powell's strategy. She should try it on Jessica Greer. Let her go. See what happens. She doesn't have much choice. For now.

8

———

DINA

Once the agents leave the break room, Dina heads that way. She trusts they won't notice. No one ever sees her as a threat, a fact she discovered as an angry, if awkward, teen. Cat-eye glasses, plaid skirts, and whimsical cardigans have been her uniform since. Still, she moves slowly. People who hurry attract attention. Her Daddy told her that long ago. Now that she's made up her mind, she has plenty of time.

The walk is short, but the tension is palpable. Phones are answered quickly, voices are quieter than on most Mondays, forget about deadline days. Even the keyboards sound muted. Every last person in here is only pretending to work while they watch Cole and Klavon from the corners of their eyes. It's truly the most excitement this office has seen since O.J.'s Bronco chase.

The lunchroom is ideally situated, naturally. She'd convinced MacCormac to put it on the interior wall—catty-corner to his office, beside the supply closet. The only area you really can't see from here is the publisher's office, which she'd sold as a bonus. In truth, nothing much happens in that luxe corner suite, the man is rarely *in* it. But the smelly old break room? Gold mine. Especially now, given that it's directly across from where she'd set up desks for Cole and Klavon.

From here she can not only see them, she should be able to hear them. She could've made other desks available, but why? She couldn't hear a thing when they were in the conference room.

Unfortunately, the pair of them have an uncanny ability to "quiet-talk." She would give anything to know what they think they have on Jessica Greer. That woman could murder a brownie, but mix up a poisonous batch? Using ricin? Not likely. Ricin wasn't something you stirred into batter like cinnamon. It required patience, equipment, and precision. Skills Ms. Greer was decidedly lacking in.

But they hadn't let her leave.

Now she's alone in the conference room, eating a candy bar. *A candy bar.* She must not be too upset; there's already an empty wrapper on the table. Dina would give anything to know what they talked about. She's not immune to good gossip.

Taking a seat at the table, Dina carefully opens her bag of yogurt-covered pretzels. Always tells herself the pretzels will keep better if she only tears off a corner. There are never any pretzels left to put away.

She wonders how long it will be before investigators talk to Kris Novak. *Who* will talk to Kris Novak. When they'll go to Ted's.

As the paper's fact-checker, Dina understands how the obvious can be elusive. It had taken her months to piece together the simplest facts while she was researching for Kris's book. Without the book, she reckons, none of this would be happening.

Cole stands, calling over one of the men in the paper suits.

Next she's heading Dina's way, bringing Ross and the hazmat guy.

Now?

Dina's only move is to angle her body toward the refrigerator and keep eating. She remains seated, glad she's still wearing her headphones.

Cole walks to the fridge and opens it. When she finds the cake Dina ordered for Tom's birthday—white frosting, blue icing, red velvet inside—she pulls it off the shelf. "This needs to go to the lab," she says.

Dina almost interjects—she'd only bought the cake that morning—but doesn't want to draw attention. Surely they've realized she's here, but they haven't asked her to leave.

The guy in the paper suit leaves with the cake. *Goodbye, cake.*

Agent Cole stops and looks directly at Dina, pointing at her own ears.

Dina feigns surprise as she slides her headphones to her neck. "Did you ask me something?"

"Do you know where they keep the stationery?" she asks.

Dina is disappointed. Figured a woman running a bioterrorism case for the FBI would know better than to assume she was a secretary. She keeps her irritation in check. Always does. "I do. Would you like me to show you?"

"How accessible is it?"

Dina tilts her chin, acts confused. She understands what Special Agent Cole wants to know—who might've taken the letterhead that was sent with Ted's brownie—but she's not sure how to answer.

"Meaning, can *anyone* get to it?" Klavon adds.

"Oh, of course," Dina purrs. Despite the age difference—he must be in his mid-forties—she finds his tall, slender build and copper skin compelling. No wedding ring. Flecks of silver in his hair add to his appeal. "And no. We keep all the supplies locked up."

"You have a lot of these, hot desks, though. Right?" Agent Cole waves toward the office.

Dina gives her a combination nod-shrug. "Is there a standard number?"

"It would be pretty easy to get some letterhead, no? For, say, a freelancer?" Cole continues.

Are they talking about Jessica Greer?

Dina makes a sound like she's impressed. "Hmm."

"Could you get your hands on a copy of an article for us?" Cole asks. "Something about bioterrorism and ricin?"

"That doesn't sound familiar..."

"No?" Klavon says. "Jessica Greer told us they talked about it on Morning Zoo?"

Dina closes her eyes. She knows which article they mean. "Yes. I mean, I'm not the admin—that's Gail—but happy to help." Her eyes widen. "But... if it's the article I'm thinking about, there's nothing about ricin in it."

They exchange a look. Dina needs to press them.

"Ricin did come up, though. Why?"

"What do you mean, *ricin did come up*?" Cole folds her arms.

"I mean, in another piece Kris wrote. More recently. About a visit from Boris Korczak. You know about him? The CIA agent?"

Klavon leans closer. Even smells good.

"What about him?" he asks.

"He was in town to speak at the Polish American Club. Interesting guy, claims the CIA tried to kill him. Sent Kris on a whole rabbit hole about Soviet suppression of the media. It's why he left. He's writing a book about it."

Cole is shifting on her feet, seemingly uncomfortable with the conversation. *Perfect.*

"Kris is kind of, well, never met a conspiracy theory he didn't repeat." Dina waves her hand in front of her pretzel bag. "He's harmless. Anyway, I'm sure I can get Gail to get you both articles."

"Much appreciated," Cole says.

Before they can leave the room, Dina blurts out what she's been trying to tell them. "You know? I don't know if this makes a difference, but Ted's ex is in town. Ben Jones? He's here for a conference."

"In town?" Klavon asks. "Do you know where he lives? When he got here?"

Dina reaches for a pretzel. "Ted told me he was coming in from San Franciso today. You can try calling him at Ted's."

"At Ted's?" Cole says.

"He's staying with him. I guess they're still on good terms?"

"So you're friends with Ted Harvey," Klavon says.

"Oh, no. I only just met him in person when he came in for his interview last week." Dina's neck flushes. "I couldn't say we know each other."

When they don't respond, Dina pushes her chair back. "I can ask Gail for those articles—"

"Finish your lunch," Klavon says. "Just have her leave them with us."

The agents return to the office without another word. Dina stays put, watching as Klavon goes to his desk and Cole heads for Jessica. This should be good.

WITNESS STATEMENTS — FBI CASE NO. 95-PGH-0047

ZIMMERMAN PUBLIC RELATIONS OFFICES

Kelley Knight, Account Director (read from a prepared statement):

Jessica Greer is an account executive who has been with the company since 1992. We have no other comment at this time but trust the authorities are doing everything in their power to bring this ordeal to a close.

Beverly Jo Marshall, Account Executive:

I saw the headline on the wire—BIOTERRORISM INVESTIGATION LAUNCHES. But you're the police, not FBI? Huh.

Carson Davis, Senior Account Executive:

She's one of my direct reports, a valued team member. I was aware she had the free-lancing job to the extent a supervisor can be.

Our employees sign confidentiality agreements to avoid conflicts of interest, but, well, local theater doesn't really rise to the level of our clients.

Marshall:

Now that I'm hearing she wrote about theater, I get it. I mean, she's a little off. Like most creative types are. I didn't know she cared about theater. But then, that's not really my thing. Unless it's touring Broadway.

But honestly, if I hadn't seen it in the news, I wouldn't have believed it. I mean, moonlighting as a theater critic for some little local? Why would someone who could get a real job want to do that for a living? But apparently somebody else got her job. Ted Harvey, right? The man who got poisoned?

The timing is definitely strange.

Davis:

I'm sure there's a reasonable explanation for all this. She's good-looking, I mean, good with clients. She's smart, you know? She can be intense, but that's normal around here. This is PR—if you're not intense, you're unemployed.

Sofia Reyes, Account Coordinator:

Yes, we're friends. She told me all about meeting her editor. Said she knew he was going to fire her. I mean, like, she had a feeling *knew.* Figured that's why he wanted to take her to lunch. But she didn't threaten anyone. Jessica vents, sure, but she's not violent. She's more likely to bore someone to death processing her feelings out loud. I mean, in a good way. Don't write that down.

9

JESSICA

I'm barely back at my mauve crypt—one of my many nicknames for my cubicle—when Zimmerman's most aggressively perky teammate pounces.

"Did you see how many people volunteered for the committee?" Beverly Jo asks.

Before turning to face her I do a quick reflection check in my darkened monitor, make sure I'm wearing my listening face—chin tilted, cheeks pushed to my eyes, no teeth. The look that says not needy, but also, not threatening.

When did I start smiling in pieces to make other people comfortable?

"What committee?" I ask, looking in her eyes as I try to keep my voice even.

"Oh, that's right. Carson asked me to tell you." She's beaming.

I go stiff. We were hired on the same day, have the same title, but she's been made team leader on a Steel Council project—a fast track to promotion. Worse, she's already acting like she's my boss, except when she goes into her closet. Today she pulled out stirrup pant leggings and a neon-orange sweater festooned with pumpkins topped by yarn "hair." Like Halloween vomited on her.

Something evil compels me to compliment her sartorial choices. "Great sweater, by the way."

"Isn't it?" She twirls to show me the design is on the back too.

Worse, I love that she believes me.

"So, yeah," she continues. "The holiday party. We're organizing the committee this year? Anyways, eighteen people signed up!"

I'm stuck on *committee*. The holiday party involves cocktails, heavy apps, and some mock awards. How does that require convening a *committee*? Pretty sure that covers the whole thing. *Done.*

"Oh no, you're upset," she says.

I need to work on my poker face.

"No, I—"

She leans in conspiratorially, dropping her voice. "I do think it's because of the murder at your little paper."

I slip off my ballet flats and wrestle into my heels, dropping into my chair as if she didn't speak.

"Where you're a suspect?" she adds.

"I am not—" I stop myself. Technically I am a person of interest. Which had meant I was free to go, so it can't be all that bad. I need to look that up.

"Bev, how did you even hear about that?"

She grimaces. "It's Beverly Jo."

That's the hill she wants to die on? Isn't Bev preferable to the more obvious shorthand?

My reply is to flick on my computer.

"We're in the business of news here, Jess." She gestures vaguely toward the bullpen, which—all credit to the cubicles—I can't really see. "We monitor all the wires. A story like that is going to spread like wildfire."

Of course it is.

"Also the police were here asking questions. Where have you been anyways?"

Damn. If this is what it's like as a "person of interest," I can't imagine how much worse it would be if anyone knew what's been going on with me. How rattled I've been. How sleep-deprived. How there was an empty Duncan Hines brownie box in my trash this morning and I have no memory of baking.

Could I have gone into a sugar coma and tossed some castor beans into the batch? Why did I remember so many details from Novak's article? More to the point, my mailman doesn't even come to my house till late in the day. How would I have delivered this package? Getting something downtown would've also required taking the T, or sleep-driving, over a *bridge*. Surely I'd remember that. Between Ethan's arrival and Carson's promotion, I haven't been that much a mess. Have I?

The minute I get home I'm putting that Duncan Hines box in the alley dumpster. I don't need the aggravation of wondering.

"Sorry, Beverly Jo. I can't divulge any details of the case."

That line is absolutely something I stole from television, but I refuse to give the Beej the satisfaction of thinking she knows more than me. "And I really have to get back to it because of the long lunch."

"Right. You said you were sick?"

Well, she's isn't stupid. I slam my shoe drawer shut. "Thanks for stopping by."

Beverly Jo wrinkles like she's smelled something questionable. I guess she needs to work on her poker face too.

Without waiting for her to say anything back, I open my email and start clicking through messages with the fury of a Minesweeper addict.

Are u okay?

Delete.

What's going on?

Delete.

Holy—

Delete.

Tap. Tap. Tap. Carson's scent hits before his voice, soap and aftershave. Clean, sharp.

A dagger to the heart.

Pump the brakes, Greer, he's your boss.

"Sorry to interrupt, Jess—got a second?"

I swivel slowly to face him.

"No problem."

That alone tells me this is not a social call.

"Just wanted to give you a heads-up," he says.

"You nominated me for the holiday party committee."

He blinks then laughs softly.

"It's like we can finish each other's sentences."

He leans against the cubicle wall, arms folded. Tie loosened, collar open.

"You don't mind then?"

I wrench my eyes away from his Adam's apple.

"Of course I don't mind," I say, after way too much of a pause.

"Good," he says. "Knew I could count on you."

But he doesn't leave. *Oh, God.*

"Actually," he says, voice lowering, "there's something else."

My stomach drops.

"This... situation," he says carefully. "With the investigation."

Oh.

Goddamn.

"We're going to need to pull you off your billable accounts for now."

At first the words don't register.

"All of them?"

"You're still a valued member of the team," he says quickly. "But we need to move you into a less front-facing role."

Valued member? "Less?" My voice is a squeak.

"What about Sterling Packaging?" It's the only account I actually run.

"Nicki can handle that," he says.

Nicki is an account coordinator. They're giving my biggest job to someone whose position is below mine?

"Just until this blows over."

Am I being demoted? "Until what blows over, Carson?"

"Jess."

The way he says my name—low, almost pleading—makes my breath catch.

"You know our business is all about reputation." He continues speaking with low urgency so, irksomely, I'm turned on even though he's shit-canning me.

"What things look like," he continues.

Three years of working together, late nights, shared jokes. That kiss at the golf outing that felt like everything and then nothing when he got promoted the next day. Now this. I want to tell him he's wrong. That reputation is about substance, track record, results. But I know better. PR is about selling what things look like. I never thought I'd be the product.

I want to argue. Tell him reputation is about results. About work. But even I know that's not true. And PR isn't about truth, it's about optics. And right now, my optics are terrible.

"Sure," I say finally. "Okay."

I stand up because suddenly sitting feels unbearable.

"I should probably notify my clients."

"No need," Carson says gently.

My heart sinks.

"We've already taken care of that."

Of course they have.

"In fact," he adds, "you might want to take a few days off."

That is some world-class spin. I shouldn't be, but I'm stunned. It makes me brave. This can't get worse.

"Who talked to the police?"

"The police?"

"Don't be like that, Carson. Not now."

"Jess," he says after a moment. "I don't really know who all they talked to, but we had statements prepared. I told them you're a valued member of our team."

That is some world-class spin. He may be the actual devil.

"But... I didn't do anything."

Even I cannot believe how lame I sound.

"Jess," he says, despite all this making my heart skip a beat. "You've worked here long enough to know the truth doesn't matter if no one believes you."

For the second day in a row, I'm staring moonily at the spot Carson has vacated. Once more, my ringing phone interrupts. Only now I wonder, am I supposed to answer? Screw that.

"Yes?" I answer. Screw the Zimmerman greeting mandate.

"Jessica? It's Mom."

Christ, her timing.

"Are you there?"

"Yes. It's not a good time."

"Not a good time? I'd say that hardly covers it."

"Mom—"

"Before you hang up, hear me out. Take a few days, come home. We'll sort this all out."

Even Mom knows what's up. "You don't think taking leave makes me look guilty?"

She sighs. "Sweetheart—"

"Because if I leave without any clients," I continue, "there won't be a place for me when this blows over."

"But honey," she says gently, "you don't even like that job."

I picture her at the breakfast nook in my childhood home, a cup of cold Nescafé in front of her. Before Dad died, she was at his beck and call—working at the insurance business, taking care of the house, managing his moods. Now that he's gone, her need to make up for what she couldn't fix for our father is bottomless. With Seth in Boston, she focuses all that frantic energy on me. I'm the only project she has left to work on, right when I want to be invisible.

"I'll figure it out," I say.

"What if you're next on this psycho's list?"

Leave it to Mom to send me down another devastating rabbit hole. "I hardly think someone is targeting Pittsburgh theater critics."

"You don't know that."

"But I'm not even the critic anymore."

"All the more reason to come home."

"Mom," I whisper, "I have access to research databases here that the library doesn't even have."

"What do you need those for?"

"Because," I say slowly, surprising myself as the words leave my mouth, "I'm going to write about this case."

"Write about it?" Mom shrieks. "You?"

"I do have a degree in journalism."

"Mmm."

Is she questioning my competence or my innocence?

"Remember when we used to watch *Rockford Files*, Jess?"

"What?"

"On TV. Maybe I can help."

Okay, time to put a stop to this. I promise I'll come for Sunday dinner—I haven't in months—and get off the phone.

Only, what now? There's nothing to work on. Except the story I pretended I'm working on. Maybe I do need to write it, to prove my innocence, not only to the world at large but to myself.

I need to find someone who knew Ted. But who? He broke up with his boyfriend a year ago, and I wouldn't know how to reach him.

Think.

Nothing comes.

A Post-It sails into my cube. *How about we meet now?*

It's Sofia—our way of communicating on the sly—and I respond immediately.

See you there in 10.

10

LYDIA

gent Cole parks the Bureau sedan against the curb, windshield framing a bruised sky over Oakland's main hill. She sits for a moment, engine ticking as it cools, replaying her interview with Jessica Greer. She'd come in all vinegar and eye contact, then started babbling like a crick. Lydia should've shut it down sooner.

She exhales and looks up the hill at Kris Novak's address. White siding, black shutters, wedged between two nearly identical structures. Novak's property is the best maintained, but this part of Oakland is a shithole. All student rentals with trash everywhere, front yards trampled flat. Hard to picture a newspaper editor living here.

Overhead, the last rays of the day seep between rowhouses and telephone wires. She's not ready for these shorter days. Never is.

She thinks of Justin down at Virginia Tech and wishes, not for the first time, he'd chosen Pitt. Closer, cheaper, safer. She could've met him for gyros on Forbes, kept an eye on him, maybe kept herself from feeling like a guest in her own home. She should've called Alice when she was at the paper, told her not to hold dinner. But Alice will have seen the news—she hopes. Always goes better if Alice works out on her own why Lydia's late. Powell knows where she is, told her to keep quiet about ricin till it's confirmed by the lab. "All we have to go on so far is the self-reporting," he'd said. "The last thing we need is public hysteria."

Was that a dig?

Doubtful, she thinks as she trudges up the concrete steps leading to the wooden porch steps. But it's going to come up if she's asking Novak about his work. Has to be quick so she can make the press conference at five. Then another debriefing. She looks at her watch. She could still make it home before seven.

She pushes the doorbell but hears no sound. *Not the start I was hoping for.* The tatty screen door creaks as it opens. Lydia reaches for the incongruently delicate knocker and taps. No response to that either. She pounds with her fist. The mailbox is labeled with a piece of masking tape that reads NOVAK in Sharpie, so she's pretty sure she's in the right place. She's about to start pounding again when the door flies open.

"Jesus, Mary and Joseph, give an old lady a break, would ya?" The woman who answers is built like a school bus, white hair piled like a crown on her head, a thin cotton smock over a faded housedress.

"Mrs. Novak?"

The woman knits her eyebrows together. Did Chen give her the wrong address?

"I'm Special Agent Lydia Cole, FBI. I'm investigating the attempted murder of Ted Harvey. Is, ah... do you know where I could find Kris Novak?"

The woman looks ready to slam the door in her face when a voice calls from behind. "I got it, Ma."

Kris Novak appears from the gloom, nudging his mother aside. He still lives with his *mother*? She can't wait to tell Alice.

"Can I help you?" he asks as he steps onto the porch.

Interesting. Most people don't want to chat with agents on their front porch, to say nothing of that little shove to his mom. But Cole has no reason to force her way into his house. Not yet. This is mostly for background. She read his articles—a lengthy piece on domestic terrorism and a recap of a talk by Boris Korczak, a former double agent who claims the CIA tried to kill him using ricin—but found little in either about the poison itself. She's only there on the off chance that Greer's story checks out.

Novak steps into the light, pale and slender and squinting as he pushes strings of hair off his face. Reminds her of a mole caught above ground. He pops open two aluminum lawn chairs. "Our parking chairs." He grins, transforming into something strangely adorable. Almost like Justin, though Kris must be twice her son's age.

"Look, Mr. Novak, I know you're no longer affiliated with the *City News*," she begins, once they've settled into their chairs. "But I'm trying to understand the dynamics of the place and I could really use your help."

He shrugs, pulling a smug, sure-whatever-you-say face. He knows something.

"You left the paper"—she pretends to check her notes— "about a month ago. That right?"

"Yeah."

"And this was right before Ted Harvey was hired?"

"Yup, that was after I left."

"But you knew he was being considered."

Novak's knee starts bouncing. "I wouldn't put it that way."

"How would you put it, Mr. Novak?"

"I... I mean he... What I'm trying to say is, the writing's been on the wall since MacCormac bought the paper a year ago. First it was the splashy new logo, decorating the office, like that. Then he starts talking about *broadening demographics*. I'm like, brother man, are you for real? I mean, we're alt news. What's alternative about that?"

"And you're saying Mr. Harvey was part of that?"

"Well, kinda. I threw his name out there at some point after I'd already decided to leave."

"Even though"—she squints at her notes again—"you hired Jessica Greer for that role. Correct?"

"Yeah. I knew she'd have a following. That girl is whack. Comes up with some crazy shit. Have you read any of her columns?"

Lydia has not read her work, needs to put someone at the station on that asap. "What do you mean by *whack*?"

"Just like, her wild takes on stuff. Unexpected angles. That's why I hired her—she sees things other people don't." His knee has stopped dancing. "Plus she has this whole Gen X slacker thing going that readers eat up."

"How well do you know Jessica? Personally?"

"A bit. We grab beers sometimes. She talks a lot about her job, some dude she had a crush on there, her mom's business."

"Did you tell her about your recommendation for her replacement?"

"Nah. For one, I didn't think they'd actually hire him. Also, Greer's been trying to ditch that column for ages. She'll find something else to write. Or maybe she'll go to the *Voice*." He shrugs again. "It's just a little side gig."

A little side gig someone committed murder over, Lydia thinks. "Did you ever talk about your work?"

"Yeah, sure. I guess." Kris tilts his head. "The thing is, I don't think this has anything to do with Ted."

"You don't think Ted Harvey was poisoned on purpose." Lydia does not phrase it as a question. She has a feeling he's going to tell her his theory.

"It's all in the book I'm writing." Novak scoots his lawn chair a little closer, lowering his voice. "It's not just MacCormac. Alt-weeklies are being bought up everywhere, corporate toadies are taking over to squeeze out critical voices in independent news."

"Hang on." Lydia pulls out her notepad, making a show of clicking her pen. "You're suggesting this poisoning was some sort of larger operation to chill voices in alternative media?"

Novak's face softens into a broad smile. "Yeah, man, that's exactly what I'm saying. Truth to power is the real threat. That's why I had to leave. I didn't want to turn out like that whistleblower, Markov. Wind up on the wrong side of an assassination attempt for my beliefs."

Lydia keeps her expression neutral. Could Novak be her killer? "Why would you recommend Ted Harvey for a job at a paper where you yourself didn't want to work? Unless you have it out for Mr. Harvey?"

"It's not like that at all. I don't really know Ted, only his work. He's a real ball buster. The perfect eff you to MacCormac."

"And that's it?" Lydia says.

"Are you asking me about the psych ward?"

"The psych ward?" Lydia repeats.

Kris's eyes turn to slits. "You don't know about her background? How after she found her father swinging by a rope in the family garage she wound up in the loony bin? Isn't she your lead suspect?"

Lydia takes a moment to consider which is the more important revelation, Greer's mental health history or the leak this case has. "Where did you hear Ms. Greer is a suspect, Mr. Novak?"

She can have Chen dig into Greer's background. No reason to let on that this is the first she's heard of Greer's alleged psychiatric stay.

Before Kris can respond, Lydia's pager belts out a series of high-pitched chirps. She pushes her jacket aside and peers at the display: 412 411. *Damn.* That's their code, means Alice wants to know where she is. *Now.*

She releases her blazer. "You were about to tell me why you think Greer is a suspect?"

Novak's knee fidgets. He scratches his head. "Ethan Silver, I think?"

She'd have to speak to Silver about that. He should know better than to discuss the details of an ongoing investigation. "Are you two in the habit of talking?"

Novak offers his signature nod/shrug.

"When did you first start researching ricin specifically?"

"I haven't been, not really." Novak shifts in his seat. "Dina, you know, she's helping research my book."

"Dina Kowalski?"

"Yeah, right. She's—" Novak's leg slows. "Are you saying Harvey was poisoned with *ricin?* Holy shit. That is something."

Lydia scowls. The cynicism in this town. "But you know about ricin, how it can be used? She was getting the information for you. Your book."

"Do I need a lawyer?"

Shit. Novak just went as cold as it's feeling out on this porch, and Lydia needs to move if she's going to make it back to headquarters for a debrief before the press conference. She'll keep an eye on him, but he doesn't fit the profile. He's got the paranoid grievance down, but then he lit up talking about Greer like he was a proud older brother. Men who try to bring down empires don't leave the research to someone else.

"That's up to you, Mr. Novak. But you're not under arrest." She stands, stowing her notepad in her coat's inside pocket and fishing out a card. "If you think of anything else—anyone who had access to Ted's mail, anyone who might have wanted to harm him—you call this number."

"Sure, yeah. Of course." He pockets the card without looking at it.

"And Mr. Novak?" She pauses at the top of the porch steps. "Don't leave town."

Back in her car, Lydia looks up toward the porch, but Novak's already retreated, the screen door clapping shut behind him. Odd guy. Between the stringy hair and beanpole body, he's not conventionally attractive, but he does have a certain charisma. Didn't set off her gaydar, but she'd guess he never thinks about sex. His only passion seems to be for conspiracy theories. Almost had her convinced.

The psych ward, though? That she hadn't known.

So much for home by seven.

11

———

JESSICA

I hear Sofia leaving her cubicle for our rendezvous. To give her a minute, and because I can't resist, I check the wires again. God forbid, but they might cut off my access. I need to get in what research I can, I tell myself.

A few keystrokes later and I'm in the *Pittsburgh Voice* archives, reading Ted's latest—a withering review of Broadway Series's "Annie Get Your Gun." Nothing jumps out there. Ted is known for his hatchet jobs. It's the tagline under his byline that stands out. "Tragedy Without Witness Is Just Suffering." I'd seen it before, so pretentious, so Ted. I write it down anyway.

Time to go. Sofia's already positioned herself on the fainting couch.

"Sorry I'm late," I begin, positioning myself against the armrest.

"Are you kidding me right now?" Sof sits up and locks eyes. "What happened? Are you...?"

"Guilty?"

"Eres loco? No!" she says. "But, I mean. Are you really a suspect?"

"I don't think? I'd be in custody if I was?" I say, but I'm not sure.

Sofia frowns. "I have no clue. What did they want?"

"It started weird. First of all, they weren't expecting me. Like, at *all*."

"You went to them?"

I nod, eager to move past this. "Then they tell me Ted's been poisoned by ricin—"

"Ricin? They haven't put that out yet."

Something in me deflates.

"What?" she asks.

I can't not tell Sof. "It's just, they freaked out when I brought it up—"

"What do you mean *you* brought it up. Brought up what?"

"They were asking all these questions, like what do I know about chemistry. Chemistry? Me?"

Sofia bites her lower lip. "But you mentioned ricin? First?"

"I know. But they were talking about Ted's condition, you know, like when they show evidence photos to elicit a reaction? Least that's what I thought. For whatever reason I remembered them from Kris Novak's article in *City News*. Remember?"

Sofia shrugs.

"Anyway, that's not even the worst part."

Sofia grabs my knees. "There's more?"

I describe how I blurted out a whole Mon body dump scene, and unbelievably, Sofia starts laughing.

"What's funny?"

"It's just..." She can barely speak for laughing. "Of course you did. That sounds like the plots to half the *Murder She Wrote* episodes we've been discussing every Monday morning for the past two years."

For the first time all day I laugh, a dry crackly thing that sounds a little desperate, even to me. Soon we're both laughing, like shipwreck survivors.

"Did we watch that together?" I ask.

Sofia sobers immediately. "Well no, I can't think of that exact one but..."

"But you know I had nothing to do with this, right? They can't convict me for nothing."

Sof raises her brows and looks to the floor. "It's good to be white."

"Okay, I deserved that," I say. "But I don't think the color of my skin matters to Agent Cole. She has a total hard-on for me."

"Well, you did mention ricin."

I bite my lip. Maybe telling Sof about this was a bad idea. Why *did* ricin come right to mind?

"Sorry, I didn't mean to..." Sof touches my shoulder. "What are you going to do?"

"I need to find out how Ted's doing."

Sof smiles coyly as she slides a cell phone out of her jacket pocket.

"When did you get that?"

"My brother gave it to me ages ago, doesn't think it's safe me living in the city."

I eye the chunky device as Sofia dials 4-1-1, gets the number and hands the phone over.

"No, you do the honors," I say. "Agent Cole would have a field day if she found out I'd called the hospital. Tell them you're a fact-checker for *Pittsburgh Daily News* and you need an update on Ted Harvey's condition."

"Ooh, that's good," Sof says. After a few transfers, she winks at me over the phone. "I can hold."

My pulse quickens. They're either looking for actual information about his condition or for someone to break the news that he's dead.

"Not out of the woods? Can you be more specific? We want to get a jump on the five o'clock press briefing—" She purses her lips. "It was their press office. The guy hung up. But the good news is, as of right now he's alive."

"Press conference? Nice touch."

Sof looks at her watch. "I've got to wrap up a few things before I head over."

"Head over where?"

"To the press conference, goof. You didn't think I made that up, did you? I'm not that quick. I saw the announcement on the ticker."

She means the large screen televisions Zimmerman keeps on all hours of the day and night, showing news programs around the world with a running ticker of local bulletins at the bottom. "They set that up fast," I say.

"They want to make the nightly news, I'm sure," Sof says. "So... I should go."

"Show-off." I frown, oddly jealous that Sofia has work to do. But also, a little tweaked. I've never thought of Sofia as *not that quick.*

"Did you hear? I'm off billable accounts until further notice."

Sof is nodding before I finish my thought. She heard. Everyone probably has. "So, are you going to come?" she asks.

"Where? To the presser? Are you nuts?"

"Suit yourself," Sof says, dark eyes flashing. "I wouldn't miss it."

I feel abandoned. I don't know which is worse: I've been fired from two jobs and am a suspect in an attempted poisoning. *Drama queen,* my brother would say. *You haven't been fired from anything, and if they had anything on you, you'd be in a cell.*

"I'll come to yours after work and fill you in," Sofia says as we head back to our cubicles.

. . .

BACK AT MY DESK, I have nothing to do but indulge my inner sadist by scrolling the wires obsessively. The one from the *Post-Gazette* is the absolute worst.

"Does Pittsburgh Have Its Own Mail Murderess?"

A nickname already?

The Mail Murderess. They don't use my name in the piece, thank God, because the moniker has a Son-of-Sam-level tabloid ring. Once you get a name like that, it sticks. The nickname becomes the story. Would Amy Fisher have garnered the same international media attention as the Long Island Lolita had?

I look down at my keyboard. The A, S, and R keys rubbed illegible from years of typing press releases about cardboard boxes and canned food. This desk was supposed to be temporary, a paycheck while I figured out what I wanted to do with my life. I should've had a better plan. Now I'm trapped here, can't pitch my client stories, can't pitch my own stories, can't do anything but refresh wires. Wait for my name to become a punchline.

I type a few keywords into LexisNexis—Novak AND ricin AND Unabomber—but the search returns nothing. I try only ricin AND Unabomber. Still nothing. No wonder Cole lost her mind when I made the connection.

UPI has more detail. Apparently the brownie sent to Ted's office was wrapped in *City News* stationery. Read, "Congratulations on Your New Job," in icing.

Reuters lists the symptoms he reported in his 9-1-1 call, which now sound like they could be anything. *I've written too many pamphlets for SmithKline Beecham.*

AP has dug up a photo. Very grainy. Judging from the clothes it's from the 1980s. Ted Harvey and Mary Beth Purcel? How could I forget about her? She's the artistic director at City Theatre, knows everyone in town, including Ted it appears.

She'll have information. If she'll talk to me. There's only one way to find out.

As I'm packing up, my desk phone rings. I almost don't answer, till I see the caller ID: *City News.*

My hand hovers over the receiver. Why would anyone from the paper be calling me? Unless Ethan's changed his story. Or it's one of the FBI people. Or they found something.

I let it ring. Twice. Three times.

What if they found another suspect?

On the fourth ring, I grab it.

"Zimmerman Public Relations, this is Jessica Greer. How may I—"

"Hi, Jessica. This is Dina Kowalski from *City News*? We've met a few times. I'm the fact-checker."

That quirky chick with the cat-eye glasses who kept hovering around during the FBI interrogation.

"I hope this isn't a bad time," she continues, her voice higher, almost apologetic. "I just... I wanted to make sure you were okay. That was really intense."

"I'm fine," I say, though I'm not sure why she'd care.

"Good. That's good."

She goes silent, and I don't know what to say, so we're both quiet.

"I also wanted to say," she continues, like that was normal. "I've been helping Kris Novak with his book, and, well, I don't think you did it. Everyone here is talking about it, but I told them there's no way. You seem too nice."

Her words should be comforting. Instead, they make my skin crawl.

"Thanks," I manage. "I appreciate that."

"Of course! Well, if you need anything—research help, or whatever—I'm really good at finding things. It's kind of my specialty." She laughs, too bright. "Okay, I'll let you go. Bye!"

The line clicks off.

I stand there, receiver in hand, staring.

She doesn't think I did it. Which means she's been thinking about whether I did it.

A fact-checker I've met for maybe two minutes in total is now thinking about me. Along with everyone else at *City News*. I hang up and head out.

How many other people I don't know are thinking about me right now?

WITNESS STATEMENTS —
FBI CASE NO. 95-PGH-0047

Chad Whittaker, Director, Three Rivers Cultural Trust:

Mary Beth called the meeting to discuss the critics pulling out of our shows. Yes, that same day. Seemed rather odd, but then, you know, needs must.

We all knew what happened. How he'd taken the new job. I believe he sent something around. I assumed everyone knew.

Mary Beth Purcel, Artistic Director, Pittsburgh City Theatre:

Can we get one thing straight though? I barely knew the man. I don't know where the photo of us at his parents' funeral came from, but it was the most time I'd ever spent with him, unless you count sitting in the same darkened theater. Which I don't. Strike that from the recording please. All I mean is, the only thing I knew about this situation in advance was that he was going to *City News*. It wasn't until the critic from the major daily called me personally to cancel that I called the meeting.

I did not set the tone of the meeting. They started without me. Other than the Prantl's almond tortes, the Trust could hardly be bothered by the poisoning. Said it was an inconvenience.

Julia Rothschild, Artistic Director, Pittsburgh Ballet:

When I suggested flowers, Chad asked to whom? Said Ted's review of their Twyla Tharp series caused Heinz to pull their advertising for the year. How was I supposed to know that?

It was all in such poor taste. Philip took it from there, said Ted would recover right away if he knew we were talking about him. Only got worse after that.

Michael Adler, Producer, Broadway Series:

I said I'd bet dollars to donuts that Ted would heal immediately if he knew he was making us squirm collectively. That was a comment on his personality. His review of our last show was worse. Said he wished Annie would get her gun already and put us all out of our misery. I think he's the violent one.

Philip Poluni, Assistant, Pittsburgh Symphony:

I came up with the joint ad campaign, "You be the judge." With all our logos. Of course there were jokes. *The show the critics are dying to see.* Like that. So what?

Russell Morris, Pittsburgh Opera:

We all feel terrible for Ted, and our condolences go out to his family. Of course we agreed to the joint ad, we're team players. But ultimately, I can't see this being more than a blip. And yes, I knew about the new job. Couldn't say how.

Bill Finch, Mystery Dinner Theater:

Poison isn't a crime of passion, is it? Not your Othello, not your stabbings in the dark. No, poison is… curated. A long game. But we're not living in a play here. Domestic bioterrorism is the threat. I—

No, I didn't know Ted personally. He refused to review our shows. But I had heard he was changing jobs.

12

JESSICA

The smell of sawdust assaults my nose as I swing open the backstage door at Pittsburgh's City Theatre Company. They're deep in prep for their upcoming show, *Crimes of the Heart*. Nothing says "make your annual donation" like a play about atonement.

I head right to Mary Beth's office, but she's not in. Odd. Especially now. Out in the lobby I can hear them rehearsing. The theater door is open. Maybe she's watching?

Onstage stand three women and one man, all holding their scripts.

"That's what I like about it, Chick, taking a drag off of death."

I try to recall the character's name. Lucinda? Lucinda takes a deep hit off her prop cigarette, and I could swear I smell it.

"Mmm! Gives me a sense of controlling my own destiny. What power! What exhilaration! Want a drag?"

Maybe I should start smoking, I think, as I feel a tap on my shoulder.

"Come with me."

It's Mary Beth, leading me back though the lobby, past the concessions and coat check, the restrooms, and into her cramped office. Place feels like a vault, file cabinets crammed behind her, stacks of scripts cover every surface, and cast photos dot the walls to offer a visual timeline of City Theater through decades of productions. She gestures to the chair wedged in front of her desk.

Despite the frumpy, matronly air she cultivates, Mary Beth is a formidable player in Pittsburgh's theatrical community. The kind of presence you underestimate—soft around the edges, from her bad perm to her scuffed loafers—because she's got the kind of authority that doesn't announce itself, more like, slithers beneath the surface. You don't see her coming before she's looped around your neck, squeezing.

She knows everyone in town too, not only in the theater community. If there's anyone with dirt on Ted, it's her. The woman has probably got a file cabinet full of suspects who aren't me.

Mary Beth leans back in her chair, looking down her nose at me as usual. "So, Jessica Greer. What brings you here?"

She doesn't offer her hand, instead, peers out toward the hallway in a way that tells me this isn't her first conversation today about Ted Harvey. Like the police have been and she's wondering if they've followed me here now.

Or the FBI.

Either that or she isn't used to seeing me in sweats. I took the T home to get my car and changed while I was there, ditching the navy pantsuit and piling my hair into a scrunchie.

"I'm sure you heard about Ted," I say.

"Yes, I..." She adjusts her glasses. "Are you going to keep writing theater?"

For a moment I think she's being kind. Then I realize she must know I'm not here about my column. My former column. The column Ted apparently had before I even knew it was gone.

"Right now I'm working on something else," I say, technically true. In my mind anyway. "I'm writing about what happened to Ted."

Something expands in my chest when I say it. For the first time all day, I feel a small measure of control return.

Mary Beth studies me. "I see," she finally says.

I lean back like this is all perfectly normal.

"You and Ted were close?" I say.

Her reaction is immediate. She drops her pen on her blotter and leans back, crossing her arms over her ample chest. The move pushes her fraying sweater sleeves halfway up her fore-arms. I notice what looks like a burn on her left wrist. But the pen had been in her right hand.

"Well, I know Ted took your job," she says.

A dull pressure blooms somewhere behind my eyes. Trying to wipe away the gut punch, I wave my hand in the air between us.

"That's all been sorted out. I... Wait, when did you know Ted was taking my job?"

Mary Beth looks down at her desk. "I don't know."

She is a craptastic liar. Worse yet, it's starting to look like everyone in town knew I'd lost my job before me. Which is humiliating. But also proves I had nothing to do with what happened to Ted. I had no motive until after he was in the hospital.

Besides, if Mary Beth thought I didn't know Ted was taking my job, she would've called me immediately to tell me herself.

"Come on, Mary Beth. You and Ted were obviously friends before you started working here."

Mary Beth frowns. "If you're referring to the photograph that has somehow surfaced, from Ted's parents' funeral, you've got it all wrong. We both graduated from Otterbein, Class of '83. But I wouldn't say we were close." She sits back in her chair. "Listen, Jessica, I'm not sure I should be talking to you."

Ted's *parents*? As in both of them? Is she trying to throw me off? She might be suspicious of me, but I have every reason to question her, too. I'm sure Ted's reviews have hurt her bottom line.

"Why do you say you shouldn't be talking to me?"

"The police came by." She purses her lips, her cheeks turning a rose color. "They were asking about you."

"Really? Just me?"

Mary Beth peels her glasses from her face. "I'm not sure what you're saying, but I'm trying to get our season underway right now. What do I know about Ted's personal life?"

Another blatant lie. Mary Beth Purcel makes it her business to know something about everyone's personal life. I wonder, briefly, if she'd helped orchestrate Ted's move.

"So the police didn't ask about your season closer last year? The one Ted panned."

Now she begins to pick at her cuffs, which must be what she does in polite

company to avoid biting her chomped-to-the-quick nails. "You both did, as I recall. But no, they didn't mention that. They wanted to know what I presume you're here to ask, whether Ted had any enemies."

Turning her back to me, she slides open a filing cabinet and starts digging in a drawer, effectively preventing me from asking.

"Remember this?" She swivels back around, page aloft. "I'd say you both have your fair share of enemies."

Before I look at what she has in her hand, I can't help but notice the organization of the file drawer—dates and names, all typed. Does the woman ever leave this place?

My eyes fall to a copy of my first review for *City News*. How that piece had tortured me. Such an awful little bunch of plays, part of City Theater's annual summer festival. I hated criticizing them—what did I know? I'd long since learned my unvarnished opinion was precisely what Kris wanted. Not the academic take. It's why I scarcely ever read Ted's pieces. They were either dull or mean. Usually both. Why bother?

"I don't have any—" I begin, but I know she's right. I've made enemies, starting with Mary Beth. She was furious about my review of their *Odd Couple* production, but it was so oddly contemporized, I had to write a *contemporary* response to the play's casual sexism. My attack was on Neil Simon, not the production completely. That whole aspect I'd ignored completely. Hence her objection, and one of the reasons I want to get out of this gig. Before I had to review them, I loved going out to see plays. I consoled myself thinking that at least my reviews got people talking about theater.

"You're right, Mary Beth. It's not possible to write criticism without attracting enemies. But theater enemies?" I grab the edge of my chair, lean forward. "We might hate hard, but we're arty people. Are we vengeful and petty? Sure. But we take our revenge in other ways. We're not *actual* killers."

Mary Beth squints at me, slams the page on her desk and leans forward, talking low. "You don't get it. Ted doesn't make enemies the way you might think. He finds your weak spot and he uses it against you." Her voice returns to its normal register. "You really should read his reviews."

It's a struggle not to react. How can she tell I don't read his stuff? And who's exploiting weakness now?

"All I can tell you is the same thing I told the police—Ted Harvey was an only child, grew up in Bloomfield, and still lives in his family's home, though both his parents passed away in a car accident when he was in college."

"That's terrible!"

"That's how I ended up at his funeral. He asked me to take him. How could I have said no?"

I nod.

"I don't know of anyone he's *close* close to. He hasn't really dated since his boyfriend moved to San Francisco without him last year, but it wasn't anything explosive. As far as I know they're not in contact. The end."

"Like I said, that's a lot more than nothing."

"Is it?" she asks. "I think it's sad more than anything."

A chill runs through me. How would Mary Beth describe me? *Lives alone with her cat. Outside of work, her main social activity is visiting her mother. Has a penchant for unrequited love.* Pathetic?

"Are you sure? Because I vaguely recall once, during inter-mission at *West Side Story*, Ted and I joked that the best thing about theater was how tragic all the love stories were."

Mary Beth purses her lips.

I'm sure the investigators asked these questions, and that the information is right there, ready to come out. But she only picks up her pen, taps it on the end of her blotter.

"Maybe you should take that to the police. I'd love to help, but I just have so much to do here."

"But you know his name, right?"

"Didn't I say? It's Ben. Ben Jones. Good luck with that."

I'm seeing myself out when Mary Beth summons me. "Jessica? Next time you want to talk—whether it's about Ted or anything else—call first. Don't show up unannounced. You're lucky I was here. I'm just back from a Trust meeting."

Her tone isn't hostile, but it's not friendly either. Message received: I'm not welcome here.

As I'm seeing myself out, I wonder if I should've told her I was going to keep writing theater. Would she have been less frosty?

I'm halfway down the block when I spot Ethan a few store-fronts ahead, pushing open the door to the Beehive.

Perfect. He has to know more than he let on at lunch.

I pass my car and hurry down the street before I can talk myself out of it.

Inside the Beehive, the air smells like burnt espresso and cigarettes. Ethan has already claimed a table by the window. A laptop sits open in front of him, and he's nursing a coffee like he plans to stay awhile.

And he's changed clothes. Again.

Now in a gray flannel shirt, he's also switched out his eyeglasses, swapping octagonal frames for a pair that's rectangular. Are they even prescription? What is this, his South Side camouflage? How many clothes can one man carry?

"Hey, mind if I join you?" I can tell he's annoyed but don't care as I pull out a chair. "Some day, huh?"

Why do I sound like such an idiot around him? I'm seconds away from commenting on the warm fall we're having.

His smile is strained as he opens his Toshiba. "I have to get back to the office. Couldn't get anything done there this afternoon, and we still have to put the paper to bed at midnight or we won't have an issue. We can't afford that so, sorry, I can't really talk."

"Real quick, while you're waiting for your machine to boot up, I just have one question."

It takes all my will not to ask about the investigation. About Ted. About why the FBI thinks I'm a suspect in a federal poisoning case.

But this is not the moment.

Instead I pull out my notebook.

"Would you email me your home address?" I write down my Zimmerman email. "I'm working on the invite list for Zimmerman's holiday party. Very exclusive event."

Ethan stares at his screen like he's trying to will it to life.

"You can just send it to the office."

Oh my God. Does he think I'm coming on to him?

"Oh no," I say quickly. "We don't do that."

We?

Who is we?

"We can only invite so many people," I continue, digging myself deeper. "So the list is... confidential. We don't send these out to offices."

He looks like he's about to protest. Then something changes his mind.

"Sure," he says.

Ignoring my paper, he scribbles an address on a napkin and hands it to me as he stands.

Then, unexpectedly, he leans down and kisses my cheek.

"Don't forget to send me that dating column idea."

Dating column. *Right.*

I'd completely forgotten about that.

13

DINA

Dina Kowalski checks her watch—4:55 pm, barely on time, the parking was a nightmare—as she flashes her *City News* ID. Cameras are lined along the back wall, the operators still setting up their sightlines. The print guys, reeking of cigarettes, are behind the radio reporters and their handheld recorders. Come Monday, she imagines, this room will be packed with national outlets.

She finds her spot on the back wall and pulls out her notepad. Her pen is dry. She's digging into her bag for a substitute when in walks Candy Watson with her expertly coiffed hair. Now why would Channel 6's vigilante reporter be here?

"Stick to fact-checking, Dina," she recalls Kris Novak saying to her once. "You don't have an eye for news." Killed her crush at least.

This had not been her plan for the day. What she'd wanted to do was man her desk, monitor what everyone said after their interviews. Soon as the agents detained Jessica, though, everything changed. These people have no idea what they're missing about Ted Harvey.

Sofia Reyes slips in thirty seconds after Candy, out of breath.

Dina clocks her the way she clocks everything. Not by staring, she doesn't need to. Always positions herself to monitor flow. A kind of tracking her father taught her about. They'd met exactly twice, in passing at the Zimmerman holiday party.

She's a possible candidate.

The room is already full. In addition to Channel 6, KDKA, WPXI, and WTAE turned out. There's a clutch of radio reporters in the front, their handheld recorders aloft. AP is here. As is Gene Collins, the *Post-Gazette*'s crime reporter, crisp in his bow tie, flipping through his steno pad like a man who never sits still. Beside him is Pete Zelinski, from the *Trib*'s newsroom. Bit of a loose cannon, that one. Dina knows them all, not personally but by their bylines. Collins is precise and relentless. He's her man. She sidles up next to him as the cameras home in on the podium.

At 5:00 pm exactly, Eddie Powell barrels in. He has the bearing of a man who's used to getting where he's going before anyone realizes he's moving—a kind of controlled momentum, like a ship. Behind him trail two younger agents, a tall Black man Dina doesn't recognize, and Lydia Cole.

Powell doesn't waste much time on his welcome. "As you all know, earlier this morning, Theodore Harvey, a local theater critic, opened mail containing a lethal biological agent. Mr. Harvey remains hospitalized in critical condition. The incident was reported to us at midday, shortly after paramedics arrived on the scene, after it was confirmed by Mr. Harvey that the lethal agent was delivered by U.S. mail."

Dina strains to hear the undertone. He's reading from a statement, but it corroborates what the hospital had told her. Though they'd said "wasn't out of the woods." Does critical condition mean he's gotten worse? No matter. A federal crime is bad enough with or without a dead body.

Gene Collins takes notes with quick, practiced strokes.

Unlike other reporters, he makes no effort to hide whatever he's writing. Dina would guess he thinks he's the sole person in the room who can read shorthand.

He's wrong.

"At this time we have several promising leads and expect swift resolution," Powell continues. "The Bureau is treating this as a targeted attack on an individual, possibly motivated by professional or personal grievance."

Professional grievance? Dina's stomach seizes. Is that code for Jessica Greer? How are they so stuck on her?

"Agent Powell?" Collins stands, pen poised. "Gene Collins, *Post-Gazette.* Do you have any suspects yet?"

Powell offers a kind of smile, but it doesn't reach his eyes. Very patronizing. That does half the work for her.

"We're exploring several lines of inquiry, but we have nothing to release at this time." He points at the *Trib* guy, signaling their importance. He might need a little help with the case, but he's good at the politics. "Mr. Zelinski?"

"Do you think there's any connection to recent domestic terrorism cases like Oklahoma City?" Zelinski asks.

The energy in the room shifts dramatically. Timothy McVeigh is fresh on everyone's mind. The FBI can't botch this one on top of that.

Powell rubs his brow, drawing attention to the perspiration dotting his forehead. "While we can't comment on specific methodologies, we can assure the public that we're applying all resources necessary and we will bring this perpetrator to justice."

He's not mentioning the ricin? They'd been told, scolded really, not to talk about the investigation. But why hide that when it could help bring the culprit to justice? Why, it's central to the case.

Outrageously, the rest of the room takes his non-comment in stride.

The floor is now open. The KDKA guy raises his hand.

"Agent Powell. Given that the victim is a journalist, are you concerned about First Amendment implications? Attacks on the press?"

Powell's face twitches, he's recalibrating. Had it not occurred to the man this would be a question?

And why is no one demanding to know more about the biological agent used? Between the World Trade Center in '93, the Sarin gas incidents in Tokyo, and the Oklahoma City bombing earlier this year, how can they not be more curious? Dina wants to raise her hand but can't risk being booted from the room.

"Mr. Harvey's work as a cultural critic is an aspect of our investigation."

Cultural critic. Not journalist. Not press. Not even theater. Powell's distancing the Bureau from any press-freedom narrative. Same as he's downplaying the terrorism angle. Dina can see what he's doing, but what are these so-called journalists doing? Kris would've come to this briefing. Ethan's at some coffee shop on the South Side, *posing* as the editor of an alt-weekly.

A hand shoots up, followed by a poof of hair. "Was Ted Harvey in a romantic relationship? Statistically, murders are most often committed by someone close to the victim."

Count on Candy to come up with the salacious angle. Though she doesn't mind if they go after Ben. The timing looks bad for him, that's for sure.

Powell repeats his non-answer about exploring all lines of inquiry, adding, "As of this time, this is not a murder investigation."

"You also mentioned professional grievance," the reporter continues, undaunted. "Are you suggesting this is tied to Ted

Harvey's job at *Pittsburgh Voice*, where he's been for the last ten years or so, or to his job at *City News*, where I believe his first day there was... today?"

Dina sits up tall to try and get a better view of Powell handling this question.

"It's like I said, Mrs. Watson—"

"It's Ms.," she interrupts.

A titter goes up around the room. Dina decides then and there to rethink her feelings about Candy.

Powell restates how Harvey's work is but one aspect of their investigation, and it's as if a pressure valve opens in the room. Even the cameras lower slightly. He peers across the assembly's heads, so relieved to be done his smile is almost genuine. "If there's nothing further..."

That's it?

On impulse, Dina scribbles on her notebook. *Ask about ricin,* she writes. Puts it in his lap.

He looks up at her.

"Then I'd like to thank you all for—"

"I've got one more." Collins stands.

Dina retrieves her note pad.

Powell extends a hand with the lukewarmest of smiles. "Mr. Collins."

"Is this another ricin case? Like the Minnesota Patriots?"

Dina's impressed. She hadn't even mentioned the Minnesota Patriots's plot to poison federal agents. Also this year. Also with ricin.

"As I say, we're not—"

"Agent Powell, poisons like ricin can be produced using basic kitchen chemistry. Should residents be worried? Are you concerned about copycats?"

Powell's glare could boil water. "As I said, the safety of our community is our priority. We will bring this to a resolution.

This is why we call these things briefings. We've got work to do. Until we have definitive lab results, we're not releasing any specifics. In the meantime, do not open any unfamiliar packages."

Powell points to a placard.

"If you have any leads, report them to this number. If you receive any unfamiliar packages, same number. This number is for any information regarding this case. The FBI is offering a ten-thousand-dollar reward for information leading to arrest and conviction."

Collins raises his eyebrows. "Agent Powell." He stands again. "That's a substantial reward to release so quickly. What happened?"

Powell's smile tightens. "As you all have pointed out, bioterrorism crimes such as these cannot be tolerated. The Bureau believes in providing incentives for public cooperation from the outset. Thank you all for coming."

With nothing further he exits, subordinates trailing behind. Dina doesn't move, but she sees Cole note her presence. Sees a flash of frustration so naked it's almost intimate. What else had she wanted to say?

"Thanks for the tip."

Dina jumps in her chair. It's Gene Collins. Before he can ask who she is or where she got it, Dina scrambles for the exit, almost colliding with Sofia Reyes. Sofia has curly hair, big earrings, and her smile is genuine. Dina steps aside and lets her pass. Sofia doesn't seem to register her at all.

That's fine. That's good.

She heads for the stairs and exits through the side door, stepping into the late afternoon chill. It's deadline day, but she's not going back to *City News*. Not now. Ten thousand dollars is a lot of money. Even if she has to split it.

14

JESSICA

"Turn up the TV, Sof," I yell from the kitchen, where I've started the dishwasher. The kitchen was a mess, but I managed to pull off a strategic clean after leaving City Theatre, before the work wife arrived. "It's almost six, and this has got to be the lead story."

I rush out to my living room. Sof is sitting on the floor behind my unfinished pine hope chest—which doubles as my coffee table—her back pressed to my sofa. I picked both pieces up in the Ikea scratch-and-dent room for fifty bucks, and I've convinced myself the read is shabby-chic as opposed to flat-broke. The fall night has turned chilly, so I flick on the little gas-fireplace heater I splurged on at Construction Junction. The pizza guy should be here any minute.

World headlines roll by on the screen—the pope's impending visit, discovery of a rare bird fossil, another stall in Israeli peace talks—before the anchor finally tees up the lead local story.

"But the big news tonight: a federal investigation here in Pittsburgh. Could your mail be deadly? Stay tuned. We'll tell you how to stay safe right after these words."

"Good Lord." I groan. "The news is so gross."

"Right? Makes me feel better for peddling stories about recycling," Sof says, even as we both stare at the TV like obedient lab rats.

The commercials aren't any better. Some luge-like cars rocket past historic landmarks while Johnny Rotten drones about getting your kicks on Route 66.

"The guy from the Sex Pistols is pimping Mountain Dew? Wow, that is lame." Sof snorts.

"This may be worse," I say, pointing at Imam shilling for Wendy's. "Pu-lease. She's never even eaten a hamburger."

"I think she's hawking grilled chicken," Sof says.

Mercifully, the doorbell rings.

"Pizza!" I leap up—only to find a tall, thin woman in a beige duster under a long silver mane on my stoop. She's lost weight since Dad died. "Mom?"

"Honey, I know you didn't ask, but—"

She's near toppling under her enormous purse, yet I drag her in for a hug. I love Sof, but I hadn't realized how badly I needed Mom until this second.

"Guys! It's starting!" Sof yells from the living room.

Mom sweeps through the sun-porch entry. "Sofia, darling! Hello!"

We squeeze together on my couch.

"Shh." My work wife points at the TV, where the anchor sets up the story.

"They're offering ten thousand dollars?" I look at Sof. "You didn't mention—"

"Shh!"

A hefty guy—ID'd onscreen as 'Special Agent in Charge Eddie Powell'—stands behind a podium stamped with an FBI seal. I wonder if they hauled the thing out of storage or if they keep it out all the time. When he brings up motive—"professional or personal grievance"—I cover my eyes. "I can't watch," I say.

But they're on to a phone number to call before a field reporter cuts in with some color.

"Ted Harvey was a local theater critic who'd recently taken a new job—"

"That's it?" Mom asks.

"That Powell was tight-lipped at the presser," Sofia says. "He denied having suspects, barely even said what kind of poison."

"... the hospital today confirmed the victim came in presenting symptoms consistent with ricin poisoning..."

"The wires had it." I look at Sofia. "That was dumb of the FBI to try and keep it under wraps."

"It's like they learned nothing from Oklahoma City," Sof says.

Mom is rummaging in her bag. "They caught that guy though."

Sofia and I exchange a look.

On the TV, they start talking about the package that was delivered to the paper.

"That's Ethan," I shout. "My new editor!"

"We can read the screen just fine, dear," Mom murmurs.

Ethan Silver stands in front of the *City News* building, grim. "I'm confident my staff isn't involved. We get a lot of visitors. Anyone could've sent that package using our labels."

"That's not true. All visitors have to sign in—" I stop when Mom shoots me a don't-say-another-word look.

The segment flashes the phone number on screen, and I click off the TV as the reporter closes the segment on the "fast-moving investigation." I want to mull over every line. Not Mom.

Pivoting like a pro, my mother jumps up and hoists a foil-wrapped pan from the depths of her bag. "I brought lasagna."

Soon we're circled around my mother's famous lasagna,

paper plates and red Solo cups spread across my white tile table. I'll still have room for pizza.

I'm passing around paper napkins, though Mom is still digging in her purse. Finally, she produces a brand-new Nokia mobile phone.

"What's that for?" I gape.

Mom looks at the box in her hand. "Making phone calls?"

"But why are you carrying around a cell phone?"

"It's for you, darling. You'll pay the monthly bill, but it came preloaded with thirty minutes. It was supposed to be your Christmas present, but you need it right now."

"Mom, I live in a duplex. My neighbors are so close I can summon them by shouting. Hell, Mrs. McMunn would be on the phone calling in anything suspicious before I could yell 'fire'. If anyone needs one, it's you out there in Murray Park."

"Well, I've had one for some time now. It's about time you get one, darling." She hands Sofia a slab of lasagna then fixes me a plate.

"Mom, stop momming," I snap, instantly sorry as I take in her revelation. "Since when do you have a secret cell phone?"

Mom puts down my plate. "It's not a secret."

"Well *I* didn't know about it."

"That doesn't make it a secret."

Sof taps the side of her water glass with a fork. "Okay, cut it out, you two. Jess, thank your mother and let's charge your new phone."

The worst part of this? I've been wanting a cell phone. Ever since I got that flat tire in the Mexican War Streets. "Fine," I say, keeping up the Luddite act as Sofia extracts my new toy and plugs it into the wall. But Mom is still foraging when out of her Mary-Poppins bag comes a PowerBook. "Jesus, Mom."

"What, Jess? This is for school." She opens to a Netscape

window already queued up. "I looked up this Ethan Silver fellow. Something about that kid bugs me."

"Okay, *Matlock*." I almost add that Ethan is not a kid, but even I can hear the elementary school in that.

Mom sweeps her hair into a ponytail, ignoring my dig. "Hush and eat."

I *am* starving. All I've had to eat all day are fries and a Hershey's bar.

"I did some searching online and found this headline, 'Staff Changes at *Prairie Call* Follow Internal Investigation.'"

"That's Ethan's old paper!" I say.

"Yup," Mom says. "But there's only a brief description of the story—'Editorial departures at Iowa City alternative weekly after competitor complaints and administrative review.' That's it."

I slump. "That story could mean anything," I say. "Ethan's slick, but I don't think he's a murderer."

"What about Kris Novak?" Jeannine asks.

"He's the nice one," I say, my words muffled by lasagna.

"Is he?" Mom points at the screen. "Did you know he donated to Rick Santorum's '94 campaign."

"Ew!" Sof and I recoil in unison.

"And why would Kris Novak leave the paper?" Mom asks. "Surely not because of that book he's writing."

"That's it! I knew it made sense!" Mom is staring, and I realize I haven't told her. "Earlier today, when I was questioned by the detectives—"

"Questioned?" Mom's jaw drops. She snaps it shut. "What did you tell them?"

"What did I tell them?" I push away my plate, suddenly queasy. It's like she thinks I'm guilty too. Might as well get this over with. "I asked if ricin was used to poison Ted."

"Oh, Jess. You didn't."

And there it is. My life's refrain to my verbal incontinence. *Thanks, Mom.*

"No, wait," Sof says. "What about Kris? He would've known Ted was coming to the paper. Maybe he's trying to scare Ethan off the job?"

Good ol' Sof, I can always count on her support. I cast a flinty glare at my mother, who's shaking her head.

"Doesn't track. Why not just send the package to Silver?"

We sit in silence a few moments.

"Ted's gay, right?" Sofia asks. "What about the boyfriend angle?"

"It's always the boyfriend, right?" I grin. "I did meet him a few times in various lobbies over the years... his name was... Ben! Ben Jones!" I sink back into my chair. "But that's basically John Doe so..."

Mom tsks. "What happened to that journalism degree?" Realizing she stung me, she winces. "Sorry—I've had too much full-sugar Coke. Have you got any Tab?"

"God, no. That stuff's poison."

"And this isn't?" She taps the can I'd given her.

"That's enough, both of you." Sofia waves her hand between us. "What can you remember about this Ben Jones guy?"

I dredge up scraps I can recall: architect, tight afro, seems nice, I wasn't totally surprised when they broke up. "You know what, I think he moved to California. San Francisco. Ted said something snarky about Mission Hill, I think?"

Quick smart, Mom has Pitt's reference library on the phone, and with that breadcrumb, she and the librarian narrow thousands of possibilities down to twenty-seven people. She cups the receiver. "What's your fax number?"

"Same as my regular number, Mom."

After she repeats it, Sof zips to my office to unplug my phone and plug in my fax.

The doorbell rings.

"Yes!" I say as I leap for the door, determined to pay the pizza delivery before Mom can. "Coming!"

Instead of my pizza guy, the middle part of a distinctive brunette bob appears in the bottom of my door's window. *Agent Cole.* Behind her I can make out Mrs. McMunn, staring at my door like she's been waiting for something to happen. *The busybody.* Even my mom dislikes her, and Jeannine Greer could make friends with a parking meter.

I swing the door wide. "Agent Cole?" I ask, looking beyond her into my front yard, which needs a mow. "Where's your partner?"

Is it my imagination, or does a look of disappointment cross her face? "Klavon's around back, making sure no one slips out. You throwing a party?" She steps inside to the sun porch but goes no farther.

I fold my arms.

"Didn't think you'd see me again so soon?" Cole smirks. "Mind if we have a look around?"

"Who are you?" Mom asks, making me startle as she materializes behind me.

Is she slipping? We just saw this lady on TV.

Cole doesn't flinch. "Agent Lydia Cole, FBI. And you are—?"

"Mrs. Frankland Greer. Do you have a warrant?"

My brows shoot up before I can contain my shock. I would've let Cole sail right in if Mom hadn't shown up and gone all *Alley McBeal.*

Cole looks from my mother to me. "You always let other people speak for you?"

"So that's a no," Mom answers, now standing beside me.

Usually I hate when my mom bulldogs on my behalf, but right now I'm psyched about it. I cross my arms and do my best to shoot a withering glare at Cole, but then the pizza guy shows.

Mom swoops between us, pays him, and wedges Cole back outside without mussing her hair. "Any concerns, you can call our attorney," she says, pushing a card at her as she shuts the door in her face and leads me back into my living room.

I'm floored. "You hired an attorney?"

"Uh, guys?"

It's Sofia, looking a little green. I'm about to offer some Pepsi when I see she's carrying a curl of thermal paper in one hand and a sheaf of *City News* stationery in the other.

"You keep this by your desk?" Sofia says.

"Yeah, of course—I send notes and—oh, shit." The implication ripples through me: the poisoned package could've come from my stash.

I stare at the crisp letterhead, then at Mom then Sof.

"I can't dump it now, right? That'd look worse."

15

LYDIA

Lydia lands on the stoop, turning in time to catch a silvery ponytail swish beyond the yellow cone of the porch light. Jessica Greer's mother is good. Too good. Spine erect, all polish and haughty attitude. The type of woman Lydia's had to learn since she left Pikeville for good. The museum-brunch type. Not someone whose skillset includes blocking an FBI investigation.

There's something off about these two. Most mothers would fall apart. Hers would, couldn't have handled this kind of pressure. One knock from federal agents and she'd have gone straight to one of her "spells"—lights out, curtains drawn, and a cold cloth in a bucket of ice. Not Mrs. Greer. She's seen mama bears, but this woman? She's beyond protective, she's prepared. Knows how to shut down a warrant request, produces a lawyer's phone number on a dime, and keeps her daughter from saying anything incriminating. Which means either Jessica Greer didn't act alone, or Lydia's looking at the wrong suspect entirely.

"Goddamn," Lydia whispers through clenched teeth as she and Klavon head back to the car. "I can't believe she lawyered up so fast."

"I can. 'Specially if she's guilty," Klavon says with a shrug. "It's why we're here, isn't it?"

Cole marches toward their car. Once she'd debriefed the team, Powell had insisted on this visit, even without the warrant. "You don't have a leak, Cole. You have a firehose. You need to get your ass over there before Greer destroys anything that links her to this."

The evidence is mounting. Chen had confirmed Novak's story about Jessica's hospitalization, but was that incriminating? She'd found her father dead when she was a senior in college, only three years older than Justin. To witness something like that at that age? The mental hospital stay is hardly surprising. More worrying is that she graduated on time. That kind of compartmentalization indicates more discipline than most people give her credit for.

This case will make her career if she can crack it.

"Powell is so far up my ass on this." Lydia kicks at a stone on the pavement.

"He's always like that, Lyd. Throw in a case this big? Where we have nothing?" Klavon moves to the passenger door, catches his partner's eyes. "That's why he gave us the Monday deadline. He's up against it."

"You're right." Lydia drapes an arm over her door. "I'm going head back to the office, do some more digging. You don't need to. Just go home."

"Lyd." Klavon's tone is whiny. He changes it on a dime. "It's all good. Fine by me. But you should go home too. Ever since Justin left for college..."

She doesn't need the scolding, not when it was starting to feel like they were bonding. Her son is pretty much her only "safe" topic of personal conversation. Far as he knows, Alice is a roommate. He's single. Never asks about any love life. Neither does she.

"I know, I know." She looks at her watch. Ten after seven. *Crap.* She never did call Alice. He's right. Her work habits have gotten so much worse since Justin left.

"I mean it, Cole. You don't want to start this on empty."

"If I don't at least try, it'll all be over before I have a chance to start," she says.

"You know what bothers me though? Powell trying to downplay the incident. He should've known the press would find out about the ricin. Especially since everyone in town already knows Jessica Greer is our main suspect. Makes us look like we're hiding something."

Klavon's expression shifts. "I'd keep that opinion to yourself if I were you."

And there it is, bonding officially over. "Okay, Klavon," she says as they slide into their seats. "Nice work today."

Before Klavon can respond, her pager goes off. She checks it, frowns. "It's Chen. Says urgent."

Klavon straightens. "I saw a pay phone at the gas station on the corner. Let's go."

16

DINA

Dina Kowalski lets herself into her apartment, drops her keys into the dish by the door.

"I know," she says, already moving. "Before you say anything."

Her coat goes on the rack. Bag right next to it. She heads for the sink, turns the water on.

"But *someone* from our paper had to go. An FBI briefing? The press, cameras, a whole circus." She lets that settle. "You would've loved it."

She dries her hands and crosses to the craft table.

It's as she left it. Yarn wound tight into perfect skeins, needles parallel to the table's edge, her pattern weighted flat beneath a glass paperweight. A half-finished sleeve waits where she stopped, the stitches even, tension consistent.

She picks it up—no sleeve island for her—and laces the yarn through her fingers.

"The whole day was like that," she says. "Ted Harvey, first day. Goes around the office, showing everyone this note he got." She slips the needle through the next stitch without looking. Muscle memory. "Wants to know who it's from. A brownie, which he ate in one gulp. The next thing you know he's calling the hospital. Claims it's ricin. Very dramatic."

She stops, listens. Her mum can be so slow.

"You're right, not surprising coming from a theater critic."

Another stitch. Then another. The soft click of the needles fills the room.

"I wasn't going to get involved." A small exhale. "But they're offering ten thousand dollars for information."

She stops mid-row, yarn pulled taut between her fingers.

For a moment, she considers her studio apartment. The silk sofa that had lived under a slipcover at her mother's house, doubling as her bed. The blue-and-white china that fools no one into thinking it was Currier & Ives. The Bunsen burner that passes for a stove. Her crafting table, the hours measured out in rows and repeats. What would it be like to leave it as is. Walk away mid-project. Let the tension go slack, collapsing into something unusable.

The thought passes.

She finishes her stitch, setting the needles down where they belong as she checks the clock.

Tomorrow has to be earlier.

She reaches for the clock. Sets the alarm for four. She'll be out by four-thirty, on campus at six, right when the archives open.

"They won't notice, Mama."

But she's wrong.

They'll notice.

The phone is within arm's reach too. She almost dials Ethan before thinking the better of it. That would call too much attention to her absence.

"Gail? This is Dina Kowalski, the fact checker. Listen, I'm coming down with something. I need to stay home tomorrow. Should be fine, I have plenty of time to check the—"

The message cuts off.

"Fine, Mama. Right again. I could've said *Dina* and gotten in my whole message. Thanks."

Gail probably won't listen to the message beyond hearing Dina won't be coming in. All she'll care about is who's covering during her lunch break, but that's not Dina's problem.

By the time anyone thinks to look for her, she'll be long gone.

WITNESS STATEMENTS —
FBI CASE NO. 95-PGH-0047

Martin Keller, former publisher, Prairie Voice

Ethan was one of the most talented editors I've worked with. Full stop. He built that paper into something people actually read. Toward the end, however, there were… concerns.

Nothing formal. Nothing that resulted in charges. But we started hearing from advertisers, from distribution partners, even from the other paper in town. Complaints about anonymous letters. Some of those letters were—allegedly—improperly addressed. Nothing was ever proven. I want to be very clear about that.

When the matter came to light, well… We both chose to resign.

Tamar Weiss, former partner

We dated for—what—nine months? Not even. What happened at that paper? It's emblematic of everything about our relationship. Which he gets from his mother.

It's like that Hanukkah. We're at Younkers, of all places, because that's where his mother gets him a gift certificate. He's looking at suits—outfits only a mother would love—and I tell him, "Get the espresso machine. You've been talking about it for months." And he's so… *relieved* is the best way to put it.

I didn't understand till we were walking out with the Gaggia and I realize, *right*. He can blame me for that.

What happened at that paper is the same thing. The falsified complaints, the letters—that was ambition. He contorted himself into whatever version of a person he thought would make Mrs. Silver proud, because he couldn't give her the life she had planned for him. He liked sleeping around too much. Never wanted kids.

Our last fight, I told him he should've tried making his paper better instead of tearing someone else down. But I'd been planning to leave before then.

I thought he heard me, but it sounds like he went back to being who he's always been.

Gordon Hale, editor, River City Weekly

Oh, he did it. You're not going to get me to hedge on that.

Our advertisers started sharing these letters—outrage, moral panic, advertisers getting spooked. All from "concerned citizens." Same language, same style, same goal. *Stop* advertising with that paper. Meaning us.

You don't need a smoking gun when the pattern's that clean.

Ethan came from money. That was always the difference. Guys like me, we screw up, we're done. Guys like him? They learn how far they can push before anyone pushes back.

So no, nothing was ever "proven." But yeah. He did it.

The thing in Pittsburgh? I have no first-hand knowledge there, but… I bet his papers are flying off the racks.

17

JESSICA

PG Plaza squats in the heart of downtown Pittsburgh—
six towers made of black glass and topped by minarets,
designed to evoke medieval grandeur. If medieval
castles had come with corporate logos. On a clear day I do love
how the buildings catch the light off the rivers, turning the
complex into something nearing magical. Tonight, though, with
the fog rolling in and that faint sulfurous odor coming off the
Monongahela, they strike me more as prison-like. Outside of
Mom's station wagon, the plaza stretches empty in every direction. The only evidence of life is the whispery thud of my tennis
shoes punctuated by the distant hum of traffic.

Feels absolutely sinister. But what choice do I have?

Once Mom had narrowed down the list of people named
Ben Jones into Ben Joneses who were architects and lived in
Mission Hill, I'd gotten Ben's roommate on the phone. If the
roomie is to be believed, Ben Jones is in Pittsburgh. *At* Ted
Harvey's. Right now. I need to talk to Ben. He'll know who'd
want to hurt Ted. Except Ted's number is unlisted, and I left his
address behind when I ducked out earlier. We're back to get it.

The building has all the security theater of corporate

America—ID scanners, revolving doors, a turnstile that wouldn't stop a determined teenager. No doorman, though, not at this hour. I swipe my card and slip inside, hyperaware of how easy it would be for someone to follow.

Now's not the time for this paranoia. That's how the good guy always trips up. I'm simply picking up work I should've taken home in the first place. The holiday guest list includes Ted's home address, and I need that to work from home.

I'm barely in the elevator before I'm questioning this plan. Actually going to Ted's house feels like crossing a line from possible suspect to probable killer. But it's not like Cole is focused on anyone else. Between her suspicious glares, my demotion, and how everyone in town knew Ted was taking my job except me, it's on me to do *something*. Prove my innocence.

Or that's how I sold it to Mom and Sofia. Deeper still, I need to prove I'm innocent to myself. I hadn't rushed home by accident to throw that empty box of brownie mix into an alley bin. It wasn't even the one behind my house.

By the time I get to the fourteenth floor, I have a plan. I'll email Carson to let him know I'll be working on the holiday party from home. They'll know I was here. I need to print the list, and that means entering an account number. The only account I'm currently authorized to use is pro-bono admin.

There are a few lights on, but I don't see anyone in the sea of cubicles. Had Carson and I been the only two who worked late all the time? I hadn't noticed. For me it was mostly about having an excuse to be alone with Carson.

I pass by the Beev's cube and can't help it. I peek inside. The main feature is a poster with a kitten clawing a tree branch that reads, "Hang in there." I'm tempted to grab a Sharpie, draw a chainsaw and add the words, "It'll be over soon!"

The next thing I know I'm poking around in her drawers when, there in the middle, I discover a veritable menagerie of stuffed animals, those mini Beanie Babies you get with Happy Meals. There's a pig, a donkey, a caterpillar. Before sense prevails, my hand is rooting in that drawer, and I've snagged a cat. "Hang in there," I whisper, shoving the wee kitty in my jeans and slamming her drawer shut before scurrying over to my desk with my prize.

After sending the list to the printer, I write an email to Carson, cc'ing the big boss, Kelley, while I'm at it, letting them know I'll be out till at least Monday. Everything will clear up once I talk to Ben, so by Sunday, Ted and I should both be out of the woods.

I'm patting myself on the back for this diligence as I head for the copier room. The door is ajar, light spilling out. I'm about to swing it wide when I spot Kelley Knight, the big boss. In Carson's arms.

I can't breathe. A burning sensation flares behind my eyes. Is he consoling her? Trying to feel her up? Am I going to weep audibly?

My first instinct is to race for the exit, but as I'm speed-walking my way toward the bank of elevators, something shifts.

It's okay if the sun shines up, eh, Carson? Last time I checked, Kelly was your *boss.*

I'm attacking the down button, and heat floods my cheeks. My hands are empty. I don't have the one thing I came for, the goddamn address list. I have to return to the scene of my humili-ation. By the time I slither back to the copier, only the safety lights remain on. The room is empty. No one slipped past me and out the elevators. Had they? Did I see what I think I saw, or was that my imagination? Am I losing it? If only it didn't feel so devastatingly familiar.

Addresses in hand, I head back to the elevators, moving slowly this time.

Those dimples. Why did Carson have to become my actual

boss? Not just a higher pay grade, but the person I report to. Not that I'd care, though it is the lame excuse he gave at the golf outing Saturday when I'd gotten tipsy at the clubhouse and I finally leaned over to kiss him and—

The elevator arrives. I look back toward the office, the mauve graveyard. Part of me had hoped I'd see Carson and Kelley. At least one of them. Some confirmation they'd been there.

On the ride down, I begin my mantra. *This is normal human stress. Everyone responds to stress. I am normal.*

Is Kelley the reason Carson rejected me? How long has their thing been going on? Why hadn't he told me the truth? Does he know I'm a basket case?

This is normal. Everyone stresses. I am normal. I am normal.

I've about convinced myself by the time I see the dome light go on in Mom's car. She's opening the door.

Damned station wagon. When we were kids she always drove coupes. "I'm not getting sucked into carpool duty when we have a perfectly good bus system," she used to say.

Right now, though, Mom's patting the seat beside her. Not smiling.

"Hurry up, get in."

18

———————

JESSICA

The night has turned clammy, and I pull the sleeves of my sweatshirt past my knuckles.

"Don't just stand there," Mom says, pushing the door wider. "We need to find that Ben fellow before he leaves town."

"Mom, I have to tell you something."

I tell her what I saw, Carson with his arms around Kelley in the copier room, serious as can be.

"You're still carrying a torch for that backstabber?"

"Backstabber? What are you talking about?"

"He takes credit for all your ideas!"

This is so her. So not my point. I flop into the passenger seat. "He's my boss, Mom."

"*Now* he is."

Her words derail me. Mom's need to horn in on my love life is grating enough without adding career advice on top. If for no other reason, this is why it would never work with Carson. "Mom, you're not listening to me."

"Shut the door," she says, putting the car in gear. "I'm listening."

"Because nothing says *I'm listening* like driving away," I grouse, giving her a moment to apologize, which of course she doesn't. Typical. I reach for the handle, but before pulling the car door shut I confess.

"What I just saw. I'm not sure... I'm starting to wonder..." My voice goes up two ranges. "I don't think it was real. What if I'm like Dad?"

Jeannine Greer doesn't lift her eyes from the road. "Why would you bring your father into this?"

I cup my elbows and look into my lap. How can she be so oblivious? "Because of what he did. Why he did that to himself."

She noses away from the curb. "I repeat, what do you think that has to do with any of this?"

My jaw drops, and I turn to her, but she stays laser-focused on the road ahead. In the five years since I'd found my father in the garage, I could count on one hand the number of times anyone in our family has referred directly to what happened. She wants me to get specific now?

Fine.

"The note he left, Mom. About not trusting himself anymore. Said he wasn't sure what was real and what wasn't. That's how I'm feeling, that's why."

We pull up to a stoplight, but she doesn't answer, simply stares ahead. It begins to drizzle. The light changes, but she doesn't move. The car behind us honks, forcing her attention back to the present moment as she pulls forward.

The edge leaves her voice. "How've you been sleeping?"

"Fine." I've never told her about my nightmares in detail, but we both know what happened the last time I couldn't sleep.

"How's your appetite?"

My appetite? I hadn't mentioned the sleep-baking either. "Normal. I guess? Why?"

"How about your memory? Dropping any balls at work?"

"Mom, I think you missed your calling. You should've been a trial lawyer." She doesn't crack a smile, so I dig in deeper. "Usually in a conversation, both people get to ask questions."

"Your memory seems fine to me. Though you did leave Ted Harvey's address at Zimmerman."

Something tightens in my sternum. Whatever Mom thinks she's doing, it has nothing to do with seeing things that aren't real. "What does any of this have to do with anything?"

"What do you think, Jess? You think your dad woke up one morning, felt a little off and took his life? Out of nowhere? That note—it wasn't about one bad day."

Her words irk me, but it's a reflex. When I think about my father's death, it *had* seemed that way. Sudden. Unexpected.

But that was a lie I'd been telling myself. Along with the one about being a good daughter.

I don't want to admit my ignorance. It would mean I'd neglected my father's suffering more than is already obvious. What if I did do this thing? Cooked up a batch of ricin along with those brownies and dropped the package in a post office box?

I sit with that a moment. Let it be true.

My mother must read something in my silence because her voice softens. "I'm sorry, sweetheart, I don't mean to sound harsh. But I promise, you're not having a breakdown."

Maybe. She'd missed the signs before.

Like me.

I should tell her about those goddamn brownies I can't remember making. The empty box I threw in the alley dumpster. How there's this thing I'm calling "sleep-baking" that could be something much, much worse.

"What's Ted's house number again?" she asks.

My head snaps up. "Right there, Mom, it's this one."

Though Bloomfield is mostly row houses, Ted's family home

is a standalone on a corner lot. Red brick. But the reason I'd seen it immediately? A single window glows like a TV screen in a dark living room. Through the living room's picture window I can see a tall, lanky fellow with dark kinky hair. In the context of Ted's house I know who it is immediately—Ben Jones, Ted's ex.

"Perfect, Ben's there!" I say.

"Is he moving furniture?" Mom asks.

I'm about to agree—Ben is bent over the sofa, shirtless, holding tight to the back—when I see a second pair of arms surround him. Someone is pushing at—

"Ohmigod, no! Mom, drive!"

"What? What?" she yells.

We don't move, and neither of us has taken our eyes from the window when an equally lanky brunette collapses on top of him.

Ethan Silver? I guess he was flirting with me. Or he's a man-whore. And Ben? The longest we'd ever spoken was during the intermission for *Rent*. He'd said something like, "Problems eliminate themselves if you're patient." I thought he'd meant the landlord character. Now I'm not so sure.

"Holy shit, Mom. Are you seeing what I'm seeing?"

"I don't know what I'm seeing!" she yells.

"Motive!" I yell back. "Drive!"

19

JESSICA

The tires screech as Mom pulls away from Ted Harvey's house. "What was that, Jess?"

"Mom, that was the new editor of *City News*, Ethan Silver. With Ben Jones."

"Ooh, that *is* motive!"

We ride a few miles in silence to the freeway, heading toward Murray Park, the windshield wipers a reassuring metronome. For the first time in a long time, I'm glad to be heading to Mom and Dad's house.

"Do you think he did it?"

"Weeelll." Mom drags the word into a full sentence. "Why move here to murder Ted? Why not move to California and be with Ben?"

"So maybe Ben did it!"

"Or better yet," she says, as if I haven't spoken, "why come to Pittsburgh at all? There's no need to travel to send a poisoned baked good through the mail."

"Whose side are you on?" I ask, though I have to admit it's a fair point. "I gotta call Sof when we get home. Let her know I'm going to stay at your place tonight."

"Call her now." Mom taps my purse.

Right. It's not like I've never used a cell phone—Zimmerman issues them when we travel—but it doesn't occur to me to call someone whenever I think of it.

I pull out the phone and dial my house. "Sof," I say when my machine answers. "Pick up."

"Put her on speaker," Mom says in a low voice.

I'm struggling with the idea that my mom is more tech savvy than I am as I explain to Sofia what we witnessed. Zimmerman doesn't come up, and I'm glad. Unless it means Mom isn't sure I'm a reliable witness.

"It's not like those two having sex means they have some kind of relationship." Sofia's voice warbles through the speaker, but her meaning is clear. They could've just met.

She's not wrong. Given the go-ahead, I'm pretty sure Ethan would've banged me in the Oyster House toilet if lunch hadn't been interrupted. Another reason—which I hate to admit—that my mom is probably right. Ethan didn't do this.

"Do you think it's odd Ben's staying at Ted's?" Mom asks.

"Maybe he needed to cover his tracks. Make sure there was no evidence at the house."

I'm getting whiplash from these two. In my addled state, I wonder if I'm letting these two make more of this situation than is called for.

"It's a thought. Anyway, no reason to stick around at my place. We just got to Murray Park. Call me back when you get to your place, Sof."

I bite the inside of my cheek as Mom pulls into the driveway, but not the garage. Never the garage. Not since Dad.

I've barely got my leg out the door before a blur of fur attacks. "Goddammit, cat!"

"Snookums, there you are," Mom coos. "You must be starving! Let me get your dinner!"

As soon as Mom says dinner, the filthy furball releases my sweatpant leg and darts toward the kitchen door. I roll my eyes. Snookums is the feral cat who started hanging around after my father died. Mom put in a cat door, but she prefers making an entrance.

Neither Seth nor I had protested the name Mom gave the little beast because we never imagined she'd stick around. But the spotted menace is never leaving. On the one hand, I'm glad she's here. Except when I visit. She's an excellent attack cat. The only person she never tears into is my mother.

With Snookums and my mother both distracted, the day's shitstorm starts pelting me. My column, my job, my dad... even this goddamn cat. I want to leave before I've even gone inside the house.

"This reminds me," I say as I walk into the kitchen. "I didn't feed Chelsea." Chelsea is my cat. She hides in the linen closet when anyone comes over. I do love cats. Just not Snookums.

"Call your tenant. Ask her." Mom says as she closes the door behind me, trapping us in the house with Snookums Scissorhands.

"I don't have her number," I lie.

"Well, Chelsea's a cat," Mom says. "She'll be fine."

Maybe this is how the little beast got this way. Only, I know Snookums came fully loaded. Any relief I'd felt at the idea of going home to Murray Park has evaporated, but since Mom drove I'm at her mercy. There's no bridge between us, that's how I ended up in Dormont, but there's no public transit either.

Da dee da daa, da dee da daa, da dee daa daa daaa.

I jump. My new phone is in my pants pocket. Has to be Sof, no one else has this number. Maybe she'll give me a ride home.

"Is that Sofia?" Mom intrudes. "Ask her to feed your kitty."

Thanks a lot, Mom, I think, looking at the number. I don't recognize it.

"Where are you, Jessica?" It is Sofia, but she sounds strange. Angry.

"At my mom's. Just like I said three minutes ago. How did you get this number?"

"I got it off the box in your kitchen, right where you left it."

"Okay?" She's so testy I don't dare ask her to come and get me. Had she stayed to do the dishes we left out? "Why are you—"

"The FBI showed up again. Right after we hung up. Apparently they got that warrant. Can you get back quickly? They're not letting me leave. That Cole lady accused me of tampering with evidence."

Tampering?

How had things gone so upside down so quickly? "What evidence?"

Sof stage-whispers into the receiver. "They found the stationery, Jess. And you know my fingerprints are all over that stuff."

Murray Park is a good twenty minutes away from my place in Dormont. "I'll be there in ten minutes."

"Mom!" I yell up the stairs toward my parents' bedroom. "We have to go back to Dormont!"

My mother hustles out of her room, wearing only the top half of her Eileen Fisher knit ensemble. "Did you hear that, Jess? On the TV?"

"We don't have time for this. Put your pants back on. Did you hear me? We have to go back to my house ASAP."

"They say Ted Harvey has taken a turn for the worse," Mom says.

Is that how the police got that warrant so quickly?

<hr>

20

JESSICA

Every ten seconds, Mom slams her foot against the station wagon's floor mat.

"You're going to put a hole in there," I say.

"Sweetheart, you're killing me. What's the rush? You have so much crap it'll take them forever—" She stops with the imaginary brake pedal, her lips forming an exaggerated rectangle around her teeth. "What I mean is, police work is slow, honey. I don't think we have to hurry."

Since when are you the expert? I want to ask, but I've got to focus. This mess should've been easy to sort out, unless I did make it. Like those brownies. Which they don't know about. Unless Sofia said something. But she wouldn't have. Would she? She did mention her fingerprints.

I can't believe I've put her in harm's way.

It's only a matter of time before they find that brownie mix box in the dumpster, if they haven't already. I can only hope they don't know about my hospitalization.

That was five years ago. Shouldn't that count for something? They don't know what a mess I am right now. Right?

Plus, what motive do I have? I didn't know Ted was taking my job. But who can prove that? I showed up at that lunch with pitches. Sounded ready. Fuck.

Then there's my encyclopedic recall of murder methods. I'd blame Kris Novak, but that only covers the ricin. I came up with the Monongahela murder mystery by myself.

"Jess," Mom says slowly. "I can hear those wheels turning."

Her eyes are boring into me, but it's better if I ignore her right now. I've got the perfect excuse not to turn my head. I'm driving.

"Come on, hon. What are you thinking?"

"Mom!" So much for ignoring. "We've just been seen driving by Ted's house."

"You don't know that anyone saw us."

"Please, it's Bloomfield. Someone's nonna is already on the phone with her sister about the suspicious station wagon, and Nonna's sister is probably related to Cole."

"So what?" Mom asks.

"You should know, Magnum P. Mom. Criminals always return to the scene of the crime. Maybe that's the real reason I wanted to go to Ted's."

"Oh, Jess. I don't know if you sound more guilty or childish when you say such..." She looks away, back through the windshield. "You used to cry when the anvil landed on Wile E. Coyote's head. You've always hated to see anyone suffer. Where's your head at?"

We lapse into silence. We've been raised in Western PA, but discouraged from sounding like it. If we say yinz or n'at or needs washed, it's understood that we're joking. But right now? Mom asking where my head's at? That's no joke. She is far gone. And I can't tell if it's blind support or because she thinks I'm guilty.

"Are you psychoanalyzing me right now?" I snap. "Or is this homework from one of your psychology classes?"

Mom turns to me, and I realize she isn't wearing her seat belt. "Those classes aren't about you, Jessica."

"Really? Because ever since Dad killed himself, you've been treating me like your personal case study."

"I was trying to understand..."

"What? How to fix me? God, Mom, I'm not one of your insurance claims."

Mom slumps in her seat, and guilt blooms in my chest. I hate that I've used my father's death as a weapon. As if it didn't hurt her enough. "Fasten your seat belt," I say, still churlish. "The last thing I need is to get pulled over for that."

My mother's near-instant compliance is somehow more heartbreaking. I am an ogre. The silence between us keeps getting louder as I try to think what to say when finally, Mom breaks it. She's so quiet I have to strain to hear.

"I thought if I learned enough about mental health, the warning signs, I could make sure nothing like that happens ever again." Her voice cracks. "Maybe I could still save you."

Like that, my guilt turns to anger. My veins fill with liquid heat. She thinks I'm guilty. Christ, if I can't convince my mother I'm innocent, how am I going to keep Sof out of trouble? She's alone in my apartment. Guilt by association.

"Sof will be fine," Mom says.

How does that woman always know what I'm thinking?

I turn on the radio so I can put all my energy into speeding and slamming the door on every thought I don't want my mother to read without my permission, a skill I perfected after Dad died.

After Dad, Mom stepped in like it was her job. Half of college, apparently, is paperwork, and she attacked it like she did Greer Fidelity, running the office while my father... didn't. My GPA even went up, which is either a testament to her or a red flag about the system. She hasn't stopped taking classes since.

Studies everything—business law, psychology, God knows what else. And Jeannine Greer has opinions about all of it. Strong ones.

People love to talk about how time heals, but that's bullshit. It rearranges you. Turns your scars into structure.

Whack. Better shut that door before she decodes that thought.

Does she really think I'm not like Dad? According to Dr. Harris, what happened to me was "situational." Not genetic. She cried when he said that. Actually cried. Like she'd been holding her breath for years and finally got to let it out.

So what's with the constant monitoring of my moods?

Thump. That's another set of ideas I want to keep to myself.

I shift my thoughts to the physical, the weight of my thighs against the gray cloth of the wagon's seat, the steady thrum of the gas pedal under my foot. I wonder if Dad ever used any tricks like this.

Before I can slam that one down, I'm distracted by lights.

Red and blue beams, strobing up and down my street. Squad cars lined up like dominoes.

"Shit."

For a second, neither of us moves. Then I cut the wheel and swing down the alley behind my duplex, tires crunching over gravel as I pull up beside my car.

"I don't blame you if you want to get in the driver's seat and turn back."

She reaches for her purse, grabs her cell phone. "I'm calling a lawyer."

"Mom." I grab for her hand, but she glowers, and I retreat. Her wanting a lawyer is worse than her faint insistence that I'm innocent. I cut the engine, snapping off the radio as she dials.

She has the lawyer's number memorized?

While she waits for someone to pick up, Mom studies my

face. I know the look. She's searching for cracks, like she did when I got home from the hospital.

"I don't need your help to..." I begin, but can't finish.

Her look changes. "Hon, you are not prepared to defend yourself—"

"But I didn't do anything," I say, but it feels more like a reflex than what I really think.

"I know, sweetheart," Mom says, too quickly. The way you reassure someone who's fragile. "I just... you've been under so much stress lately. And..."

She doesn't finish, but she doesn't need to. We both remember the kitchen. Seth. The knife. When I couldn't tell what was real.

The service picks up, and she leaves a message. "He'll call back," she says. "This is a prominent case." As if she's reassuring me.

Stowing her phone, she crosses her hands in her lap. "In the meantime, say nothing."

That's when I know. This isn't her first call to this lawyer on my behalf. Now I want to drive away, but I can't leave Sof alone in there with the horrid Agent Cole.

"Come on, Mom. We have to get this over with."

The walk to my front door feels biblical, like the Red Sea crossing. Because of the tape, we have to take the neighbor's cut-through. Up and down the street, heads duck behind gauzy curtains. My front yard is trampled, muddy footprints crisscrossing the lawn. For once I'm glad I haven't gotten around to mowing it lately. Mom and I link arms, but she's mostly holding me up.

Out front I see the door is ajar.

Chelsea! I think, panic squeezing my lungs. "Mom—"

My mother's eyes widen as she nods toward the house. There on my stoop is Agent Klavon, walking toward us from inside. He's not smiling, but his face is so trustable, I want to ask what they've found. What happens now.

Then I see what's in his hand. An evidence bag with my *City News* stationery inside. Another decision made for me.

Before I can say a word, Mom is pulling me back.

"Mom, no." I slip through her hold and break free. "Agent Klavon, I can explain the letterhead. I see you found my *City News* stationery. Like I told you, I work from my home office and I correspond with theaters all the time. In fact, we just pulled it out. Sofia's fingerprints will be all over it too. Meaning my friend, Sofia Reyes? She's in there now." I try to see inside my house. Is she still in there?

"Jessica!" Mom warns. "Not without the lawyer here—"

"No. Not if Sofia is about to get in trouble for something I did." I jerk my head back to Klavon. "Not that I did anything." *Dammit.* Mom is right. I am ill-equipped for this, but Sofia shouldn't pay for my mess.

"Where were you two?" Klavon asks.

"With our attorney," my mom says.

Klavon's eyes harden. So much for the friendly face.

I consider mentioning the cat for leverage, but they're not going to let me disrupt their search for her. They'd probably tear up the place more trying to find her, which they won't. Poor girl, she's got to be terrified.

"Can't we at least stand in the sunroom to regroup?" I ask. "It's about to start raining again."

Klavon hesitates.

"It's fine, we swept it," a man I don't recognize says as he tramples across my yard from a van.

My "sunroom" was likely a porch at one time, it has no vents. I keep meaning to use it for yoga but never get around to it. It is completely empty. *Good work, guys.*

"Alright then," Klavon says. "But you can't stay. We're going to be here awhile." With that, he disappears inside.

Can't stay? It's my house. I'm thinking of a smart comeback when—

"Thank you, Agent Klavon," my mother calls after him.

The Judas.

Folding my arms, I look inside to find Sofia sitting in my prettiest, least comfortable chair. She is pissed.

Once Mom and I are alone in the sunroom, I want to shut off the lights so the whole of Dormont doesn't have a front-row seat to this humiliation. I don't dare touch anything. Mom fixes me with a look and pulls a steno pad out of her bag.

Something else must have happened, she writes.

I shrug. *Duh.*

She scratches out her words, writes: *They wouldn't have let you leave the house if they knew a warrant was forthcoming when we saw them.*

"Thanks a lot, Lacey," I mutter.

Her bag vibrates. Out comes her phone, which she holds at arm's distance to read. Too vain for readers still.

"Remember, not a word," she hisses before stepping outside.

I'm debating whether to follow when I hear someone call for Klavon. I put my forehead on the door's glass panel to get Sof's attention. *Where is Cole?* I mouth. She doesn't acknowledge me but stares, eyes full of spite, before turning to face the wall.

This is going sideways. We should tell them about Ben. And Ethan. At least Ted's vicious review of the Public's last show. Saying nothing feels like agreeing that no one else could be guilty. That I am the most likely suspect.

I reach for the French door handle, grip the lever—then stop. I know why I'm letting everyone else call the shots. Not because everything I say or do can and will be used against me, but because of what Mom is thinking—I could be guilty.

Maybe I shouldn't let her hire my lawyer. But where would I get the money? Also, I'm wondering about the same thing.

Mom returns.

"Did you talk to the lawyer?" I ask.

She nods then starts straight into the house.

I reach out to stop her. "Mom... We're not supposed to go in there."

She's through the door before I finish my sentence, her beige duster swooping past Sofia, and she strides toward my dining room. I want to scream. But also—she's so confident. And I'm, well, unsure. And cranky. And scared.

Has Carson been having an affair with Kelley this whole time? How did I miss—

SLAM. Don't need that thought intruding.

Forcing my mind elsewhere, I wonder what it looks like in my house now, what they've done. I was so proud when I bought this duplex. So what if I had to cash in my retirement? I'm still young enough to make that up, and I couldn't resist the bargain. It's barely been updated since it was built in 1910—the wiring is still knob and tube—but it also came with crystal doorknobs, a gas fireplace, and so much built-in storage.

In my mind's eye, I see drawers overturned, underwear strewn across the floor. Knickknacks everywhere. Mom's right, this is going to take them a long time.

Someone in a white paper jumpsuit, carrying a giant camera, walks into my field of vision. This is my worst nightmare come true. I don't want to be here for it.

Then Mom reappears, Sofia in tow. They're walking toward me. I'm thrilled to follow. When we get to the car, I feel free to speak.

"What about Chelsea?"

"Get in," Mom barks. Sofia and I comply straight away. "Without evidence, they can't compel you to stay. Or answer questions. We can head back to Murray Park and meet with them tomorrow."

Compel? Must be the attorney talking. "What about the stationery?"

Mom glares through the rearview as she turns the ignition. I don't want to go back to Murray Park with her, but the way Sof is acting, I doubt she'll let me stay at her place. Not that I blame her.

I could call Carson—

My mother backs out slowly. "There's been another ricin drop."

My jaw drops. "That's amazing! I have an alibi for the entire evening. Where?"

Mom hits the gas. "Your office. Zimmerman. For Carson."

Her words hit with brutal clarity. I grip the door handle so hard my fingernail breaks. So much for my alibi of running into Zimmerman, alone. Did Carson or Kelley see me though? *Dammit.* Even the Beev knows I have a thing for Carson. I can't slam these mental doors shut fast enough, because they aren't doors. They're lids to a jack-in-the-box, and that box belongs to Pandora.

"Jess, you're shaking," Sofia says softly.

I look down at my hands, now in my lap. She's right. But I don't feel scared anymore. I feel rage.

21

LYDIA

PPG Plaza is lit up when she arrives, three squad cars angled at the curb, an ambulance idling for no apparent reason. Lydia cuts the engine and sits.

Some small part of her knows she should call Alice, should've called the minute she left Greer's. Every other fiber of her being has already moved on. This case really could be the one. Not only a conviction, Powell off her back. A case that rewrites what a woman with her particular profile, a gay woman from the hollows of Appalachia, is allowed to be in this Bureau. And she'd do it by identifying a family bioterrorism operation that defied every known profiling model. The file would be passed around Quantico for decades.

She lets herself want it for ten seconds, then gets out of the car.

The lobby has been cleared—a pair of uniforms keeping a small knot of PPG employees behind a cordon, still in their work clothes, some of them clutching their coats, hopeful. Lydia badges through without slowing down.

Murphy waits at the elevator bank, already looking like he resents her. They've worked together enough times, Lydia knows it's a posture. Murphy's family tree lines the walls at the down-town station. Policing is in his blood. If anything, he should be grateful. They needed the manpower, had to involve Pittsburgh PD. Plenty of his relatives retired from the force without ever seeing the inner workings of a case like this.

"What've you got?" she asks.

He walks her through it: Kelley Knight called 911 at 9:47 PM, building evacuated, package isolated in Carson Davis's office. Says nobody touched the package this time, but it sounds like a match to what the vic described in the earlier drop—bakery box, cellophane window, congratulations note on *City News* stationery.

Lydia winces at the mention. That damn stationery. What they'd found at Greer's was old—wrong red, wrong font, wrong logo. Though it did show she had access. "Is it bagged?"

"Yeah, and sent the brownie to the lab."

"We got preliminary statements from both Knight and Davis before you got here," Murphy says, handing over his notes as if to say, *We did this part for you.* He knows damn well she can't leave it at that.

"Where are they now?"

"Zimmerman's conference room. Fourteen." He jabs the elevator button for her.

"And it came by courier?"

Murphy nods.

The mismatch is slight but significant. If the first package had been delivered by a courier, she would not be involved in this case at all.

A slender woman in a business suit is pacing the walls when Lydia walks in. A man sits at the long table in front of a cup of coffee he isn't drinking. The woman extends a hand.

"Officer? I'm Kelley Knight, Accounts Strategist for Zimmer-man. This is my colleague, Carson Davis. Whatever we can do."

Lydia motions for her to sit. "Special Agent Lydia Cole with the FBI." She shakes Kelley's hand then Carson's. "You've both given statements to the police, but I have a few additional questions." She looks at Davis. "The package was on your desk when you came back."

"That's right."

"Back from where?"

He pauses before answering. "The copy room."

Lydia matches his hesitation. "How long were you gone?"

"Twenty minutes. Half an hour?" He wraps both hands around his coffee cup. "I didn't see it being delivered."

"Was there anyone else from Zimmerman in the building?"

Knight answers before Davis can. "I was here. Working late." She halts, measuring her words. "And Jessica Greer. She's been asked to work from home while the investigation is active, but she was here. Near the copy room."

"You saw her."

"I did."

Lydia turns to Davis. "You as well?"

His jaw shifts. "Yes."

"Did she speak to either of you?"

"No," Knight says.

Davis looks at the table. "No."

"Did she see you?"

Kelley looks at Carson. She offers a barely perceptible nod.

"Yes," he says. "She did."

"But she didn't speak to you either? Seems odd, no?"

Carson looks back to Kelley. She ignores him this time.

"She might've felt like she'd be in trouble?" Carson coughs. "For coming in when we'd told her not to?"

Trouble doesn't begin to cover the hell Jessica Greer has landed in. Two drops makes it serial. She can get the letterhead. Now the woman is seen scurrying around a building where a copycat package has materialized. Lydia keeps her breathing even.

Then Kelley reaches for the coffee mug, and Carson slides it over.

A tad intimate for colleagues, but does it matter? So what if they're bumping it in the copy room after hours? What difference does that make to her case?

"Agent Cole?"

"What?"

"I asked if I need to call my husband. It's getting late."

For one sickening moment Lydia considers the possibility that Greer is being offered up. As if Zimmerman has decided they want nothing to do with her so they invented this whole thing to finish her off.

"Just a couple more questions first." Cole flips through Murphy's notes. "Why would someone send you a welcome gift? Says here you started five years ago?"

Davis scratches his ear. "Oh, right. I just got a promotion."

Kelley puts the mug on the table, all *cut-to-the-chase*. "Carson's an account supervisor. Jessica's boss."

Lydia gives Knight a good look. Her composure is real, which isn't to say it's genuine. From her French manicure to her pearls to her low heels, her polish is manufactured. Her words are deliberate. Practiced. Having a domestic terrorist on your payroll can't be good for the bottom line. So, no, Lydia reckons. The only thing they're trying to hide is their affair.

"Has Jessica Greer given either of you cause for concern before this week?"

Davis opens his mouth to speak, and Kelley puts her hand on his forearm. "We have nothing but good things to say about Ms. Greer's employee record. She's a valued member of our team."

"But she's been here, what? Almost three years without a promotion?"

Davis straightens. "She's good at her job. Very good. But I don't think she's fully invested."

"Fully invested?"

"Right. That column of hers for the paper. How can you be available as needed to your clients if you're tied to a local weekly performance schedule? She never volunteers to go out of town."

"And that's a job requirement?"

"Pretty much."

"What's your relationship with Jessica Greer like, Mr. Davis?"

"Agent Cole," Knight interrupts. "It's late, and we may be overtired. Our families will be worried sick. We have no comment on the case or the investigation. We were simply here when the package arrived."

"And is that normal, packages arriving at all hours?"

"Absolutely," Knight says.

"To answer your question, though," Carson interjects, "we get along great. I can't imagine she'd do this to me."

I can, Lydia thinks.

Carson Davis looks younger than Kelley. Closer to Jessica's age. He's got standard-issue good looks—strong jaw, square shoulders—but he's too thin in Cole's mind, though she couldn't say for sure what most women would find desirable in a man. Mostly, he seems like an arrogant little jagoff.

When she departs she offers them each a card and her warning about not leaving town. In reception she finds Murphy, who falls into step beside her. "Keycard log is being pulled. Building security says they can have it in the morning."

"I want it tonight."

He doesn't argue. Means he wants this too.

Downstairs the lobby is empty, the ambulance gone. Only the police cars remain. Lydia stands out front, smells the dark, menacing scent of the river. Quiet and mostly out of sight from the city, they roil through the landscape, hiding secrets far worse than Jessica Greer's.

She turns the evidence over one more time, because that's her job. Two drops. Two similar packages. All in Greer's orbit.

One question she can't answer yet: when was the Zimmerman package mailed? She will have to wait till tomorrow on that. If it went out before the first drop—or was meant to go out at the same time—that changes the shape of the narrative entirely. It could mean the targets were incidental.

She pulls out her notebook and writes that down. Underlines it twice. Snaps the notebook shut.

22

DINA

Dina Kowalski has been awake since 4 AM, which isn't unusual. Always rises with the birds, gets in her hour of calisthenics before she starts her day. Not this morning.

This morning it's straight to Carnegie Mellon's archives, not even a detour to her crafting table. She does love the stone archways, rustling papers, even the moldy book smell that permeates the air. It's unusual, but news of the second package makes this visit different. Urgent, considering there's been no news of an arrest.

After claiming the corner table near one of the bulky microfiche viewers, Dina plots her next moves. She overheard them. They wanted a "quick arrest," and that was before the latest bombshell. *We don't have enough to arrest her*, Agent Cole had said. Surely there is something in these archives that can help. She can't have them looking in her direction.

Which means they should be, *technically*, looking at anyone who's been researching ricin. They should have already found the Harveys' research. Her footprint could not be far behind that.

But I'm no Fanny Price.

Dina Kowalski had never had the luxury of an Austen heroine, letting others decide her fate. It would be her luck to wind up on the wrong side of things. The FBI won't care about the elegant thesis she developed for Kris Novak's book. Or that college hadn't been an option. Not after what happened. Or before then, for that matter. She never had any money growing up. Her skill as a researcher was the only currency she had available. If that currency offered any protection, the library was her secret artillery. She would arm herself. For Kris, too.

She'd made it too easy for him. Worked so hard to prove herself indispensable, to show she was more than her typing speed, it allowed Kris to remain oblivious to the fact that his book wasn't his idea, let alone his work. It would've taken him *years* to dig up the story on Georgi Markov, which wasn't even on his radar. *Simpleton.*

Mere keystrokes had led Dina down the Markov rabbit hole. The KGB-driven assassination was part of the government's vast propaganda machine, meant to suppress dissent.

Dissent was being suppressed now, too. At alt-newsweeklies, Dina contended, finding the perfect audience in Kris Novak. Only this time, corporations were driving the silencing, buying up every alternative paper they could get their greedy capitalist hands on. Not that Dina was a communist. Or even a socialist. No, her interest was the ricin angle—which had become obvious when Kris needed background for the Polish American Club talk he told his mom he'd get comp tickets for. The speaker had survived an attempted assassination by ricin-tipped bullet. The FBI should've found this easily enough. Patent records are public. First you had to look.

She would have to steer them. If these cloddish agents ever got to digging, they were likely to see more suspects.

She starts with the Harveys' research—Novel Applications

of Ricin-Based Compounds in Agricultural Pest Control—a bound run of departmental publications no one had opened in years before Dina had come along. She feels the spine, cracked from where she's eased it flat, and starts skimming the pages, glossing past yield, mitigation, and controlled exposure findings. All of it clinical and academic. Small wonder no one was looking for this.

She copies what matters—co-authors, grant numbers, sponsors—onto her pad. Surely the FBI has all this. Patent records are public.

On a hunch, she moves to the microfilm readers along the far wall. The machine hums to life as she threads the *Post-Gazette* reel, fingers steady from habit. She fast-forwards past classifieds, sports scores, election coverage—noise—until the headline snaps into place: **Carnegie Mellon Researchers Die in Suspicious Accident.**

She leans closer, scanning quickly—no tampering, light snowfall, alcohol, investigation to follow. She cranks forward, looking for more. Nothing the next day, or the day after that. She fast-forwards through December, January, February... nothing. The story disappears.

Rewinding, slower this time, Dina finds the obituaries. "Dr. Michael Harvey, 58, and Dr. Patricia Juergen-Harvey, 52, both of Bloomfield, died November 29 in an automobile accident. Survivors include one son, Theodore Harvey, a junior at Otterbein College, studying theater arts..."

She sits back, the machine ticking softly as the reel idles.

The FBI should find all this too—the accident, the absence of resolution. If they haven't already. Maybe this is why they have yet to arrest Jessica Greer. What if none of this will redirect them?

Dina's gaze flicks to the clock. Already 6:00 a.m.

She ejects the film with practiced care, wondering at the

investigators' incompetence. If she hadn't brought up ricin at the press conference, would they even be aware it's as simple as mashing up castor beans to make the stuff? Anyone could have done this.

When it comes to research, however, there is something Dina knows that most people don't. The most revealing materials often aren't hidden. They're overlooked.

Her chair legs scrape softly against the worn marble floor as she rises to head deeper into the stacks. Personal papers are never where they should be.

Back here, between the rows of crowded metal shelves, it's a full degree cooler. All appears tidy, the boxes upon boxes of Hollinger cases, their edges soft with age and neglect. But inside each box is a time capsule, brimming with donated research notes, correspondence, and other academic ephemera. Everything from conference badges to uncollected term papers.

She scans the labels until she finds what she's looking for, a smallish box marked simply "Juergen Family Papers—Donated 1983."

Pulling on her white gloves, Dina slides the case free and carries it to the table. There she lifts the lid gently. Before the familiar smell of pencil shavings and something metallic makes its way to her nose, she pictures the manila folders, edges curled, tabs fading. One space slightly off, a small gap where something once sat. Her fingers slow.

She knows these contents by heart—a file marked "Correspondence—Harvey, Michael & Patricia, 1976-77." Teddy would've been fourteen. Fifteen tops. A difficult age, she knows. But those letters. Page after page of symptoms—violent retching for hours, could barely lift his head—all coinciding with the Harveys' experiments. Her hands shake to recall the pages. She's barely able to contain her fury.

She could've missed it herself, though the information had

been there for anyone to see. How 'novel applications' was code for weaponization, how 'agricultural' meant live animal experimentation. And finally, Ted's symptoms.

Not that she could take full credit. Though his parents danced around the question in some of their letters—*Dr. Morrison insists it's Teddy's sickly constitution*—it was her father who'd first uncovered the link.

But he'd missed something as well. And that had all been here too, in young Ted's own hand. A notebook that had been swept up with these papers, showing clearly—Ted had poisoned himself.

Dina wonders if his parents ever knew. If his mother blamed herself for the rest of her life.

This is what the FBI needs to find, to truly understand the man's depravity.

Out of habit she flips ahead. There's no quenching the researcher's thirst once she's on a roll.

More correspondence. Grant applications. But nothing that connects the Harveys to current events and then—

A report, dated October 1982. *Safety Concerns Regarding Unauthorized Research Methodology.*

She knows this report. Seeing it now though, the name... something caves in behind her ribs.

Chester Kowalski, Safety Inspector, PBOS.

Her father.

Without warning, Dina is transported to the Carnegie, her sixth grade field trip. She's walking through the dinosaur bones with her classmates, all in matching yellow name tags. The fossil in front of them, her teacher had just told them, is 150 million years old. She is staring, trying to understand that number as time, when under Dippy's knobby neck, she spies her father. He's sitting on a bench beside a woman with platinum blond hair and two children. The boy is maybe nine, the girl about her age. The woman is scraping something off the boy's face with a Kleenex while her father is in animated conversation with the girl. The girl he calls his daughter. He looks happy. Relaxed. Nothing like—

She cuts herself off.

She'd never said a word about this sighting. Not to her mom. Not to him. And most especially, not to herself. Not since the trial. All that's sealed.

Dina forces herself to breathe normally, though her heart has jumped to her throat.

Turning her attention back to the report, she scans it quickly, a typewritten summary of his report on their work. Attached to it, however, is something she hadn't ever laid eyes on before. A letter from an insurance company, marked up with her father's careful block lettering, underlined instances of Ted's suspicious childhood illnesses, and his recommendation for immediate review and termination of their work. But his name is not on the attachment.

How had she missed this?

With one deft movement, the memo is in her satchel while the attachment is moved to the front of the box, and the box itself left in a more prominent position.

Time to find Jessica Greer. If she's going to take control of this narrative, that's where she needs to start.

WITNESS STATEMENTS — FBI CASE NO. 95-PGH-0047

Stanley Wierzbicki, Events Coordinator, Polish American Club of Pittsburgh (Oakland Chapter)

I'm going to be honest with you. When your people called, I thought it was about the parking situation on Atwood. We've been going back and forth with the city on that for eighteen months.

Anyway, Boris Korczak. Yeah, he was here in September. Part of the speaker series we do. Polish history, culture, heritage. That sort of thing. Mr. Korczak came to talk about his career experiences. Sixty-three people attended, which for a Tuesday is excellent. We served pierogis. The man can hold a room.

Did I know anything about ricin before that evening? No. I knew nothing about Korczak's story. Ex-CIA, double agent, claims the KGB tried to kill him. Wild stuff.

I did hear, when it was on the radio later, there was some other guy the KGB did get to.

Now with all this news about that theater critic I know you can make it from a bean. I wish I didn't know that.

Kris Novak? That was the guy's name? Sounds like a nice Polish kid. What do I know. I was pumped when the story blew up. Not that I mean anything by that. Yeah, no, I'm not trying to book terrorists if that's what you're asking.

Whatever happened with that newspaper critic is somebody else's business.

If there's nothing else, I got a Wigilia planning meeting in a few.

23

JESSICA

I'm late.

I told Mom and Dad I'd be home for dinner, but Kendra wanted to grab one more beer at the Mad Mex, and then it was midnight and I still had to pack my laundry and—

The steering wheel feels wrong under my hands. Too smooth. Too cold.

The Fort Pitt Bridge stretches ahead, cables rising like ribs against the dark sky. Friday night traffic is light. I should make it home by one, maybe one-thirty if I'm lucky. Dad will wait up. He always waits up.

Something's not right.

The bridge is closer now. My foot presses the brake pedal, but I can't feel it. Can't feel anything except the weight in my chest, pressing down, making it hard to—

The car tips.

The railing is gone and I'm falling and the river is rushing at me and my car is bubbling underwater. Sinking.

As the Monongahela closes over my head, thick and cold. Through the windshield I watch the surface recede—lights overhead fracturing into something distant and unreachable. My hands claw at the seatbelt but the mechanism won't release. Won't. Release.

The door won't open and I can't roll down the window and the water keeps rising, filling my nose, my throat, turning everything to liquid darkness—

If I can hold my breath until the car is fully submersed I should be able to open the door. Shouldn't I?

The pressure builds in my chest. I'm panicking, gasping for air, but I can't breathe water.

I can't.

Breathe.

I—

I gasp.

My eyes snap open. My hands shake as I touch my face, my arms. My clothes are damp. It's dark. For a moment I can't tell if I've narrowly escaped. But that's a ceiling. Not the Mon. Not drowning. Not 1990.

I'm dry. Mostly. My sheets are soaked through with my sweat.

The alarm clock glows green: 4:32 AM.

It's Thursday night. No! Friday morning. That was five years ago. That was just the bridge dream.

This is stressful. Everyone responds to stress. I am normal.

Only this time it wasn't the normal dream. It started differently. Usually I'm on a bridge that starts swaying, I think I can make it to the end. But the road keeps getting longer until I'm almost there and... snap!

This time the dream started before the bridge. That night. The night. Me, driving home late from IUP, feeling guilty that I'd missed the family dinner, thinking about Dad waiting up. The memory bleeding into the nightmare, or the nightmare bleeding into the memory, until I can't tell where one ends and the other begins.

The plunge always feels real, the sinking always the same protracted moment: the bridge, the fall, the water closing in. The suffocating certainty that I will never breathe freely again.

I swing my legs over the side of the bed. My feet find the floor—solid, real. Where am I? The heating vent starts blowing, familiar and ordinary. Through the window I see the backyard at Mom's. I'm in Murray Park. The guest room. Everything where it should be. Except inside my head.

Pulling on my IUP sweatshirt, I pad toward the kitchen, flipping on lights as I go. The house feels too quiet, like it's holding its breath. Mom won't be up for hours. Snookums's empty food dish sits beside the cat door, no sign of the beast. Two things I don't have to deal with at 4:30 in the morning.

I fill the kettle, set it on the stove. While I wait for the water to boil, I lean against the counter and let my eyes drift around the familiar kitchen. Mom's collection of rooster fridge magnets. The wall calendar, still turned to last month. The basement door, slightly ajar, leading to the stairs where Dad's office sits untouched.

In the darkness beyond that, past the laundry room, and another door—the garage.

Stop.

I try to slam the mental door, but it's too late. The memory is flooding through, vivid as the dream: Dad's car in the driveway. Me coming home later than I'd intended, opening the garage door with my remote because I'd forgotten my key. Calling out "Dad?" because the lights were on.

And then—

Something hanging from the beam. My brain scrambling for explanations—a Halloween decoration? A punching bag? One of those weird art projects Mom was always threatening to start?

But it was April. We weren't a family that "worked out." And

Mom didn't do art projects. And the shape was wrong, was familiar, was—

Him. Swaying slightly. The rope creaking against the beam. Dad's face—not his face anymore, something slack and wrong and gone.

I couldn't move. Couldn't breathe. Couldn't process what I was seeing.

I don't know how long I stood frozen like that before I heard my mother in the distance. Screaming. The sound is so vivid I feel it's going to pierce my eardrums right now, the shrieking.

I jump, nearly knocking over the sugar bowl. It's the kettle.

My hands are unsteady as I flip off the gas, pour the water, watch the tea seep into the water and darken the cup. Steam rises, a barrier between the fear and the calm, between now and then.

Five years ago. The dreams started then.

For a while I slept so little, the nightmare blurred into my waking hours. I was seeing things. Hearing things. Convinced that I was about to die. I still can't sleep through the night when I'm stressed. Five years, and I'm still organizing my entire life around avoiding every goddamn bridge in Pittsburgh. Most nights, that's enough.

But I've barely slept in three nights.

The tea is too hot to drink, but I wrap my hands around the mug anyway, letting it ground me. The clock on the microwave reads 5:07. Too early to call anyone. Too late to try sleeping again.

The Duncan Hines box flashes through my mind. The one I found in my trash yesterday morning. The bloated, sick feeling when I woke up. Sofia's voice, "You were sleep-baking!"

But what if it wasn't only brownies I was baking?

My eyes drift to the butcher block. Mom keeps it obsessively stocked, a knife for everything, each slot filled. Except one.

I don't finish the thought.

The FBI knows I have access to *City News* stationery. They know Ted took my job. They must also know I was institutionalized. What they don't know—what I can't tell them—is that I can't remember Wednesday night. Not all of it.

I think about going back to bed with my tea, but my sheets are still damp, and the thought of lying there in the dark—

A sound from deeper in the house jolts me. A creak, someone shifting their weight on the floorboards.

My breath catches. I freeze, mug suspended halfway to my lips.

Another soft shuffle of movement. Coming from the direction of the dining room.

A jolt runs through me. Is this real or imagined? Is my sleep-deprived, traumatized brain conjuring danger? Or is someone really there? The only defense I have is my mug of chamomile tea and, well, Mom's butcher block. Again.

The floorboard creaks in another spot.

I slide the chef's knife from its slot, the satisfying whisper of metal rasping on wood accompanies the movement. "Stop right now or I'll slice this through your throat," I bark.

The light flicks on in the dining room. I spin around so fast I knock into my tea cup, causing the brew to jump the rim and burn my torso. I curse.

I look up, see my mother standing in the archway to the kitchen. Her eyes go to the knife first. My gaze follows. My arm is still raised, knife poised to strike.

"Jessica."

My mother is using her *calm down* voice. The same one all the nurses used on me at the hospital. Do they teach that in some class?

"Put down the knife."

"What are you doing here?" I ask.

Mom is still in the living room, wearing her robe and fuzzy slippers, readers on her head. Under her arm is the newspaper. She must have retrieved it from the front porch.

"I live here," she says, her soothing tone replaced by annoyance.

The absurdity strikes me, and I almost laugh, except this isn't funny. Not for her or me. "I thought—I heard—"

I press my hand to my chest, feeling my heart trying to beat its way out. "I thought—" But I can't finish. Can't admit I wasn't sure if someone was really there or if I was hallucinating. Can't admit that for a moment I was more afraid of what I'd do than what an intruder might. Can't admit I'm terrified I poisoned Ted Harvey and my brain erased it like an Etch-a-Sketch.

Mom glances at the clock—5:11 AM—then back at me. "You had the dream again."

It's not a question. She knows. Of course she knows. Enough about the nightmares to connect it to my anxiety. She saw what happened after Dad died, sat through all those hospital meetings, heard all the prognoses, from "significant impairment" to "expected to stabilize."

I've tried to keep the dreams hidden, how they never fully stopped. They're nothing like the frequency of five years ago. Until now. Complete with holes in my memory where something terrible might be hiding.

Nothing about me right now is stable.

This is stressful. Responding to stress is normal. I am normal.

"I'm fine," I repeat, but my voice cracks on the last word.

Mom's expression shifts. She crosses to the counter without a word and slides the knife back into its slot. The sound of metal sliding on wood fills the kitchen. She pours herself a cup of tea from the kettle, takes her time adding honey. When she finally speaks, her voice is firm. "We're going to get you through this."

Not *you didn't do this.* Or *I know you're innocent.*

Through this.

She sounds so certain, but this isn't a college exam, or hospital paperwork, or crime TV. Mom thinks my sense of justice would stop me from killing someone. I worry it could be the very thing that makes me capable of it.

I blow onto my tea and say nothing.

24

LYDIA

Lydia takes in the evidence board, the crime scene photos pinned in neat rows, pausing to feel the impending win before she snaps on the overhead fluorescents. The lights cloud the vision, returning the Bureau's conference room to its corporate drudgery of light blue—the carpet, the walls, the chairs. It already smells like burnt coffee in here. That and whatever industrial disinfectant the cleaning crew uses on the linoleum floors. In spite of all that and a lack of sleep, Lydia is energized.

The night before, Alice had slept through her late arrival, then this morning she'd complimented Lydia's resourcefulness. She'd even fixed the wiper blades, left a note. *You need all the time you can get.* Either she's proud of me, Lydia thinks, or right now she's cleaning out the checking account.

There was no stalling to find out. The second drop necessitated a full in-office briefing. She's in before seven, losing brain cells to the dry erase marker fumes as she arranges the timeline and Agent Campbell wheels in the evidence cart, metal wheels squeaking against the floor tiles. Behind him trails Sandra Chen from Intelligence, clutching a stack of computer printouts fresh from the dot-matrix like a shield. Klavon slides into the seat beside Cole and flips his legal pad to a fresh page, completely at ease.

"Morning, Cole." It's Detective Murphy from Pittsburgh PD, looking like he'd rather be home in bed. There's more to his hostility than having to work with the Bureau. Cole suspects he knows about Alice.

Lydia is about to start when in storms her boss, Eddie Powell, head of the Bureau's Pittsburgh office. In one hand is his trademark green Thermos—he refuses the office dreck—and in the other, a manila folder thick enough to choke a horse. Powell doesn't attend routine briefings.

"Okay, Cole." Powell drops into his chair. "Walk us through what you've got. And it better be more than yesterday."

Dizziness overtakes her as she moves toward the evidence board at the head of the room.

Klavon leans in her direction. "You ready for this?"

This is what she's been working for, owning the outcome instead of following someone else's lead. *Authority*. It's unfamiliar. She looks down at the top of Klavon's head, his close-cropped curls, still black. Her own hair is flecked with silver. She grins at Klavon. About fucking time, she thinks.

"Alright, people. Let's walk through what we know." She whacks a photo with her pen. "This is Ted Harvey. Thirty-two-year-old white male. Lived alone. Has been a theater critic for the last nine years. Yesterday around noon, he calls nine-one-one, complaining of nausea, vomiting, dizziness. The EMTs arrive eight minutes later, right before Mr. Harvey goes into a seizure. The hospital confirms ricin soon after his arrival."

"How about we move on to the updates, Cole?" Powell takes a swig of his coffee. Lydia suspects he spikes it.

"The biggest update is that the Zimmerman drop sent to"—she checks her notepad on the table—"*Carson Davis*—had no ricin. None of the major toxins. They're still testing, but it's either unrelated or a copycat. My hunch is copycat."

"This is why I hate press conferences," Powell says. "While we profile this thing to death, the press eats us alive. Gene Collins is already running stories about kitchen formulas. Every lunatic in town who can find the Food Co-Op thinks they can craft a lethal agent in their own home."

Klavon shifts uncomfortably. Lydia feels heat crawl up her neck.

"So let's talk evidence." She nods at Campbell. "Tell us what you found."

Mike Campbell stands, tugging his left ear, which means he's nervous too. He is easily her favorite evidence tech—sticks to the facts and never tries to explain her job to her. She's glad he's in the room.

"We only have the package from Zimmerman—"

"You said the building's garbage was picked up Thursday morning?" Powell interrupts but is looking at Klavon. Not Lydia. Which means they've been talking about the case without her.

"That evidence was in a Westmoreland County landfill before anyone was looking. Great."

Campbell continues. "The letterhead and messages match. Different fonts but standard, Arial and Times. There was no printer in Jessica Greer's home, but that's not saying much. These were both printed on a LaserJet. They could've come from any office, or Kinko's, or library with a public terminal. The first package was logged in the *City News* mailroom, but we don't know how the second package was sent."

"It just appeared?" Powell pours more of his sludge. "And the letterhead at Greer's. Didn't match the congratulatory notes, correct?"

"Right, but we do have Greer entering One PPG shortly before the second drop was reported," Lydia says, fighting to sound certain. "And she did have the stationery. She could obviously get her hands on it if she wanted." It sounded reasonable to her.

"It's flimsy, Cole." Powell knocks the table with his knuckles. "This is domestic bioterrorism we're talking about, and Pittsburgh is bursting with tension. We can't have another drop."

Before Powell can push further, she moves down the board. "This is Ben Jones." She taps his picture. "Ted's ex-boyfriend. Flew in from San Francisco day of the poisoning."

Chen clears her throat. "Return ticket Monday. Claims he's here for a conference, but no hotel record."

"He makes no sense for a number of reasons," Cole jumps in. "For one, he didn't have to leave California to poison his ex by mail."

There's a slight release of tension. She's been running the scenarios all night and still thinks Greer is her strongest lead, but she has to eliminate the others. "And this is Ethan Silver. Left his last job over harassment complaints."

"No one was prosecuted," Chen says. Sandra is always precise too. Lydia has more than a little bit of a crush on her. Alice would mind if she knew.

Powell snorts. "Define harassment."

Lydia hears the derision in Powell's voice when he says harassment. Knows ever since Anita Hill, you can tell a lot about a person from the way they say *harassment.*

Color climbs at Chen's delicate throat as she explains how letters were sent to the competing paper's advertisers, complaining about adult ads. Whoever did it made the mistake of using real names and addresses out of the phone book.

Klavon looks up from his notes. "Another mail case? Could he have been trying to bring attention to his new paper?"

"It's an interesting coincidence but even more unlikely considering Silver's past experience." Lydia feels like she's chopping down trees. "Another angle we're looking into is the theater community. Sandra?"

Agent Chen rustles through her accordion printout. "His reviews were blistering. We talked to a number of arts administrators with grudges, but none have any prior records or chemistry knowledge."

"Greer's the only person we talked to who mentioned ricin. Before the media got a hold of it," Klavon adds.

So why don't I trust that he's with me?

"I don't get the sense he was well-liked by local artists," Chen continues. "To the extent anyone thought about him at all. Before this. But I'm still going through the list."

"We'll keep looking, sir. As of now, our prime suspect is still Jessica Greer." Lydia doesn't have to believe it. Only has to say it like she does. "She works for *City News* and Zimmerman Public Relations. A ricin delivery at each location."

"We also have a prior on her," Murphy says. "The girl pulled a knife on her brother. This wasn't long after her father offed himself. No charges. Family sent her to the loony bin instead." Lydia frowns. *Pitiful.* Much as she wants to seal this case, she hates that Greer's breakdown helps her. She knows what people said about her mama's spells.

"Our suspect has a confirmed history of violence? Why do we not have her in custody?"

Lydia's jaw tightens. "The evidence points to her, but—"

"But nothing. You've had twenty-four hours to deal with an amateur. Either she did it or she didn't."

"There is one more thing." They need to talk about this as a team, not as a bunch of runts vying for the top dog's attention. "Ted Harvey's parents."

Powell's lips part, but before he can speak, Lydia shuts him down.

"They were researchers at the university, figuring out how to use ricin. We figure that's how Mr. Harvey recognized his symptoms."

A vein on Powell's forehead bulges. "And?"

"And there's not much else on them. They died together in a car accident in 1982. It's nothing but a coincidence, but the former editor of the paper thought it could be related. We have to run it down. I bet the press would have a field day with it."

Powell's laugh is sharp. "What's that, another hunch? Jesus Christ, Cole. I don't pay you for your womanly intuition. I pay you to find evidence."

Womanly intuition. Like she's reading tarot cards instead of crime scenes. Around the table, no one meets her eyes. Chen's gaze is fixed on her printouts. Klavon has found something fascinating about his pen. And Murphy—Murphy's smirking.

Powell squeaks shut his Thermos lid. "You want psychology, fine," he says. "I want names on paper by the six-o'clock update. If Greer so much as sneezes, I want it logged. No more hunches on my watch, Cole."

He leaves, the door slamming behind him. For a long moment, no one moves. Klavon exhales. "You realize he just told us to arrest somebody by dinner."

"Good thing we're skipping dinner," Lydia says, gathering her files.

As the team disperses, Klavon hangs back. "You really think it's Jessica?"

Lydia pulls her folders to her chest, considering. She tends to favor Occam's Razor over conspiracy theories, but as her mom would've said, *It ain't paranoia if they're after you.*

"The ricin connection suggests there's more here than

revenge," Lydia says. "Whether Greer's our killer or extremely unlucky, we'll find out soon enough."

She exhales, returning her gaze to the evidence board photos. What if the best way to hide a conspiracy is to make it sound too crazy to believe?

Then she kills the light.

25

DINA

The midnight-blue Mercury wagon in the driveway is unlike the rest of the neighborhood. It's shiny and clean, no dings or dents, but older. Probably paid off. The people here know which car belongs in Mrs. Greer's driveway. A strange car parked will be noticed, but Dina trusts the Greers will welcome her inside. It will all be discussed in the Giant Eagle checkout lanes.

At precisely 8:30 she rings the doorbell and waits, courier bag nestled at her hip. She'd found the address easily enough. Once she'd called Zimmerman and confirmed Jessica Greer wasn't in.

The woman who answers is tall and elegant in a silk robe and fuzzy slippers, hair swept back gracefully. She's so nothing like Jessica Greer that Dina falters. She is, in fact, very much as Dina pictures her future self, priestess of her domain.

Has she come to the wrong address?

She begins, "May I help—"

"Come on in, Dina," Jessica yells from inside.

She's in the right place, Dina thinks, snapping back to her purpose as Mrs. Greer steps aside.

"I'm so sorry to interrupt at this hour," she says as she sees that Jessica is also in her pajamas. At least she's risen to her feet by the time Dina enters the front room.

The house smells of books and coffee and spaghetti sauce. Lived-in.

"Jessica, hi. I'm so glad I found you. I need to speak with you right away."

Jessica stares, uncomprehending. "But how did you...?"

"Know where to find you?" Dina smiles broadly, doesn't care her snaggletooth is showing. "I thought it was better if we spoke in person, but you weren't home when I stopped by."

Now Mrs. Greer is looking on, jarringly curious.

She gestures, a rolling motion with her hand. "We keep an emergency contact list for all employees." Dina keeps both lists. "When you weren't at your house, I took a guess you'd be here."

They're still looking more alarmed than pleased.

Dina scopes out the room. Stone fireplace to her left. Green-striped couches surround a low coffee table. A wall of Reader's Digests, spines all aligned. Another wall, all family photographs. She averts her eyes quickly.

"I've been in the library all night and have something here that I think you'll both want to see."

"I'll get us fresh coffees. How do you take it?"

"Black," Dina says. "Like my soul."

They laugh. Mercifully. She finds humor can be tricky.

"Sit," Jessica says, returning to her spot on the sofa, a plate of half-eaten lasagna on the coffee table in front of her.

How does she stay so skinny?

Her hair is mussed and greasy this morning, and shadows have appeared under her eyes. She looks almost strung out. Frightened maybe. Good. Frightened people are easier to point in a direction.

Once they're settled with their coffees, Dina digs into her bag to spread its contents—mostly—across the table and squats in front of them. Some reports will stay in her satchel. All she needs is for Jessica to catch on, and her compulsive tendencies will take over. She won't be able to leave it alone until she discovers the truth. Then Dina can step back. Ten thousand dollars isn't worth this heat.

"Ted's parents." Dina pats the pages on the glass-top table. "They were researchers at Carnegie Mellon. Studying ricin."

She watches Jessica's face go through several calculations at once. *What?* registers first, then something more complicated. That's the thing about Jessica Greer—she's not stupid, she's undisciplined. Her thoughts arrive on her face before she can stop them.

"Dr. Michael Harvey and Dr. Patricia Juergen-Harvey. I came across these records while I was researching for Kris's book and—"

"Who's Kris?" Jeannine Greer asks.

"God, Mom." Jessica rolls her eyes. "Do you never listen?"

Did Jessica really speak to her mother that way? Dina won't have that. "That's Kris Novak, Mrs. Greer," she says before Jessica open her big fat mouth again. "Previous editor at *City News.*"

"Oh, of course. He's the one who just left." Mrs. Greer takes a sip of her coffee. "But please, call me Jeannine. Or Jeannie!"

Dina smiles, tighter this time. She will try.

"So anyway, they were developing ricin-based compounds all through the 1970s and early 80s, but they only ever filed one patent. 1976. Then their work just stops." Dina pushes at her glasses.

Jessica leans over the papers. "Like, no explanation?"

"Exactly," Dina nods, brushing her flop of platinum bangs to the side. "Then I found out his parents died in 1982. Car accident. Initial reports described the wreck as suspicious, but there weren't any investigations or court proceedings."

Jessica rubs her eyes. "Are you saying they were killed on purpose? For their work?"

"Oh my gosh, no," Dina says, placing her hands over the photocopies. "I haven't turned into Kris."

Jessica smiles, nods. "So..."

"So back then, it took about two weeks to get autopsy results. Nobody writes 'natural causes' in an initial report, but by the time they figured out whatever killed Dr. Harvey—given his age he could've had a heart attack, lost control of the car—and by then the case was cold."

Jeannine nods. "'82 was about the time Agent Orange started seeping into public consciousness. CMU probably took it as an opportunity to shut the work down altogether."

"It's possible." Dina's going to have to bring them along. "But you know, Ted still lives in his parents' house. I don't know what they're waiting for. They need to go search his house."

Dina sits back. It's all in her satchel, but that might've been too much. She looks between Jessica and Jeannine. They're sitting there, waiting for her to spoon-feed them. This is the bane of every fact-checker's existence, but also the reason they exist. Time to pivot. Ben Jones was never plan A, but he's convenient. Until these morons finally see what happened.

"You know who else lived at Ted's house?"

The Greer women stare at Dina now, agog.

"Ben Jones."

"I knew it," Mrs. Greer says, putting her cup on the end table so hard some coffee sloshes out. "You said as much last night, Jess. You had the same idea."

Dina's steely eyes brighten behind her glasses. "What idea?"

"It's always the boyfriend! We saw him last night at Ted's house last night," Mom begins. "Ben J—"

"Hang on, Mom." Jessica raises her palm like she's directing traffic. "Why are you bringing this to us, Dina? Instead of the police."

Dina offers a mirthless grin. FBI, she thinks, looking down at her papers. Not the police. "I heard some of what those federal agents were saying. They sound desperate for a conviction and..." She looks at Jeannine purposefully. "The only name that came up was Jessica Greer."

She doesn't see Jessica's reaction to this information, only Jeannine's as she reaches for Dina's hand and squeezes. It's as if Mrs. Greer is her mother, from before the cancer treatments turned her mute and incontinent. Dina leaves her body briefly, unmoored by maternal adoration.

Jessica elbows her shoulder.

"So sorry." Dina shakes her head. "Would you say that again?"

As Jessica relays the scene she and her mother had witnessed through Ted's picture window, Dina grows still with shock.

"When Jess said it was Ethan Silver, I hightailed it right out of there," Mrs. Greer finishes for her daughter.

"So you're saying..." Dina is speaking slowly, afraid this fortunate turn will derail. She hadn't even mentioned Ben was in town. They hadn't noticed. "Ethan Silver was at Ted's house last night? With Ben?"

Surely this will be the thing that moves the investigation to Ted's house at long last. "But Ben Jones lives in California, according to our emergency list. I tried to reach him when, you know, after the ambulance."

"If his roommate is right, he left late Wednesday," Jeannine says.

"You talked to Ben's roommate?" Dina must contain herself, ask follow-up questions she already knows the answers to, just to keep still. People who are good at finding things out love being asked how they found things out. It's the most reliable thing about them. "How did you find him?"

"On the internet." She's beaming. "Same as the flights. There's a red-eye that gets in Thursday mornings."

Dina inhales sharply. That is surprisingly good work.

"It does mean Ben would've been in the air when Ted was poisoned," Jess adds. "But not when the package was delivered to Zimmerman."

The phone rings. Something passes between Jessica and her mother that Dina can't quite read. Jealousy?

"Fine." Jess stands. "I'll get it."

Dina smiles at Mrs. Greer, somewhat cowed to be alone with her now. "I'm impressed, Mrs... Jeannine. Most of the country thinks *you've got mail* is the extent of the internet."

"It's for you, Mom."

"That was quick," Mrs. Greer says. "Pardon me."

Dina takes the opportunity to stand, stretch, and move toward the wall of photographs, starts with family of four around a Christmas tree.

The father has Jessica's coloring, the brother too. He stands, one hand on his seated wife's shoulder, the children at their feet. The frame is wood, the kind you buy when you intend to keep a photograph for a long time. It's dated by the clothing—late seventies or early eighties. They'd had years after this.

There'd been a similar photo in her mother's house once, the three of them—her, Marge, and a man Dina had understood, even at six, was a visitor. Her mother had kept the picture on the nightstand year-round until Dina was eleven or so, when it moved to the back of the closet, until it disappeared entirely. It was the only photograph of the three of them. Dina never asked where it went.

She thinks of Marge now in the way she tries not to—the IV

pole, the particular yellow of her skin, the way she apologized for things like being cold on the hottest day in August, as if cancer were a social imposition. *Don't fuss, Dina. I'm fine.* She was not fine. Had not been fine for a long time.

Dina straightens the frame slightly. It doesn't need it.

"This is such a beautiful family picture," she says over her shoulder. "Your parents look so happy together."

She moves on.

"Is this your brother?" she asks, though she already knows. The resemblance is unmistakable—same jaw, same set to the eyes. Same father. "He's very handsome."

Something flickers in Jessica's face. Proprietary. Interesting.

Mrs. Greer returns beaming, something about the brother getting married. She's heard families bicker. Usually it's background noise. Not today.

Today, the photos perhaps, she feels caught by their drama. It hurts to hear them fight. They expect they have time. Have no idea what it costs, not having it.

"Must be nice," Dina says, touching the Christmas photograph as she speaks, letting her fingers rest, feeling the smooth grain. "Having that everyone-together-for-the-holidays kind of family."

No sooner has she finished than she knows she's put a foot wrong. *The father*, she thinks. For Pete's sake, Dina, the man killed himself.

She turns, dropping her head. If it comes to it, she can produce tears. "My father passed when I was sixteen. I know what it's like to, to... to lose that. Sorry. My mom always says I'm too sentimental about him."

They stand in silence a moment, Dina reaching for a bridge. *Too sentimental?* That wasn't quite right.

The phone rings. Again. It's like these people live in a train depot.

"I've got it," Jeannine says.

"Well," Dina says, moving toward her papers, not looking at Jessica. "I should probably get going."

Jessica tries to intervene, reaching for the table. "Let me help."

"No, no," Dina insists, pushing her off with her voice. "I mean, I have a certain order is all."

"Suit yourself," Jess shrugs, grabbing her plate of lasagna as she plops into the love seat. "Are you taking that stuff to the police?"

Dina stops sorting the pages. "I, ah…"

"Guys." Jeannine races into the room. "That was the lawyer."

Jess looks up sharply. "And?"

"He said you need to stop investigating. Immediately." Jeannine's voice is tight. "Anything you find could be used against you in a trial. It makes you look more guilty. *Guilty.*"

"How?" Jessica asks.

"You could be tampering with evidence?" Jeannine looks at Dina. "But I bet the two of us can keep digging."

She stops fiddling with her bag, feels Jessica's eyes on her. On the one hand, she could keep an eye on things. On the other, it would put her at the center of the investigation. Attention she wants less than she desires Ted to pay for his crime. Crimes.

"I don't know." Dina rises to her feet. She's about four inches taller than Jess, easily half a foot taller than her mother. "But that second ricin drop should help."

The Greers look at each other, wide eyed.

"How so?" Jess says.

"You two were at Ted's. Then here, right? That's an alibi."

"Actually—" Jess begins.

"*Actually,*" Jeannine cuts her off, "that's a good point."

Dina shifts her courier bag, hugs it at her midsection. Whatever Jessica had been about to say, it wasn't *that's a good point*. So much for her new chum. "Okay then, Jeannie. Well—"

"Great!" Jeannine puts her arm around Jessica. "I'll just run up and get changed, then we'll head out. Jess, you'll stay here where it's safe."

"But—"

"No buts, darling. With everything that's happening, the last thing we need is you being spotted somewhere you shouldn't be."

"Where are we going?" asks Dina.

"To the police, of course," says Mrs. Greer. "We have to tell them everything."

FBI, Dina thinks.

She can hardly not go now.

26

JESSICA

After Mom and Dina leave, I can't sit still. Try Mom's HBO, land on *The Price is Right*, but can't get into it. I end up wandering through the house, searching through rooms I haven't really looked at in years.

Mom's *Reader's Digest* collection still sits across from the kitchen, stacked neatly by volume. One of them looks slightly off flush? I scan the titles—*The Tower, Incident at Hawk's Hill*—till my eye lands on *Stay of Execution*.

Was she studying up?

But no, turns out it's a memoir from some journalist who had leukemia. A real problem, to be sure. I flip through the pages in search of hope until the spoiler hits: he dies. *No thanks.*

I head toward my old bedroom. What used to be my old bedroom. The air smells like powder and old perfume. Mom has claimed every inch of the space, from the sewing machine where my desk was to the vanity ringed with bright bulbs like a stage set to my closets, filled with boxes of God knows what.

At the vanity I paw through her cosmetics. Our coloring is completely different, but in the fancy mirror, it looks like I can get away with Mom's foundation. Eyeliner too. Even a lipstick.

For a moment I look like someone who has her life together. Someone with agency. To this mirage I add a spritz of her perfume, letting myself disappear behind her scent.

Without thinking, I head down the stairs. All the way to Dad's office. His reading glasses are folded on a stack of *Insurance Today* journals, the top one dated April 1990. *Right before—*

That's when it lands, that suffocating weight pressing down, the one that started after I found him in the garage. When reality became tenuous, every conversation a code I couldn't crack.

I am. Sick. Of this.

Anger blooms in my chest, soft at first, like I might cry. But I don't want to cry. Don't want to be this victim. Don't want to be sidelined. I look at my watch. It's after 11. Could be lunchtime.

I pick up the phone and dial the office. Sofia answers on the first ring.

"Can I borrow your car?"

Forty-five minutes later and I'm still waiting for Sofia to get to Mom's already when the knock comes. Not a polite tap-tap— this is sharp, urgent. For a split second, I think: cops.

Before answering I automatically turn to my reflection in the front hall mirror, startling. The woman looking back isn't me but Jeannine Greer, wearing a younger face like an ill-fitting mask. For a moment I can't remember which of us chose these clothes. I blink hard, trying to summon Jessica back to the surface, but she feels far away.

Gripping the doorframe, I peer through the screen to find Mrs. Galletti, the picture-perfect suburban mom in high-waisted jeans and a maroon turtleneck, balancing a Pyrex on her hip like an offering. Her kids were a couple years older than me and Seth—a lifetime in high school—so I never really knew her, but I pull the handle to welcome her in.

"Jeannine! I—" She stops cold, dropping her parcel.

Glass explodes against the concrete porch with a loud crack. Bits of beige explode, a geyser of noodles and cream. Steam curls from the casserole remnants like breath in cool fall air. For a split second I think Mrs. Galletti is bleeding, but it's only a nimbus of cream and noodles tinged with pink, spreading at her feet.

Then I see her face. Mrs. Galletti is looking at me, through me, with horror-movie recognition. She thought I was my mother. Not in a "genes are wild" way. No, like she's seen a ghost. Or a crime scene.

I swing the door open, but Mrs. Galletti doesn't budge. The rising steam is already dissipating when Snookums launches from nowhere. Rather than go after the spillage, she sets on Mrs. Galletti.

Go, Snookums!

Only, Mom will go ballistic if so much as a sliver of glass makes its way into that cat's digestive system. "Snookums, no!" I yell, but it's half-hearted. I'm not sure she won't lunge at me.

Snookums hisses—how dare I interrupt?—before returning to Mrs. Galletti's jeans. I plunge my hand into my pocket, where it latches around something small and squishy, the stolen Beanie Baby cat. He swats it away with barely a second glance, quickly returning to his real enemy—and mine too, truth be told—Mrs. Galletti. The stuffed toy bounces into the creamy puddle. What now? I don't know how long that stonewashed denim can protect her.

As if hearing my thoughts, Mrs. Galletti screeches, yanks off her Reebok, and whacks the cat like she's a piñata. Snookums bolts.

Though I've wanted to do the same many times, I am indignant on the cat's behalf. "Jesus, lady—" I start, until I see it in her eyes. Wide. Unblinking. Pure fear.

She doesn't speak. Doesn't attempt to pick up her broken dish. Spins on her heel and runs.

Snookums is long gone, but I'm still bent over a dustpan on the porch when Sofia rolls up.

"Look at you, domestic... What did you do to your face?"

"Is the makeup that weird on me?" I ask.

"Yes?"

"I didn't have anything else to do, so I used my mom's makeup."

"Were you planning on running off to vaudeville?"

I twirl for her, modeling one of my mom's old tracksuits to a cacophony of rustling. "Joining the circus as a matter of fact."

"I'm thinking freak show's a better bet. *One of us, one of us...*"

"Har har." But I feel disgusting. Sticky. After explaining the casserole incident, I tell her I have to jump in the shower. "I'll be quick. I won't wash my hair."

"You better be. Some of us still have to work."

She doesn't mean it, I know, but the remark stings as I jog up to the bathroom.

I'm not done toweling when I hear Sofia. "Jess! Come quick."

My heart slams. I race out dripping. She's frozen in front of the TV. Channel Six. Six on Your Side.

Candy Watson, blond and lacquered, standing in front of my house like it's a crime scene. It *is* a crime scene. Crime tape flutters in the wind.

"This quiet Dormont neighborhood has been rocked by revelations that the woman suspected in the ricin poisoning of theater critic Ted Harvey lives here on this street."

My vision tunnels, the edges of everything all soft and blurry.

"Suspected?" I can only whisper. "That's not reporting, that's a verdict. I—"

"Shhh!" Sof grips my knee.

"...lifelong Pittsburgh resident has lived in this house for four years..."

They show my porch. My door. My goddamn welcome mat.

I can't hear Candy anymore. My pulse is roaring in my ears. Footage of my neighborhood rolls as they describe the facts of the case. "...as Ted Harvey lies in critical condition..."

"Critical?" Sofia says. "I thought he was doing better."

"Well let's face it, Harvey's always in critical condition." I attempt to laugh at my joke but it sounds more like I'm hyperventilating. Sofia is glued to the tube.

Ross Klavon appears onscreen. "Sending ricin through the mail is a federal crime carrying up to 20 years..."

Twenty years? Voluntary manslaughter gets less. "Note to self, next time I want to kill someone I'll have to remember I'd be better off straight up murdering them."

Again, no smile from Sofia.

The camera cuts to file footage of Ethan standing outside the *City News* building, looking appropriately mollified under his severe eyewear.

"Ted Harvey was excited to join our award-winning team," Ethan says. "*City News* has always been Pittsburgh's premier alternative newsweekly, and Ted's expertise would have elevated our already stellar arts coverage—"

"Oh my God, he's turning this into a sound bite for the paper," I groan.

"Hush!" Sofia squeezes my knee. "I want to hear..."

On screen they cut to a thin man under a principled tangle of dreads. I don't recognize him, but onscreen he's identified as DEREK PAULSON - PITTSBURGH VOICE STAFF.

Great.

"Look, Ted jumping ship was a betrayal, especially for *City News*, basically a corporate shill masquerading as alternative media. But that Jessica Greer, she knew nothing about theater. Ted had his theories on how she even got that job."

"Wow, harsh," Sof mutters.

"Okay, Derek. At least buy me dinner before you screw me on camera—"

Sofia gives me a look that reads, *things a murderer might say.*

"...I'm saying I'd be surprised if it *wasn't* someone in the theater community," Derek says. "But yeah. Huge rivalry between the papers."

The camera returns to Candy Watson. "But some in Pittsburgh's tight-knit theater community say Harvey had made enemies with his sharp reviews."

"Finally," I say. "Someone is sticking up for me."

Cut to Mary Beth Purcel onscreen. She's standing in front of a pull-up banner for their next show, *Crimes of the Heart.*

Sofia gives me a look. "Ethan's not the only one using this for publicity," she mutters.

"I'm not surprised this would happen to Ted." Mary Beth sounds harried, as if she should be somewhere else. As usual. "He had a way of making enemies. I don't think he and Jessica Greer got on, not after she trashed his play. Only play he ever wrote, as far as I know. Though I'm not sure what Ted ever did to her. Besides take her job."

Her words slither into my ear and coil there. *I guess Mary Beth hates us both.*

Mary Beth's expression shifts, as if she's caught herself speaking out of turn. "What I mean is, Ted's a passionate critic. That kind of intensity can elicit extreme reactions from people. It's the reality for everyone in our business." Mary Beth casts her gaze to the ground, shaking her head. Her chin is still tilted downward when her eyes travel to the camera.

"Please, that is some world-class CYA." Sofia is frowning at the tube.

But I can't stop thinking about what Mary Beth had said to me the day before. How Ted finds your weak spot. The way her voice had dropped, like she was remembering something specific. It reminds me of how we talk around Dad's death, my breakdown, and now how Mom feels about Seth's fiancée. That careful dance of half-truths we perform around the things we can't say out loud, even to ourselves. What is it Mary Beth isn't saying?

What is it I'm not admitting to myself?

"Troubled," I hear Candy intone, and suddenly Mrs. Galletti is on the TV, decked out in a mauve power suit, lips pursed in martyrdom. My stomach drops. She has prepared for this moment.

"Yes, I'd say the whole family is... But Jessica especially has always been a troubled girl." Mrs. Galletti shakes her head, a pantomime of pity.

No. Please no.

"Mental problems run in that family. Her father..."

I jump to my feet. "Lady, we've barely traded two words in the last decade."

Next the Zimmerman offices appear. A ringing sound fills my ears. Sof's hand finds mine. Carson Miller, my boss, is talking. About me.

Jesus.

"...a sterling reputation in this office and in this community. I have seen her handle challenges with grace and fortitude for years. These insinuations are baseless."

Hugging myself, I drop back to the couch and let out the breath I'd been holding. My heart melts. My sweet Carson, defending me on camera. Calling me sterling. Baseless accusations. My throat closes. Maybe he does care—

Maybe I really didn't see what I thought I saw at the office last night?

The program cuts back to Candy Watson, now standing closer to my house.

"Maybe don't stand in front of my house while you're talking about suspects," I yell at the TV.

"Stop," Sofia says. "I can't hear—"

"And there are questions about the suspect's lifestyle and the constant stream of male visitors to her home," Candy Watson is now saying.

"Male visitors?" Sof snorts. "What is this, 1955?"

Mrs. McMunn appears like a ghoul, clutching a Trapper Keeper of all things.

"That woman has it out for me."

They're talking to her in her front yard, but positioned so that *my* house is in the background. As if I am the epicenter of this story, which, I hate to admit, I am.

"...comes and goes at all hours," she's saying, holding that binder like it contains state secrets. "She's either dressed like she's homeless or ready for the red carpet. I showed you my log, all the different cars. Different men. I had to start a record for safety purposes, you understand. A neighborhood watch situation."

"She keeps a LOG of your visitors?" Sof's voice climbs an octave.

"I had no idea I had a lifestyle, let alone *male* visitors." I sink deeper into the couch cushions.

"She must mean the pizza delivery guy."

"Stay tuned to Channel 6 for all pertinent details as we have them, or if you have any information, be sure to call this number," Candy announces as the Channel 6 hotline flashes. She closes, promising weather after the break. Like this is just so much gossip that fits nicely between cats stuck in trees and society weddings.

"That was insane," Sof says. "She's making you sound like—"

"I'm guilty of being batshit crazy or running a brothel," I finish.

We sit in stunned silence, the weight of what aired settling over me like a heavy blanket, suffocating me with the smell of cold casserole. It's that stupid Beanie Baby. I reach into in my pocket, about to hand the toy over to Sof to return, but change my mind. The last thing she needs is more guilt by association.

"Well," Sof says finally. "At least it can't get worse."

I laugh, sharp and hollow. It can always get worse.

27

LYDIA

Lydia is pushing aside the Purcel file to page Alice—a quick '143' to say *I love you*—when in walks Mrs. Greer and that quirky admin from *City News*, the one with the wet sneeze and the appliquéd cardigan. She notices two wobbly initials stitched in red thread at the hem: DK. No machine stitch, that. Too strange. Wide D at the base, lassoed shut with a looping oval.

What in the hell brings Jeannine Greer and Dina Kowalski together?

Something spikes in her belly. Like something she missed. Had her suspect's mother strong-armed the secretary? Beneath her plaid skirt, Cole spots a pair of knee socks and penny loafers. Some people dressed for the job they wanted. Dina looked the type who dressed for the parental approval she'd never gotten. Considering Jeannine Greer's ability to reduce grown adults to stammering children with a raised eyebrow, for someone like Dina, her attention could be intoxicating.

Or maybe they hadn't come together. Cole collects her files, snaps her folder shut, and waits.

"Agent Klavon told us to come straight back," Jeannine says. "He said we wouldn't be bothering you."

Bang. Jessica's mother hits passive aggressive out the gate. "Good morning, Mrs. Greer and… Ms. Kowalski, is it?" She doesn't wait for a reply. "What brings you here?"

Jeannine sits and pats the chair beside her. "We've learned some very interesting things. Right, Dina?"

Dina stands frozen, clutching an old-fashioned leather satchel under her arm, wheels turning. She's either weighing the risks or resenting being managed like a child. Possibly both.

"Stand if you prefer." Lydia forces herself to uncross her arms and throws a pointed once-over at Jeannine. "The chairs can make it feel like you're back in the principal's office."

Dina's forehead softens a titch. She not only sits, she pulls the chair closer. "I was researching Ted Harvey's background," she says, her voice measured, "and I discovered that his parents were ricin researchers at Carnegie Mellon in the 1970s and 80s."

Lydia's coffee cup stops halfway to her lips. How the hell— "Come again?"

"Dr. Michael Harvey and Dr. Patricia Juergen-Harvey. They—"

"Back up, Ms. Kowalski. You were doing what? Researching?" Lydia doesn't like to be thrown like this. It's disconcerting and worse. What else doesn't she know about Dina Kowalski? She attempts to regain control. "How… I mean, what made you start looking into Ted Harvey?"

Dina looks at the floor, the pale skin of her ears going crimson. "I'm a fact-checker. Research is what I do," she says, still looking at the floor.

Jeannine cuts in. "Someone has to conduct a thorough investigation."

This is perfect. Ms. Marple and Nancy Drew are here to solve her case too. As if Powell breathing down her neck isn't enough, now she's got amateur detectives questioning her competence. "And you think Ted's dead parents—?" She stops herself, can't believe she almost let these yokels get her to reveal anything about the case.

Dina brightens. "As a matter of fact, we have found a number of other angles to pursue beyond Jessica Greer."

"Ms. Cole." Jeannine shifts in her chair. "I think what she means is—"

"It's Agent Cole."

Dina moves her forearm in front of Jessica's mother. A not-so-subtle *shut up, I got this.* "What I mean, Agent Cole." She focuses on Lydia, who notices her eyes are a startlingly icy blue. "Is that I'm a researcher. It's my profession, but I think of it as a calling, really. That's why I was helping Kris Novak with his book. I already had some information, and I went back to double-check."

Lydia watches as she prattles on about her discovery, the wonders of microfiche records, how you could uncover something you weren't even looking for, how the Harveys died before getting their patent.

By the time she's pulling photocopied documents from her bag, she's glowing. Lydia has to hand it to Dina—she's shut Mrs. Greer down.

"Ms. Kowalski, this is all very interesting," Cole says, cutting through the monologue. "But I can assure you both—"

"Oh, but I haven't gotten to the interesting part yet." Dina straightens. "Ted's parents died in a car accident in 1982. The initial reports called it suspicious. Then the investigation disappeared. Like someone buried it. Maybe whoever went after the Harveys is going after Ted too."

Lydia scans the photocopies, more to buy a second than to read. Another whack-nut conspiracy theorist? She would be working with Kris Novak. And yet—Lydia's impressed she made that connection so quickly.

"So you think two scientists dead thirteen years somehow tie into this?" Lydia keeps her voice even. "The thing about conspiracies"—she sets down Dina's pages—"is that they always sound airtight until you start adding up the number of people who'd have to keep secrets. For decades."

The room stills. Lydia waits for them to take the hint.

"I have something," Jeannine blurts.

Of course she does. Lydia resists the sigh rising in her throat.

"Two things," Jeannine corrects herself, brightening. "Your editor, Ethan Silver? Left Iowa after competitor complaints—harassing people through the mail. And Ted's ex-boyfriend, Ben Jones? Flew in Wednesday night. So..."

Cole's jaw tightens. She already knows about Silver's Iowa exit—come to think of it, hearing about that case a few months ago had primed her to pounce on the scanner lead—but hearing it from Jeannine makes her stomach clench. She doesn't like witnesses comparing notes.

Then Jeannine adds, "He was having relations with Ethan Silver. I saw them."

That stops her. Lydia's pulse ticks once. The harassment, the timing—she's on it. But this? Two men tied to Ted, now tied to each other? That's new. And it changes things.

"You what... you *witnessed* this?"

"They were in plain view of the street. Standing in front of the first floor window at Ted's house. I was—" Jeannine stops herself. "Saw the whole thing."

Before Lydia can press, Klavon appears in the doorway with a fresh cup of coffee. "Thought you might need this."

They flirt—lightly, predictably. Lydia can tell Dina notices because she catches the flicker of an eye-roll. The woman misses nothing.

"Thanks for sending these two back, Klavon. They've brought some interesting information. Apparently Mrs. Greer witnessed an encounter between Ethan Silver and Ben Jones. A sexual encounter."

"Yes." Jeannine nods. "Through the living room window at Ted Harvey's house."

"Really," Klavon says, but Lydia can read his expression. He was out in the hall listening the whole time.

"So what's your next move?" Jeannine asks, smiling as she tilts her head at Klavon.

A spike of irritation hits Lydia again, but sharper this time. They're investigating an attempted murder, not hosting a coffee klatch. Also, it's her case.

"We'll look into it," Cole says.

"That's it?" Jeannine asks, looking between Klavon and Cole.

Lydia scratches her ear. "How did the two of you connect?" she asks, waggling her pointer finger between Dina and Mrs. Greer.

"I know Jessica from the paper," Dina says, not really answering the question. "And—"

Jeannine scooches forward in her chair. "I'm sorry, are we ignoring the bombshell?"

Lydia looks at her, then lifts a brow in Klavon's direction as in, Do you want to take this? He gives the slightest shake of his head.

"Mrs. Greer, I said we'd look into it, and we will." Lydia stands. "Thank you so much. Now if you'll excuse us—"

"This is outrageous," Jeannine says, her expression hardening.

Something flashes behind the mask. This woman's not sure her daughter is innocent either. Then the moment passes and she's back to being outraged.

"My lawyer will be contacting you."

"We do understand how you feel," Klavon says, cupping his hand around Mrs. Greer's elbow. "The process can feel slow, but to do our jobs..."

He's already got her out the door with Dina following, and Lydia has never been more grateful.

She's not moved by the fact that her suspect's mother brought damning evidence, but it is a genuine lead. Powell will hate it—maybe more than Lydia even—but she needs to follow up. Even if it complicates her beautifully simple, beautifully high-profile case.

"Chen," she barks into her phone. "I need you to dig up some flight manifests."

28

LYDIA

Lydia takes the fourteen flights down the stairs instead of the elevator. Too still in the elevator. Too much time to picture Powell's face, Jeannine Greer's outrage, Dina Kowalski's pale-gray eyes lighting up at her own cleverness.

She could take a car. Should, probably. But it's only a fifteen-minute walk, and for once it's not raining. Lots of people in the street to watch along Liberty, men smoking under awnings, women in heels clicking along like they're about to be late for something.

At Wood the light catches her, and she waits, seeing her faint reflection in the bank window—overcoat, badge clipped at her waist. The female version of Klavon, essentially. Why do people open up to him more easily?

She knows why. Knowing how folks tick is the job. So is withholding. Maybe hiding herself is what makes her *good* at the job. She hopes not. She hopes she's going to change things for women like her, women with the sense to fall for women.

The light turns. Lydia steps off the curb.

Ben Jones.

Ex-boyfriend. Moved out of town. Shows up the day of an

attempted murder. Seen that *same day* having relations with Ethan Silver in Ted Harvey's living room window. Like they're in a goddamn play.

The thing is, nothing in Ethan's profile—not even the so-called mail fraud case—had struck her as particularly damning. Sounded like a bunch of amateur operators thinking they're slick. It's like she told Powell, he'd know better. Right?

She'll talk to Ethan next. She needs to find Ben before he skips town, if he hasn't already.

The Hilton lobby is a wash of marble and hushed conversations, conference badges swinging from lanyards, men in blazers with flushed cheeks, apparently unaccustomed to midday drinking. Not so surprising for architects. They can't afford sloppy work.

At the front desk, she flashes her badge. He's not a guest of the hotel—Chen was right—and they point her to registration. On the walk she scopes out the layout—exit and entry points, snack tables and coffee urns—and who prefers which spots. The crowd itself looks a cut above the average downtown conference attendee, lots of pointy glasses and flashy colors. Nothing like the conservative corporate types who generally flock to Pittsburgh.

She doesn't see Ben Jones.

"I'm looking for a Ben Jones." She flashes her badge again. "He's a registered attendee?"

The man behind the table registers her ID. "We don't know which sessions our guests choose at any given time"—he paws at the schedule—"but you're in luck. The keynote plenary is in the ballroom right now. Most of our guests would be—"

"Thanks."

She doesn't wait for directions, knows right where to go.

The ballroom doors are propped open, a spill of voices and the thrum of a mic'd speaker. Chen had also dug up a description—tall, lanky, bespectacled—and as Lydia scans the room she's confident she'll spot him quickly.

And there he is, the only black man in the room. She's familiar with that math.

Ben Jones is standing near the back, off to the side like he hasn't decided whether he wants to belong. He's watching the stage, but not really focused.

Lydia steps in beside him.

"Ben Jones?"

He turns. There's a flicker—surprise, calculation—but it settles fast.

"Yes?"

She shows the badge, quick. "Agent Cole. FBI. Mind stepping out with me for a moment?"

People nearby shift, pretend not to listen.

Ben nods. "Sure."

No protest. No performance. Noted.

Out in the hallway, the ballroom noises are muffled instantly.

"We haven't met before. I'm Special Agent Lydia Cole." She extends her hand.

Ben looks at Lydia's palm, adjusting his glasses before taking it. "I didn't realize the FBI was attending the conference."

"We're full of surprises."

He gives a small smile, not quite warm. "You're here about Ted."

"Among other things."

She lets that hang.

Ben folds his arms, then seems to think better of it and drops them to his sides. "How is he?"

"Alive."

Relief flickers across his face. Real enough to note.

"That's... good."

"When did you arrive in Pittsburgh, Mr. Jones?"

"Thursday morning. Red-eye from San Francisco." He doesn't hesitate. "I left California early yesterday morning."

"And you're staying with Mr. Harvey?"

He nods. "I am. I told him about the conference, and he said we should celebrate."

"So you knew he'd gotten a new job?"

"No, actually. Not before I got in town."

"And you used to date?"

"Yes. We lived together for a short time but..." Jones almost shrinks into himself, likely reassessing the wisdom of trash-talking his ex at this particular time.

"But what?"

He looks at her, eyes searching. "But we broke up. Last year."

"And you haven't been to the hospital yet, to see him?"

Jones shakes his head.

"Even though you're staying at his house."

Another, smaller shrug. "He insisted. *So* Ted. Of all people, he'd understand."

"What do you mean, *of all people*?"

"The man's obsessed with work."

"What about Ethan Silver, Ted's new boss?"

Ben's gaze shifts, briefly, down the hall. Not away, more sideways.

"What about him?"

So much for getting him wrong-footed with a quick subject change. "When did you first meet him?"

He lets out a breath that could almost be a laugh. "Last night. I forgot how small this town is."

"Depends who you ask."

Ben studies Lydia for a second, like he's deciding something.

"We ran into each other earlier," he says finally. "At the paper."

"And then you ended up at Ted's house together."

"Yes."

"Why did you go to *City News*?"

He hesitates now. There it is.

"I had some leads I thought he might be interested in," he says.

"Leads on what?"

"The case. People who might have had it out for Ted."

"And you took those to *City News*, and not the FBI?"

Ben's jaw tightens slightly. "You think I make a habit of going to cops?"

Lydia doesn't mind being called a cop in this moment because Ben is right, and the reality of it is far worse than mixing up law enforcement. She not entirely sure it would be better at the Bureau if she's being honest.

"Well, you did fly across the country overnight, head straight to your ex's house, and fail to visit him at the hospital. All before ending up in bed with his new boss."

Silence.

"May I have a copy of your list, Mr. Jones?"

"Sure," he says.

And like that, she knows he didn't do this either. Though she's not particularly interested in his names, Chen's list was comprehensive.

"I didn't hurt him, you know," he says, his cool slipping.

"I didn't say you did."

"You're thinking it."

"I'm thinking a lot of things."

He presses his palm to the side of his head, smoothing nothing on his perfect fade.

"Ted... he liked to orchestrate things. People, situations. You'd think you were making your own choices, but somehow you were always exactly where he wanted you."

Lydia watches him carefully. "What are you trying to tell me?"

Ben shifts his weight uncomfortably, like he's already said too much. "It doesn't matter."

"It might."

He's slower to answer this time. Then, quieter, almost like he's talking himself into answering. "He asked me to drop something with a courier box for him."

Lydia doesn't react. "What kind of something?"

"I don't know what was in it. Small package. He'd prepaid, had a label and everything. Said I just had to give them the parcel."

Lydia wonders if Jones has heard the news yet, that the second drop was harmless. "And that didn't strike you as odd, considering?"

"It was normal. Normal for him. He gets off on getting me to do things for him." He frowns. "I needed a place to stay, what can I say?"

Lydia considers his words. Given what she's learned about Ted, she would've guessed his love language was words of affirmation. But who *didn't* like acts of service?

"He was always having me do things like that. Errands. Calls. Whatever he didn't feel like dealing with himself."

"Where was the package going?"

Jones sighs. "I didn't even look."

She decides against telling him the package was nonlethal. She needs him nervous.

"When is your departure?"

"Monday. We were going to hang out this weekend, see a show. Celebrate our new jobs. I also just got the job I have now. That's why I had to foot the bill for this conference. I signed up before I had it. But I wouldn't miss Frank Gehry."

"I see," Lydia says, though she does not. "Mr. Jones, I'm going to need you to stay in town while we verify your story."

His shoulders stiffen. "Am I under arrest?"

"No."

"Am I a suspect?"

"You're someone I'm not finished talking to."

He exhales, tension bleeding out of him in a way that reads more like exhaustion than relief. "Okay."

"And I'm going to need that list." It is due diligence. "Today."

He accepts her card and she's about to turn away when he says, "Jessica Greer's on it. That list."

Lydia stops, coolly tips her head. "You think she had reason to kill Ted?"

"Oh, she had it out for him long before he took her job. That could've been the last straw."

"What do you mean?"

"I mean from her very first theater column, she eviscerated Ted."

Lydia knits her brows. "She criticized Ted's column?"

"No, his play. He wrote a play back in '93 that she went after like she meant it. They've hated each other ever since."

Lydia wants to hug Ben Jones. "In print, you mean. She wrote an article about Ted?"

He nods.

Lydia waits till she's out of sight to fist bump the air. Finally, she's found the missing link.

She stops at the lobby to ask for a phone. Her first call is Chen, get her to dig up that article. Then Campbell, talk to the long list of theater people Ben provided. Then off to *City News*.

WITNESS STATEMENTS —
FBI CASE NO. 95-PGH-0047

Vincent Caruso, Playwright

You don't want to see anyone harmed. That's not—I don't wish him harm. What I will say is, I only just found out he wants to write plays. That he's always wanted to write plays. And suddenly his reviews make a lot more sense. Did I hold a grudge? I'm not sure what bearing that has on anything. He's a critic. Who cares what he has to say?

Annette Shrop, Actress

I heard he was sick, and I'm sorry, obviously. God. I just hope when all this settles down they find someone who actually likes theater. Someone who comes in wanting to love it. That's all I'll say about that.

Professor Gerald Fein, Otterbein College, Department of Theatre (ret.)

I had young Theodore for three semesters.

I've had students with more natural ability than Ted Harvey. Most of them, frankly. But he wanted it. He wanted it in a way that's genuinely rare. Sometimes that's all you need. I'll be curious to see how he comes through this.

29

LYDIA

I t's lunchtime, and the *City News* office is dead. Even the receptionist seems to be at lunch, so Lydia breezes right in. She hopes Ethan Silver is at his desk. The timing is ideal. In her experience, hungry people say things they might not on a full stomach.

As luck would have it, he's there, visible behind the glass walls, seated in front of an open laptop, staring at the screen like he's lost an argument with it.

She takes a breath before she barging in. Call it her *womanly intuition*, call it her gaydar. But Lydia knows that Ethan and Ben are not the Bonnie & Clyde type. She's there to get the article Jessica wrote about Ted. She does not need Ethan calling a lawyer.

"Mr. Silver." She keeps it warm. Cordial. "Sorry to drop in. I tried to reach you this morning."

He looks up, and she clocks it immediately—the wrinkled shirt, the hair not quite right. Whatever kind of night he had, it was unplanned. "Agent Cole." He closes the laptop but she catches his pursed lips. "Of course. Come in."

She sits without being invited, another small calculation. Not aggressive. Familiar.

"I won't take much of your time. You mentioned when we last spoke that Jessica Greer had been pitching you story ideas before you got the call about Ted."

"That's right. Dina called at 12:37." He sits forward. "I can see it in my phone log."

"I see," Lydia says, surprised by his childish enthusiasm for the technology. "But she's been your theater columnist since the paper launched. Isn't that right?"

Ethan's eyes narrow behind his glasses. "That's right. I think we went over all this yesterday."

She ignores his pushback. She has him now. "Oh, that's fine. Would you be able to get me a copy of her first review for the paper?"

Ethan tips back in his seat. "That might take a minute. Those articles haven't been digitized. But I bet Dina could dig it up."

"That would be fantastic, Mr. Silver. Thank you."

"Oh, you mean now?" He plunks forward awkwardly. "Okay, yeah. Sure." He stands, looks around, unsure what to do.

Lydia would guess he's not used to being given tasks at his paper.

He gestures toward the door, lifting his brows. "Would you...?"

Lydia knows he wants her to accompany him. Get out of his office. "That's all right." She smiles. "I'll wait right here."

As soon as he's out the door, Lydia scoots forward, scanning his desk. It's not strictly protocol, but that's never stopped her.

His voicemail light is blinking. The flashing red light would drive her to distraction, but it's the clearest signal in the rampart of paper—stacks of *City News* mockups marked with grease pencil line his desk, article printouts covered in red ink dot every surface, the bent edges of Post-It notes stick out everywhere—and the only thing with an off switch. She's squinting at a "Missed Message" note—*City commish wants you ASAP*—when Silver returns.

"Excuse me." He sounds annoyed.

Again, she ignores it. "Did you find the article?"

"Not yet," he says, sounding wary as he returns to his seat. "Dina isn't in today. Hopefully Gail can do it."

Ethan fixes his gaze on Lydia. "Why are you so interested in that one?"

She smiles. "Ben Jones mentioned it."

Ethan visibly jolts.

"You know him," she says, giving him a chance.

She can see him sorting—wondering what she already knows, what's safe to offer. When he lets the silence hold, she fills it for him. It's mostly curiosity. What she really wants, Jessica's article, is making its way to her.

"When did you meet him?"

"I don't think that's relevant."

"You don't? You just slept with him last night, the same night his ex-boyfriend is poisoned, a man who also just so happened to start working for your paper that same day, and you don't think that could be of interest?"

"Well, I would've said if you'd asked. I haven't seen you since..."

"Since you met him yesterday? That's either a terrible coincidence or one hell of an onboarding process."

Ethan opens his mouth to speak, but Gail arrives, carrying a curled sheet of thermal fax paper. "From the archive system. It's a little rough."

"That was fast." Lydia takes it. "Thank you."

It's a short piece she scans quickly. The review is harsh—Ben had gotten that part right—but Ted Harvey isn't named. There's no mention at all of any playwrights, or actors, or directors. The coverage centers on a "New Works Festival," something experimental that the City Theater puts on to, according to the article, "spark bold experimentation."

Either Ben Jones lied to her, or Ted Harvey lied to Ben Jones. And somewhere in there, Jessica had become the subject of a years-long blood feud. Ethan is inconsequential, like the rendezvous they'd had.

She stands, tucks the fax pages into her coat.

"Thank you, Mr. Silver." She offers her hand. "You've been helpful."

He takes it, and she feels him wanting to ask about Ben, whether he's in trouble. She doesn't give him the opening.

At the door, her pager goes off. She glances down at the number. *Klavon*. She turns back to Ethan. "May I?"

He gestures to the phone on the edge of his desk. "Let me get you an outside line."

She smiles at Ethan, gestures toward the door. "Would you mind? FBI investigation and all."

His mouth opens briefly before he shoots out the door, grateful to be relieved of her questions, she imagines.

Klavon picks up on the first ring.

"Cole, you won't believe what she's done this time."

"Who?" she asks, hoping she knows.

"Jessica Greer," he says.

She knew it.

30

JESSICA

Sofia reaches over from the passenger's seat to give me a hug. "Oh my God!" she cries out.

"What?"

"You... your face. You didn't wash your face?"

"I was hurrying for you," I remind her.

"Okay, well"—her earring presses cold against my cheek as she squeezes me—"call me from the fire lane at five."

Then she's gone behind PPG's black glass, leaving me alone with her car. I couldn't stay at the house after the Channel 6 ambush. Not with Mrs. Galletti phoning every neighbor, Mom and Dina out there doing God knows what, and nothing to do but flip through the channels, waiting for news updates.

My car is still at my house, right where Mom and I left it. Besides, there's plenty to do without ever crossing a bridge on the east side. I'm only borrowing it till Sof gets off work. My car feels too conspicuous. I can picture Mrs. McMunn on the phone now. "The Mail Murderess is on the loose in her car, free to commit all manner of crimes and misdemeanors!"

Mail Murderess. Jesus. The taunt ricochets in my mind as

Sofia's Chevy roars to life. The city feels hostile—every bill-board, every face at a stoplight turned toward me, jeering. Without being aware I've steered toward the river, where I hop onto Boulevard of the Allies. I don't have a plan. More like a general destination, Bloomfield. *Ted's house.*

Dina is right, the FBI isn't looking at anyone else. If those two were able to dig up so much dirt on Ben Jones, how hard can it be? Nobody else might be interested in talking to him, but I am. How had Candy Watson *not* talked to him? The spurned lover angle feels very on brand for her.

Before I realize it, I'm nearing Schenley Park. I'm turned around, still on Boulevard of the Allies when I meant to turn on Forbes. Yet as I wind through the park, the midday sun glowing in the canopy of oak leaves overhead, I have no desire to turn around and leave this otherworldly dome. Such a stark contrast to the chaos of my morning.

By the time I'm passing Phipps Conservatory, I'm actively telling myself I'm driving to clear my head. Then I recall the Planned Parenthood fundraiser here last year, when Ted had sidled up to me, eyebrows lifted, lips pursed, studying my wrist like he was appraising it. "Interesting choice, a man's watch. Daddy issues much?"

I had to leave the gala. Had he known it was my father's?

If that attack showed me anything, it was that Mary Beth was right. Ted did love to exploit people's weaknesses. He was also the one with the grudge. Against *me.*

But why?

The trees blur as I pick up speed, heading deeper toward the inevitable. Squirrel Hill. *Carson's house.*

He'd be at work, not at home. It's not like we're going to finally clear the air or talk about what I saw in that copy room. Or thought I saw. But I do want to do something for him. Carson was the only person who'd stood up for me on that program.

He'd looked so sincere, so protective. Like he actually cared what happened to me. I want to show him how much I appreciate that. I still have that invite list for the party, too. The least I can do in return is drop it off for him to give to Beverly Jo on Monday.

What I wouldn't give to be a fly on the wall for that. See the look on her face.

"You want me to do what now?" she'd ask, petting whatever weird themed sweater she'd be sporting.

Or maybe I shouldn't do this. I could give the list to Sofia when I return her car, and she could take it in on Monday. This is what I always do. I try too hard with men.

As I'm turning on Negley, I remember that Bluebird Bakery is up the road on Shady. Carson loves their Whoopie Pies. I could get him one. Dropping off the list really *is* the minimum I can do. Why not stop? He won't be home.

A bell tinkles overhead as I enter, greeted by the smell of fresh bread, marzipan, and coffee. Weaving through the lunch crowd, I grab a pie from the cooler, my mind racing ahead to the note I'll write as I pay. Should I ask forgiveness?

I grab a takeout bag and, after catching the eye of the man at the register, drop three dollars on the counter. "Thanks," I call over my shoulder as I head for the door.

Outside the air is bracing, snapping me back to reality. Why am I always attracted to relationships where I feel like I'm the underdog? Like I need to prove myself worthy.

I know why.

Ms. Cleo swears I will meet a man. "But first there will be a reckoning." Even she knows I must atone.

"Is that her?"

My head jerks to a knot of Bluebird customers gathering by the door. Are they staring? Judging? Did I hear right?

"I can see it," another person says.

The sidewalk tilts beneath my feet. Mrs. McMunn's voice cuts through: "I had to start a record for safety purposes... a neighborhood watch situation."

I heard them all right.

Hospital smells flood my nostrils—antiseptic mixed with fear. The doctor's voice: "Sometimes people break under pressure."

The car keys go slippy in my sweaty palm. The rational part of my brain knows this is from everything that's unfolded. But the irrational part whispers that maybe this is something deeper. Darker. Maybe I am my father's daughter in all the worst ways.

Slam! Thud! Whack!

If ever there was a time for my compartmentalization skills, it's now. If only the doors didn't rattle on their hinges, crack, and lead to another gaping portal. My thoughts scramble, like a radio tuner when you can't find the station.

Kerplunk.

Why isn't this working? I need activity, some way to externalize.

Pulling my journalist's pad from my purse, I tap it with my pen like I'm shooing away the distractions. *Hope this sweetens the inconvenience!* I scrawl. Re-read.

It's Saran Wrap-level clingy. What about word play?

Oopsie! Took this with me. Or, *whoopsie* like the pie.

Worse.

In the end I go with *I had the party planning list with me, thought you might need it.* Simple. Professional. Not desperate?

I put the key in the ignition and head down Walnut toward Carson's place, shaking off the paranoid spiral from the bakery. The tree-lined streets of Shadyside calm me some—all those grand Tudor houses with their perfect landscaping, like something from a magazine. Here, even the sidewalk cracks look intentional. Money has a way of making surfaces look good.

But as I cross into Squirrel Hill, the scenery shifts. The streets narrow as I near Carson's, where graduate students and young professionals squeeze into converted houses that have seen better decades. He could own a much nicer place if he was willing to move outside the city. Instead he rents here. I'd only been once, last Christmas when a group from work went caroling—Beverly Jo's idea, naturally—but I know the place as soon as I see the building. An old Victorian mansion chopped up into apartments, sitting at the intersection below, wrap-around porch sagging under the weight of commuter bicycles and old sofas.

It's that moment, idling at the top of the hill, I see movement behind Carson's second-floor window. A blond head pressed against the window, hands tangling in her curls.

My eyes drop to the driveway. If I didn't know whose hair that was, the car is undeniable. Kelley's silver Saab. Parked right out front like she belongs.

It's Friday afternoon. Since Carson's promotion, those two aren't working the same accounts. So why would they need to meet now?

The memory of last night crashes back—Carson's arms around Kelley in the copy room, her face buried in his shoulder, his hand stroking her hair. Had he pulled her closer because he saw me watching?

Why am I here? I could have easily brought in this list on Monday. If I still have a job on Monday. If I'm not in prison.

The crushing weight of how unfair this situation is makes it difficult to breathe. Whether I did try to poison Ted Harvey— which I have no memory of one way or another—the news media has convicted me. Meanwhile, my boss who knows I'm totally smitten with him is literally fucking me over. He wasn't protecting me, he was protecting the goddamn company.

My hands tighten around the steering wheel. I should leave. Drive away before I do something I'll regret.

Instead, I aim for the Saab and hit the gas.

31

LYDIA

Sofia Reyes is already waiting for me in Zimmerman's reception area. That's too bad. Not that Lydia was going to surprise her. When the police called to tell her that Sofia's car had been in a hit-and-run, they said Ms. Reyes had asked for Lydia by name.

She'd liked hearing that.

"Agent Cole?"

The woman greeting her bears little resemblance to the woman she'd met at Jessica Greer's house. She's standing in the lobby with her hand out, smart in a silk blouse and heels. Pretty earrings.

"Ms. Reyes, we meet again." She takes Sofia's hand, small and soft but with a firm grip. "Is there somewhere we can talk?"

To Lydia's surprise, Sofia presses the down button on the elevator, takes her to a server room.

"This used to be Zimmerman's secretarial suite," she says, sidestepping cables snaking between metal racks of humming servers, patch panels, and backup drives. "They ditched it when everybody got their own computer, sometime in the '80s."

The ladies' lounge Sofia guides her to is like another world, with a plush seating area that features a long, backless sofa and stuffed chairs with matching upholstery. The space is long and narrow and has only one exit.

"Could we do this in your office?"

"Agent Cole, my office is a cube that doesn't have a spare chair. This is the most private spot in the building." She takes a seat.

"Fine, then." Privacy isn't what Cole is after, but there's no need to antagonize this person. By all accounts she's Jessica's closest confidant at work, and apparently close outside the office as well.

"How exactly did Ms. Greer come to be in possession of your car?"

The professional facade cracks. Reyes speaks to her lap. "She asked to borrow it."

"I see." Lydia pulls out her notebook. "Did she say what for?"

"Not to hit our boss's car, if that's what you're asking." Sofia rubs her brow. "Sorry, I'm stressing. I don't know. I should've asked."

"The last time I saw you, you seemed pretty upset with Jessica Greer."

"It was a misunderstanding, Agent Cole. It wasn't even the same stationery at her house, so..."

"So?" Lydia taps her pad. "That only proves she can get *City News* stationery."

A look crosses Sofia's face, reminding Lydia of her son Justin about to put on his best Christopher Robbins and say, *Silly old bear.*

"I get it." Sofia waves her hands in the air. "I got caught up in it all, too. But here's the thing. Last night, before I went to bed, you know what I realized?"

Lydia raises her eyebrows.

"Before yesterday, I never even heard of Ted Harvey." Here

she makes an expansive gesture, her hands an extension of her words.

Lydia fidgets on the backless couch. "And?"

"Don't you see? Jessica tells me everything. If she wanted to kill someone, I'd know about it. How much she hated him. But that guy? She never mentioned him. It makes no sense."

Lydia lets Sofia sit with this. She'd sat across from dozens of people who would've said the same thing—and been wrong. But she needs to go gently, keep this witness on the sweet side.

"Before today, would you have thought she'd use your car as a weapon against"—she flips through her notes—"Kelley Knight?"

Sofia's eyes widen, and Lydia thinks, briefly, she's made her point. Then her eyes shift left and her cheeks lift—an unmistakable wince. The idea of Jessica Greer attacking someone is not altogether foreign to Ms. Reyes.

"After that news segment, I should've... I should've been more careful," Sofia says.

"News segment?"

Sofia lets her jaw fall open. "You haven't heard about it?" she asks. "Candy Watson from Channel 6. That vigilante reporter. She did one of her reports today. Full-on profile. The *killer next door* type of thing."

Christ on a cracker, the media's going to ruin this case for Lydia. She makes a note to have Murphy call Candy Watson, see if she can slow this down by scaring the living daylights out of her. She keeps her response even.

"That would be upsetting." Lydia wonders if Sofia knows about Jessica's psych history, if knowing that would've made her less willing to lend out her car. "But tell me this, what does Channel 6's report have to do with hitting Kelley Knight's car?"

"Well, I couldn't say exactly, but... her and Carson, she

always thought they had, you know, a thing. But I think he and Kelley have been at it awhile."

"A thing? Are you suggesting she hit Kelley Knight's car because of a romantic rivalry?"

"Well no, but, maybe?" Sofia's voice cracks, tears she's been holding back threatening to spill. She's not crying for the car. She's crying for what's happening to her friend. How she might be condemning her.

"Has she contacted you?"

Sofia shakes her head.

"Thank you, Ms. Reyes. If Jessica contacts you..." She pulls out a card.

"I'll call you immediately," Sofia volunteers. "But there's one more thing." Sofia leans closer, dropping her voice despite that they're alone. "You know about Jess's mental health history, yeah? I'm worried she might be having some kind of episode."

Cole stiffens. So she does know. "Thank you, Ms. Reyes. We'll let the professionals handle any evaluation."

She needs to get back to headquarters.

Lydia slows as she crosses through PPG's lobby. She's passed through several times now without seeing the atrium, the palms, and the glass pyramid overhead. She looks up, allows a moment of gratitude. The case had been mushrooming, too many threads, too many grudges. Ethan Silver. Ben Jones. The Harvey parents and their thirteen-year-old car accident. And she'd let it all happen at the same time she was letting Jessica Greer slip through her fingers.

The evidence is circumstantial, but it all adds up. The stationery. The motive. The targets. Now this—a woman who borrowed her best friend's car and weaponized it.

Seen all together, it's clear she's been unraveling since her father hanged himself in the family garage. Twenty-eight, stuck in a dead-end job, and spurned by her unrequited love, her writing was the one area where she thought she was excelling. Now she's been pushed out at her paper and her job. She's spiraling.

Powell was right to push. A person in freefall doesn't always know they're falling. She needs to catch her before she does something worse.

Lydia stops at the light on Fifth.

Glad is the wrong word for what she's feeling. Lydia is never glad when she sees the ugly human truth behind a case.

What she is, is finished.

She pulls out her notepad, makes a note for the arrest warrant.

32

JESSICA

"Jess? Where are you calling from?"

"Seth, I'm in trouble."

"Where's Mom!" He's shouting now. Demanding.

The volume is only adding to the disoriented feeling I'm calling him about. I need to know what he remembers about that night. "I can hear you fine, Seth, you don't have to yell."

"You sound weird." He's still loud. "There's a lot of noise."

"I'm outside!" I say. Now I'm raising my voice too. "Mom got me a cell phone."

"Are you *driving*?"

I look around. I'd driven blind into Smithfield cemetery and parked Sof's car in front of somebody's mausoleum. The place is empty.

"No, I parked. I'm..." I exhale and try to regulate my voice. "Inspecting the damage."

"Damage?" he asks, calmer, almost normal.

I'm not sure how to answer. I'm looking at the front bumper, and there is no damage. Not a scratch. Even the headlight's still intact. Had I imagined that whole incident? Impossible. I'd *heard* that sharp crunch of impact, felt the jolt in my hands and body as Kelley's door buckled, and seen that satisfying scrape in the paint. And after, when I thought it was all over, something hit the ground. I saw it from the rearview—plastic door trim rocking on the pavement.

Or had I?

"It's nothing. The car's fine."

"The car?" he asks, but doesn't wait for an answer. "Mom's worried you are in deep shit. She also told me you guys saw your new editor having sex with the boyfriend of the guy who was poisoned. How is neither of them in deep shit?"

His anger on my behalf blurs my vision. "I don't know, Seth. They're saying I poisoned Ted Harvey because he took my theater critic job. But that's not why I'm calling. Not exactly."

"What do you mean?" he says. "Tell me what's happening."

"Seth, they aired that stupid crime watch show with Candy Watson. As far as she's concerned I'm guilty." I put on a mock newscaster's voice. "Because we care about your safety."

"God, I hate those." Seth deepens his voice to a baritone. "Could a killer be lurking at your door? More at 11!"

Despite everything, I laugh. But the sound turns desperate, reminding me why I'd called in the first place. "The thing is, that fuckwit Mrs. Galletti said how I'm obviously guilty because it runs in the family."

He's quiet, and my heart fills with dread. "I know, Jess," he says. "The story's everywhere. It made the *Boston Globe*."

My stomach drops. That means his fiancée, Yuna, must know too. She was around when everything happened with Dad five years ago, but more at a distance. I'd so hoped for a clean slate with her. I've not been taking this seriously enough.

But Seth isn't finished. "They specifically mentioned Dad's suicide. Made it a whole mental health angle." I can hear him slow breathing, the way he does when he's trying not to go emotional. "They even mentioned Western Psych."

His words hit like a physical blow. I'm on the ground now, fetal position, phone to my ear as I am faced with my deepest fear that yes, I have inherited my father's darkness. Now it's my turn.

Again.

Memories flood back, scattershot. First in Mom's kitchen, knife in hand. Strangers asking stupid questions. Stupid questions I can't answer. *What day is it?* The last day I'll let a man abandon us.

Then that weird urine smell permeating the walls. Everything white. A psychiatrist explaining how sometimes people break under pressure. And I had. Broken. It was the only way to live with what I'd seen. When my words come I don't recognize the voice.

"That's just it. Seth, I'm starting to wonder if I actually did this thing."

"Oh my God, Jess. Can you find the off switch? Just, stop. Please, Jess. Right now." His voice hardens. "First, Dad suffered from depression. Depressed people don't plan complex murders, that takes a level of mania. Yuna confirmed this."

They'd talked about this? Of course they'd talked about this.

"Seth." It's my turn to sound soothing. "Yuna's studying to be a trauma surgeon, not a shrink."

In the silence that follows I hear the "noise" Seth mentioned, static on the line that makes it sounds like I'm in a wind tunnel. I picture him, straining to listen, paused over a kitchen drawer he's probably organizing. Somehow, the cramped studio he shares with Yuna is always immaculate, his doing and not Yuna's. In that way, he's like a carbon copy of Jeannine Greer. Finally he speaks.

"No," he says. "Mom says you're fine. And I don't care what they're saying. Our family is not unhinged."

I shoot upright. Our *family*? Meaning me *and* my mom and brother? Something crystallizes in that moment—a shift from the spiraling fear I've been drowning in to something sharper, cleaner. Something beyond rage. Clarity.

The worst thing imaginable has, in fact, already happened to me. I know what it looks like—a father, gone before anyone could reach him. I know what it smells like—sharp antiseptic that doesn't cover the stench of anxious bodies—and what it sounds like—clueless doctors explaining your experience back to you. Breaks can heal, they said. But I didn't break, I cracked wide open. And I survived.

Let them come for me all they want, but not my family. They will not become collateral damage. I won't let the papers drag my family through their carnival of speculation and amateur psychology, turn my mom and brother into footnotes in their true crime narrative about "hereditary mental illness."

Especially not Seth. "They can't do that," I protest.

"They're going after everyone. They even mentioned Ted's ex being in town."

"Seth," I start again, but this time I'm insistent. "You listen. This is not going to be like then. I will not hurt you again."

"Hurt *me* again?" My brother sounds confused. "Are we talking about the same thing?"

"You know. The kitchen. With the knife." My blood goes cold. The knife. I'd blocked it out so completely I'd almost convinced myself it never happened, but just now I'd seen the blade flash in my hand.

More of the memory floods back—finding Seth in Mom's kitchen at 2 AM during Christmas break. Angry because he was so mad at our father. My hand raised. "I'll kill you before I let another man abandon us!" I'd screamed, thinking Seth was leaving us too. Then his voice saying my name, falling to the floor, my weapon clattering harmlessly across the room.

"I could have hurt you," I whisper, not sure he can hear me. Not sure I want him to hear me.

"Hurt me? Jess, do you even remember that night? You always blame yourself, you're such a dork—" Seth stops himself. "Everyone made such a big deal of it afterward, but you were just scared. Mostly of yourself, I think. I mean, you were—"

The line goes dead. I stare at the phone but the display is blank. The numbers are still lit. It's not the battery. What the shit? I try dialing back, get a recorded message telling me I need to purchase minutes and did I have a credit card?

I shut the thing off and toss it in my purse. Sit staring into my bag. Long-distance calls eat through prepaids like candy, and my card is maxed, none of which changes the desperate urge I have to talk to someone. I should return Sofia's car and take the T as close as it'll get me to Mom's.

I push against the headstone I've been leaning on, rising.

Your memory is a blessing.

Or not, I think. Even Seth is questioning my memory.

Or is he? He said I always blame myself, like I shouldn't. What if I shouldn't? What would I do differently if I wasn't beating the crap out of myself right now?

Find Ben Jones.

The thought barely forms before I've decided. He shows up—and then the packages start. Not one. Two. And he's *at* Ted's house.

I'm going to Ted's.

WITNESS STATEMENTS —
FBI CASE NO. 95-PGH-0047

Caller 14-1007 (Female, declined to identify)

I work downtown, always take a walk at lunch. Even if it's raining, or I'd never do it. Anyways, not saying it's her, but I saw a blond woman put a package in the courier box on Wood Street. Around lunchtime, maybe. I don't know if that helps, but I hope you catch her.

Caller 14-1041 (Male, identified as "Tom," no last name provided)

You should talk to the girl's coworkers. People at that PR firm. I dated a girl over there a few years back—those types, they're high-strung. Competitive. Wouldn't surprise me if any woman working there snapped.

Caller 14-1072 (Anonymous, male voice, possibly distorted)

Check the editor. Silver. He didn't leave his old paper for no reason. You don't just walk into a situation like a second time by accident. Yeah, I said a second time.

Caller 14-1136 (Female, identified as Betty McMunn)

I've already spoken to someone about this, but I want it on record. I keep a log of activity on our street. For safety. That Jessica Greer comes and goes at all hours. Always entertaining different men. I have license plates if you need them. I don't trust that kind of behavior.

Caller 14-1120 (Male, declined to identify)

Have you ever seen his byline? *Tragedy without witness is just suffering?* The little drama queen. I'd bet dollars to donuts he did this to himself. You should look into that.

Caller 14-1078 (Female, declined to identify)

I live over in Greentree. Saw a blond woman matching that description in a track suit whack a guy with her car. In broad daylight! Right near the tunnels, the South Hills side. Around lunchtime, maybe. That woman is on the loose, and you need to find her.

33

DINA

A line of brake lights stretches as far as Dina can see. They have yet to reach the Greentree exit.

Jeannine grunts in frustration. "I should know better than to take 376 on a Friday afternoon."

"Hmm," Dina mutters. But it's all the same to her. If anything, the car is a best-case scenario. So long as they're inside the station wagon, the variables are limited. Jeannine can't go off saying or doing something Dina will have to walk back later. She's contained.

Jeannine reaches for the radio, but Dina stops her. "Do you think we did the right thing, going to Cole?"

Jeannine shoots her a sidelong glance. "I don't know."

Dina leans against the passenger door and studies her. Jeannine Greer charges forward without asking permission. *I don't know* are three words Dina would bet she rarely utters. All facts that could make her a threat. So Dina pivots to something safer, Jeannine's grievance.

"Was it just me, or, did it seem to you like Agent Cole was hardly interested in what we had to say?"

"Absolutely not! Not you at all." Jeannine grimaces, takes a noisy breath. "That woman has made up her mind. She's ignoring evidence to prove her pet theory, that my baby is guilty."

Dina shifts, the vinyl seat squeaking beneath her. "I probably shouldn't have encouraged you to go. I hope we didn't give Lydia anything she could use against... any ammunition."

"Encourage me? Going to see Lydia was my idea." Jeannine's voice is firm. "They probably knew all that stuff anyway."

Not everything.

A roaring honk snaps their attention back to the road. Apparently Jeannine had failed to advance a couple of feet and the guy behind her wanted to correct her.

"For the love of God, this is ridiculous," Jeannine snarls as she rolls forward, squeezing the steering wheel like it's a stress ball. "And I'm starving."

"I can unwrap your sandwich," Dina offers.

Jeannine looks at her, smiles like she's the only bright spot in her world. Dina revels in the attention.

"That's okay, dear. I couldn't eat a thing. You go ahead."

She doesn't need to hear it twice. After leaving FBI headquarters, they'd picked up lunch at Primanti Brothers—coleslaw, fries, mystery meat—and its thick perfume has been making her dizzy ever since.

"Maybe a beer though?"

Dina hands her one of the bottles.

"Did you get any IC Light?" Jeannine asks.

Dina shakes her head. "No, just regular Iron City."

"No thanks. I want to hear what they're saying now. See if our visit had any impact at all." Jeannine flicks on the radio before Dina can stop her.

For Chrissakes, is this woman that naive? Dina wonders. She'd been enjoying the break from the news.

Static crackles as Jeannine adjusts the dial. A KDKA news-caster booms into the car.

...Ted Harvey continues to improve as investigators continue the search for Jessica Greer. The former theater critic fled the scene after ramming a parked vehicle outside a residence on Shady Avenue. She is now wanted on federal bioterrorism charges as well as felony hit-and-run. If you see Jessica Greer, do not approach. Call 911 immediately. She should be considered armed and extremely dangerous. This is KDKA NewsRadio—

Jeannine snaps it off.

"Armed and—Jesus..." She points to her purse. "Give me that."

A deep-pink flush blooms on Dina's face as she reaches for the handbag, her hands trembling enough that she drops it. "So sorry, I—"

But Jeannine is dialing already, already moving past it.

"Goddammit," she says when the call doesn't go through.

"What?"

"Jess must have turned her phone off."

Dina bites her lower lip. She's frustrated to lose the spotlight of Jeannine's attention so quickly, sick of hearing about Jessica. Jeannine's *real* daughter.

Before she's stowed the bag, Jeannine's phone rings. She reaches for it, not even looking at Dina, plucks it from her bag, and checks the number.

"Seth? He never calls during work unless something is wrong." Without waiting for Dina to respond, she answers.

"Slow down, I can barely—"

Dina looks out the window. Jeannine's *other* real child.

"You talked to Jessica?" Jeannine asks.

Dina has been fully replaced.

Behind them, the same guy lays on his horn, inches his car forward.

"She said what? ... This morning? When this morning? ... No, I didn't see it. They said hysterical? Bastards. No, don't call the station, that will only make things worse."

She hangs up and slumps back in her seat, oblivious to the guy still pounding his horn. Dina watches her, waiting.

Jeannine's voice tightens with fury. "The Six on Your Side people did a real hatchet job on Jessica. Used her father's death, interviewed our neighbors..." She exhales sharply. "When this is over, Jessica is going to have to write a book. Once she sinks her teeth into something, she doesn't let go. She gets that stubbornness from me, you know. They both do."

"Your kids must be really close," Dina says quietly, staring at the empty bottle in her hand.

"They are now but haven't always been. After Frankland died, I was barely keeping my head above water, trying to run his business, dealing with the funeral, the whole mess." She takes a long sip. "Seth was just about to move to Boston for grad school, but Jessica had a nervous breakdown. Right when she was supposed to graduate."

So the stories about Jessica are true. "That must've been very hard."

"It was." She shakes her head. "But then Seth deferred his admission. Stayed home to help me out."

Dina's grip tightens on the bottle. He took a year, she thinks. Just... *decided.*

Jeannine's voice softens. "Made me think I'd raised them better than I thought. Now..."

Dina stops paying attention, turns her face toward the window, staring at the red smear of brake lights stretching into rain.

Parents these days. So *involved* with their children. Asking what they want for dinner in the grocery aisle. Her mother never asked, only had time to do. Thanks to Chester Kowalski.

He never knew she took his name.

Jeannine straightens, snapping back to business. "You know, the more I think about it, the more I think we need to call Cole back. I don't care what she thinks, the ricin connection is too much of a coincidence. You said you got all that info from the CMU archives?" Jeannine's already reaching for her phone. "I bet they haven't even checked them. I'm going to call and tell them they need to go over there and look around."

"No." The word comes out sharper than Dina intends, but she can't have Jeannine learning about Ted's childhood that way. She would feel sorry for him. That's what always happened—the scales tip, and suddenly the monster has a mother, a childhood, an excuse. Happened with her father. Jeannine would be no different. She's already proven it. "We can't."

Jeannine pauses, phone in hand, studying her. "Can't?"

A loud banging at the window interrupts. Jeannine jerks around. It's the man from the car behind them. Through the windshield, Dina sees a six-foot gap in the lane ahead.

He motions for Jeannine to roll down her window as the rain spatters his suit, darkening the shoulders. "Listen, lady, if you're gonna just sit there—"

Jeannine throws open her door, knocking the man backward. "You listen to me, you pointy-headed pencil. You think I'm a pain in your ass now? Keep carrying on like you are and you'll see what a pain in the ass I can be, because I'm about to have a hot flash. And you do not want to see what happens then. So I suggest you step away from my car—"

As she listens, Dina is awestruck. Never before has she been defended like that. Not by her mother, forever too exhausted by living, nor her father, who forever cared too much about appearances. Mrs. Greer wouldn't betray her. She's a woman, for God's sake. She would see the monster for who he was.

"I have a daughter to save, and you're about to be in my way."

The man retreats, water slicking his hair flat, fury contained by glass and weather and someone else's refusal to yield. Something twists low in Dina's chest—recognition, sharp and unwanted. Sooner or later, everyone disappoints her.

Jeannine is back in the car, damp and glorious. She turns to Dina. "I'll take that beer now. Calories be damned."

But she'd chosen a side.

Dina faces Jeannine, beer bottle in hand. Jeannine's grin falters. "Dina, what—"

34

JESSICA

In the fifteen minutes it takes to get to Bloomfield, my mind gets even clearer. It's as if the fog that's been clouding my thoughts for days lifts and suddenly everything is in sharp relief.

Of course I rammed Kelley's car. Back when I'd first started and she wasn't the big boss, I'd mentioned thinking Carson was cute. She looked me straight in the face and said I wouldn't find it in an HR manual, but Zimmerman frowned on interoffice romance. I know what I would find in an HR manual about supervisors and their employees though.

And of course Sofia's car doesn't have a scratch. The Chevy is a tank, and the Saab is a tin can. If someone saw my regrettable hit-and-run, at least there wouldn't be any blowback on Sofia. She's at work. Better yet, her car is fine. Whatever they throw at me won't be as bad as a murder rap, I didn't damage anything that actually matters. Though people could be looking for this car. Looking for *me*. I can't just roll up to Ted's house.

Bloomfield follows a grid, at least for the few blocks south of Liberty where Ted lives. Unlike most of Pittsburgh, this little section is more sloped than hilly. About three blocks away from

Ted's, I squeeze into a narrow alley and ease into a gap in the line of parked cars. The unbroken terrain makes me feel exposed. Rain has started to fall in earnest, so I check the glove box. Tucked inside, Sofia has stashed one of those teeny umbrellas. Jeannine would be proud. I'm never that organized, making do with a mad dash and my Columbia shell. But I'm in one of Mom's blazing tracksuits—a teal number with bright-pink accents—and have those three blocks to walk. The umbrella offers some cover, from rain and prying eyes.

Still, I take a circuitous route to Ted's, the brisk October air biting my cheeks as I go. Once his place is in my sights, I keep to the opposite side of the street and slow my pace. I circle the block, checking for signs of surveillance. Nothing.

The picture window—in vivid color the night before—is dark. The house looks empty too, abandoned almost. Had Ben gone back to San Francisco? Maybe he and Ethan are off somewhere, planning their next rendezvous. Or they could be going at it right now. Hopefully not in the house.

I'll sneak up to the back door from the alley, see what I see.

Behind Ted's house the alley is brick, lined with garbage cans and overgrown weeds. I slip through the gate in the chain-link fence, my heart hammering as I approach the back door. I peer through the window, see nothing. A light's on in a distant room, but no sound coming from inside. My mind turns to possibilities, namely, where would Ted hide a spare key?

Under the mat seems too obvious, but I check. Nothing. I run my fingers along the door frame then check the flower pots flanking the steps, all filled with dead marigolds.

There—taped to the underside of a ceramic planter—I find my prize. Very Ted, hiding something in plain sight but making you work for it.

The key turns easily in the lock. Inside the eat-in kitchen, I wait for my eyes to adjust to the dim interior. Flowered wallpaper, pale-olive appliances from the '70s, all very tidy. The only thing on the counters is an old-fashioned canister set with handwritten labels—flour, sugar, beans. Dishes are stacked in the sink. No dishwasher. Either Ben left in a hurry or Ted left his mess behind for Ben. Both feel equally plausible.

Across from the door is a set of steps. To my left, a formal dining room. I can't see beyond that. Can't see the picture window. Anyone could be hidden in this maze. My heart is pounding now, drowning out other sounds. They say in dreams you have to charge the monster, force your legs to run like you can choose. Only this is no dream.

"Hello?" I call out, aiming for casual, professional. "Cleaning lady! Anyone home?"

A clattering sound echoes from deep within the house, followed by what sounds like a muffled curse. My blood turns to ice. I am not alone.

I dive between the chairs as footsteps pound on the stairs, the kitchen table's Formica surface the only thing standing between me and whatever's about to go down in this kitchen.

"Jesus Christ," a familiar voice mutters.

From between the chair legs I spot hands brushing jeans over very skinny legs. That's not Ted, or Ethan. And though I only met him a handful of times, it's not how I remember Ben either. I crane my neck further—

"Jess?"

My head bangs against the tabletop as I start, followed by the screech of chairs across linoleum as I fumble for purchase. Apparently the stairs also lead to a cellar, where my former editor seems to have been hiding. His long hair is pulled into a firm top knot, but otherwise his appearance is disheveled—shirt smeared with dirt, untucked, and what looks like cobwebs billow from said man bun.

"Kris Novak?" I hoist myself up. "How did you get in?"

"The front door was open." He's brushing dust from his forehead. "Jesus Christ, what are you wearing?"

I look down at my mother's matched running set then back at Kris. "Long story. What are you doing here?"

"What does it look like?" His eyes go wide as if it's obvious. "Come with me. You need to see this." He jerks his head toward the stairs.

Much as I'd like to, I can't not follow him down the narrow wooden steps. We wind up in a finished basement that smells of old carpet and mothballs. The decorating was probably done around the same time as the kitchen, wood paneling, a chartreuse shag rug balled up in knots, mismatched furniture. There's even a component rack stereo and giant speakers.

But Kris is urging me along to the laundry room. The door is open, revealing a barrel-bodied washing machine—no dryer—under a fluorescent shop light. Beside that stands a stainless steel work table like you'd find in a chemistry lab. It makes sense when my eyes travel up the wall to the glass-fronted cabinets, jammed with an astonishing array of equipment—beakers, test tubes, a small centrifuge, precision scales.

"Can you believe this shit?" Kris says. "Ted's parents must've been doing some of their research here, at home. What psychos. Jesus, no wonder Ted is such an odd bird. Can you imagine growing up with this in the basement?"

I run my fingers along the steel surface, noting how it's all curiously dust-free. Impossibly so if this was the Harveys' home lab. Someone's been down here. Recently. *Ben.*

I look over at Kris. "How did you get so filthy?"

Pulling a slim notebook from his back pocket, he announces proudly. "Finding this. Lab notes. I found it in a crawl space behind the water heater."

My heart skips a beat. I snatch the journal from him and flip through a few pages, chemical equations, random notes, and some kind of poetic ode to ricin, all in a childish scrawl. *Ted's?*

"Should we be touching this stuff?" I ask.

"Good question. Dina told me about Ted's parents—"

"When did you talk to Dina?"

"She called me from the road. I guess she and your mom were stuck in traffic. Anyway, I'm starting to think there's something much bigger going on here."

"Like what?"

"I mean, his parents just so happen to be studying ricin. Then *boom!* They die right before they can go public with it, convenient car accident. At first it's suspicious, then it's not?" Kris takes the notebook back and waves it in the air. "Now it turns out there's a whole lab at the Harveys', and their son almost dies from ricin poisoning?"

I look at my feet and notice Kris and I are both wearing Doc Martens, wonder briefly if his personality is also categorized in the *DSM-IV*. I shake my head, waving the thoughts away. He's going off half-cocked without all the information. *All* the cop shows would agree, it's always the boyfriend. "Here's the thing though. Ted's ex is in town. I think—"

"This smells like a government cover-up. Like the feds wanted that research classified, buried." Kris is now pacing the tiny space, ignoring me. "And me? *Fuck me.* I'm writing a book about how corporations silence dissidents using bioweapons like ricin. I've got to be—"

He stops and turns to me. "Ben Jones is in Pittsburgh? Why would…? Oh, shit. You think he tried to kill Ted and hang you for it. Like, after living in this house he figured out how to do it. Whoa."

Whatever else describes his behavior, Kris is quick as a whip. "Was Ben here when you got here?"

"No. *Damn.*" Kris tucks the notebook back in his pocket. "I knew Ted had a fucked-up childhood. You remember that review he did of *Arsenic and Old Lace*?"

My cheeks flush. I should have read Ted's columns more, but with what time? Does Kris not sleep?

"He wrote something like... 'What makes this story delicious isn't the body count—it's the idea that your most charming relative might serve death with a smile and a cookie. Evil is no guest; it lives in your kitchen, wearing oven mitts.'"

"Kris," I say, already heading for the stairs. "I need to check something."

I race back upstairs, and there it is, hiding in plain sight. Flour, sugar, and the one that struck me as odd—beans. Not *coffee* beans, just beans.

"Kris," I yell down. "Do you remember what kind of beans ricin is made from..." Before I can finish, he's in the kitchen with me. I point to the jar. "Are they poisonous to the touch?" I ask, reaching for the can.

A pounding at the front door interrupts us. We stare at each other, eyes wide.

"Police! Open up!"

35

DINA

Dina's knuckles are white as she steers the station wagon off 376 at Banksville Road. Beside her, Jeannine Greer slumps against the passenger door, breathing but unconscious. The Iron City bottle rolls somewhere on the floor, proof of how quickly this got out of hand.

Pressure point behind the ear—she'd read about it once, tucked into an article she'd pulled for Kris. Quick. Precise. Effective.

But Jeannine had fought. She was stronger than she looked, nails digging into Dina's arms. Then the bottle—too hard, too loud—and the second impact, her head snapping forward into the steering wheel. That sound is what stays with her.

According to the article, she should've been rendered unconscious immediately.

She wasn't.

Why had she kept nattering on about the FBI? Hadn't Dina shown her enough to make it clear how inept those people were? She didn't expect Jessica to understand such subtleties as the suppression of independent oversight, or how DOD research could disappear when it became inconvenient. But Jeannine? Such a letdown. She'd thought they were in on this together.

Her thoughts are pushed aside as the wealth of Mount Lebanon unfolds before her—large, pristine lawns with circular drives, BMWs nestling beside Volvos. She hadn't noticed before how much it's like Fox Chapel, where her father had lived with his other family. Not that she'd ever been invited, but she'd seen his house, seen his whole family, wife and children, many times. They'd moved years ago now but were probably still collecting insurance money and social security benefits that should've been hers.

It must be garbage day, because bins line the street. Everything else manicured and expensive, the exact opposite of the neighborhood she'd grown up in. In her mind's eye she sees herself driving straight at the giant pails, an exploding flurry of trash in her wake. Then Mrs. Greer stirs. That woman is going to come to long before they get to Murray Park.

The Giant Eagle looms on her left, and Dina pulls a sharp turn into the lot. Around back, she knows, there's an enormous dumpster. She drives to it and cuts the engine, checking Jeannine's pulse. Steady. Good. This was not the second dead body she'd hoped for.

Someone will find her. She could even call an ambulance. Mrs. Greer will wake up with a headache and no clue how she got here.

As she struggles with Jeannine's dead weight, reality hits. She checks the time—Ted could be discharged any minute.

Once he starts talking to reporters, his parents will come up. He'll tell his made-up sob story. He'll win again.

But a story like this won't end there. Her father's name could surface, along with questions about his death. That cold case would crack right open.

Not on her watch. Move.

One determined heave and she clears the vehicle. The duster Mrs. Greer is wearing makes it easy to slide her body to the dumpster. The coat's ruined, but Jeannine will be fine. These people always are, Dina thinks.

The Primanti's bag goes into a dumpster down the lot. The beer bottles—after a wipe-down—go into separate trash cans.

The hospital is only twenty minutes away now. Ted Harvey had spent thirteen years building his reputation as Pittsburgh's most feared critic, savaging everyone from high school drama teachers to Broadway touring companies. But he'd never written about his parents' work. Never mentioned them at all.

Dina would make sure it stayed that way.

36

JESSICA

My hands are still shaking as I pull into Allegheny General's parking garage, Sofia's Nova coughing like an old smoker. The escape from Ted's house plays on repeat in my mind. "Go," Kris had said as he pushed me back toward the cellar. "There's a coal chute on the side of the house. It's our best shot."

The last thing I heard before I landed in a hedge was the sound of splintering wood as the police kicked in the front door. We took off in opposite directions, a mad dash through the alleys until I reached the car.

It's on my second spin around the garage that a news bulletin interrupts the stream.

This is a KDKA News Radio update. Local theater critic Ted Harvey, the victim of yesterday's ricin poisoning, has been moved out of intensive care at Allegheny General Hospital.

I HADN'T EVEN THOUGHT about Ted being in ICU.

*...Harvey is now listed in stable condition and expected to make a
full recovery. Police continue their search for Jessica Greer in
connection with the case. We now return—*

Someone else must have something.

Did you see this one, Jimmy?
Looks like the Mail Murderess is on the loose in Squirrel Hill now.
What?
Yeah, she hit a car—

I yank the dial to OFF. Give myself about one second to enjoy knowing I was right. I did hit Kelley's car. The victory is short-lived, as it should be.

There is almost certainly an APB out on me, probably on Sofia's car too. I can't believe I made it this far.

If I do manage to sneak into Ted's room, I'll be the last person he wants to see.

I should leave. Drive straight to the FBI office and turn myself in. Tell them what we found, except I have nothing to show them. Kris has the notebook.

"Whatever you do, stay away from the hospital," I can hear my mother shouting, though of course she's not here.

And yet I'm driving deeper into the garage. I'm going to ignore every rational warning.

Someone has to warn Ted.

As I circle the parking levels in search of the darkest corner, I can't help but think about what Kris said. That there's no coming out of a childhood like Ted's unscathed. Difficult as he is, no one deserves to have their life ended.

And this is when I know—I didn't try to poison Ted. I might

not remember making a batch of brownies, but that's not the same as having a personality transplant. What I am is the only person who's actually going to have their life ended if I take the fall for this.

I'm jabbing the elevator button when I notice—my hands are filthy. Damn coal chute.

The elevator dings its arrival, reminding me—my father had a few stays here. There's a staff lounge with showers in the basement. Hopefully scrubs, too. Beyond personal hygiene, I need the disguise. I have no clue where Ted's room is.

I'll have to clean the inside of Sof's car too, but I can worry about that later.

The elevators drop me into a maze of corridors. Fluorescents buzz overhead, the only sound as I dart through deserted halls. There's no signage, and I'm starting to worry they moved the lounge when I turn a corner and find a hamper full of scrubs. Putting germs out of my mind as I try to avoid the bloodstained pieces, I grab the first matching set I can find as voices approach.

I bolt in the opposite direction with my prize and spy a bathroom. Forget the staff showers. Industrial strength hand soap will have to do. The end result isn't quite right—the surgical cap doesn't match the top and pants, which are too big, and my fingernails are a disaster—but as long as I keep moving, I should be good. No one will see me as a threat.

The tracksuit gives one dying swish as I ball it up and drop it in the trash. Another item I'll have to replace when this is over.

Tucking my hair completely under the cap, I take on the hurried, purposeful stride of nurses everywhere and set out to find this asshat.

At the elevator I hesitate. The last thing I want or need is to bump into one of my nurse "colleagues," so I change course for the stairwell. From there I head to the top floor, thinking I'll work my way down till I find him. I'm about to hit the fourth floor when a cop busts in. There's a moment of sheer panic before I realize he's holding the door open. For me. "I guess everyone but me knows the smoking lounge is on three." He smirks.

I smile back. He's handsome in that chiseled-jaw way. But a *smoker?* Maybe I could convince him to quit?

Jesus, Jess. Focus! Police don't hang out at the hospital. He's clearly posted for Ted Harvey. This must be Ted's floor.

"Yup." I smile but keep my gaze trained on the floor. "Thanks."

Soon as I hit the corridor, I spot another cop. This one's standing in front of the duty station, one elbow on the desk, chatting up a nurse. Ted's room must be right there.

My heart is hammering, but there's no considering my options now. I charge at them with a brisk pace, about to turn for the door when—*ding ding*—the elevator bell rings again. A flurry of nurses and police spill out, flanking two orderlies pushing a gurney. On it, under a thin blanket, is none other than Ted Harvey.

Keeping my head down, I change direction as if I'd forgotten something in the stairwell.

37

LYDIA

Lydia Cole regards the open file in front of her, aligning the pages so they're tight and neat. Like her case. She's handed the affidavit for Greer's arrest off to Powell, who assured her he'd have it signed in a matter of hours. Even if it has to wait till Monday, the APB will ensure Jessica Greer is in custody soon.

The phone rings, and she slams the folder shut.

"Agent Cole, FBI."

"Lyd, it's Ross. We picked up Novak."

"Novak?" She pushes the file aside. "What for?"

"Pittsburgh PD grabbed him two blocks from Ted's place. I'm calling from there now. You're not going to believe what we found."

"At—where? Ted Harvey's place?"

"There's a chemistry lab, Lyd. In the basement. You need to get over here right now."

Lydia's already on her feet, swiping her keys into her coat pocket.

TED HARVEY'S house is on a corner lot. Red brick. Looks enormous. Much too large for one person. Whatever's in there, there's no fitting it within her tidy case file.

She takes the stairs two at a time, sees the picture window before reaching the porch. At night you'd see inside from the street easily. Mrs. Greer had her wits, that's sure.

What Lydia sees now are evidence techs, ghosts in white paper suits, moving behind the glass. Then inside, Campbell's voice. "Be sure and get a shot of that before you move it."

Klavon is in the living room, gloves on, one of the uniforms hovering nearby with a notepad.

"Glad you could make it," he says.

He's joking, Lydia knows he is. But she's not one for banter at a crime scene. "What am I looking at?"

"Police arrived on the scene around 3:30, alerted by neighbors who saw someone break into the rear of the house. They caught up with Kris Novak a block away." He gestures toward the kitchen. "He's in there. Says he found the chem lab. Won't shut up."

Lydia moves past him. Past open drawers. Cabinets rifled through. A trail of knickknacks and gewgaws, all cast aside. The place is what she would've expected and not at all—spotless ashtrays, old phone books, everything slipcovered. Like the house has been waiting for its former owners to return.

THE KITCHEN DOOR is across from a set of stairs that goes to the basement and the second floor. Novak sits at the table, a white Formica that predates even the seventies appliances. The uniform sitting beside him is attempting to take notes while Novak talks, words spilling over each other, both knees bouncing.

"—it's bigger than Ben though. I mean, he's clearly too good for him, so that's suspicious right there. And both his parents die in a car accident? Now he's also poisoned by ricin? Honest to God—"

"Mr. Novak," Lydia cuts in. "Start again."

He turns to her, eyes bright, almost relieved. "Castor beans were sitting right there." Kris gestures to the empty spot on the laminate counter. "It feels on purpose. Like anyone who knows anything about ricin. Is it my fault? Did that story bring too much heat?"

"Your article about domestic bioterrorism?"

"Yeah, man. That one."

Lydia lets *man* slide. Novak is the type who calls everyone *man.* "Why did you come here, Mr. Novak?"

"I just told you." His knees go still. "Ted's parents die in a car accident, he gets poisoned with the same—"

"Today. Why come today?"

He opens his mouth. Closes it. "It felt right? Everything's breaking open. I heard Ben was in town, so I thought I should talk to him."

"So you broke in?"

"Nah, man. Door was open." He says it like it's obvious.

She doesn't pursue it. "But Ben wasn't here. What made you look around?"

"Agent Cole."

She looks up sharply at Klavon. *This better be good.*

"The officers who apprehended him found this." Klavon drops an evidence bag on the table.

A composition notebook with a marbled cover. Old.

"You were stealing evidence? Mr. Novak, this is not a good look."

Kris Novak jerks forward to speak, thinks the better of it and slouches back. "We just ran. It was instinct."

"We?"

Something shifts in his face. "Jessica Greer was here."

Now it's Lydia's turn to go still. She might save her case after all. "Jessica Greer?"

"She showed up just before the cops showed. Said she was going to the hospital." He pauses. "To see Ted."

The rest of the story assembles itself. Greer, inside the victim's home, handling evidence, now alone with a man who can't call for help from a hospital bed.

"Klavon, you stay on him." She's moving toward the front door. " Get everything you can from this scene."

"Where are you going, Lydia?"

She stops, flashes a rare smile. "Allegheny General."

38

TED

My eyes flicker open. It's not the movement that wakes me—it's the silence. For the first time in what seems like an eternity, it's silent. The beep and buzzing of my life-saving apparatus has ceased. Blessed relief! But... Where are they taking me? Fluorescent lights scroll overhead, sandwiched between what look for all the world like asbestos tiles. I shall have to speak to someone about that.

This concern is soon relegated as the stink of industrial disinfectant and despair penetrates my nostrils. I cough. Lightly only yet it's as if someone has set fire to my larynx. The agony! It must be from the vomiting. Or the ventilation tube. Still, the orderlies keep pace. No one rushes to check my vitals. The wheels keep turning.

Oh, the indignity.

What is that from? Shakespeare? Funny, I don't remember any diminished intellectual capacity from childhood. Then again, isn't stupidity the condition of childhood?

Well, I can amuse myself at any rate. Now that I'm being— released? God, I hope not. Everything feels less urgent now, but it feels far too soon. The relief I felt at the machine's absence is outweighed by this loss of oversight. The constant parade of concern from doctors and nurses checking my heart, my lungs, my bowel movements... it's over. No more the star of my own medical drama, I'm simply another patient on a gurney. How pedestrian.

On the elevator, though, I see it. The looks. Not from my companions, whoever they are, but from others. Patients. Visitors. Doctors, even. Word about me must have spread—the ricin victim. The theater critic who survived a bioterrorism attack. That has a nice ring to it, doesn't it? Much more interesting than *sallow-skinned son of university researchers*, though of course, my story was always going to turn out better than my parents'. Theirs had no arc.

Maybe I'll get a book deal. That would make up for the fact that no one has visited. No flowers.

We're rolling down an identical corridor when all of a sudden we slow. Turn. My new room. Beige walls, a single window overlooking the parking lot, and—God help me—a roommate. Some elderly man who appears to be sleeping off what I can only assume is something thoroughly uninteresting. A heart attack, perhaps. Or diabetes complications. The sorts of ailments that don't make the evening news.

The evening news! My eyes travel to the wall across from my bed, where, small mercies, there *is* a television! I'll be able to monitor this situation, see what people are saying about me.

They wheel me alongside the new bed and begin the mechanical process of transferring me from the gurney. Up, over, down. No "How are we feeling today, Mr. Harvey?" Instead, they offer all the ceremony one might afford cheap luggage. But their practiced choreography is belied when the burly fellow with the unfortunate overbite lifts the bed rail into place, jarring my shoulder.

"Watch out," I try to say, but my voice is scarcely a whisper. It feels like I've been gargling with Comet.

Then they're pulling the curtain between the beds shut and leaving. No "Would you like water?" Or "Here's how the bed works." Or even "Here's the television remote." No. I'm flat on my back, the television mounted opposite, taunting me with its blank screen. I open my mouth to ask for their assistance, but all that emerges is a pathetic wheeze. I am alone with the old man and the now-maddening silence.

Do they even have a remote control for the TV in this sterile purgatory? Is there not a nurse's call button?

I crane my neck to survey my new domain. I'm quite weak yet, but beside my bed I do spy a rolling tray table pushed to one side, putting the water pitcher and plastic cup a hair's breadth outside my reach. Then I see it, the flowers. So many flowers. Actual bouquets.

The theater community I've spent years needling with my reviews has rallied around me like a martyred saint. On the window sill I spy an arrangement from Mary Beth Purcel. Lilies, naturally, the theater person's flower of choice. Very dramatic. Here, finally, is the recognition I've long deserved. Naturally there have been no visitors. I've been in the ICU. Not even Ben would have been permitted. Family only.

A tear rolls down my cheek, and I turn my head to wipe it against my pillow, where I spot a coiled cord snaking from the bed toward... somewhere. I follow the line to a rectangular device clipped to the bed rail, also out of comfortable reach. Surely, the same sadists who designed hospital gowns chose this setup. I stretch, shoulder protesting, grasping for this lifeline to the outside world.

I must see the news. Must know how my story is being told. When at last the elusive device is in my hand, I bring it near but see only incomprehensible markings. The first button I push raises the back of the bed. That's actually much better. The next button, however, nothing. For heaven's sake. This is as bad as being at home alone. Or with my parents.

The scene returns to me, as it has repeatedly throughout this stay. How could it not from a hospital bed? I'm in the basement with Mother, playing paddleball, watching her as she bends over her microscope, notebook beside her, shifting her eyeglasses into place when she makes notes.

Why didn't I merit that sort of close attention? For a long time I thought it was because of her beauty, her dark hair always in a neat chignon, never a run in her pantyhose, no makeup. Perfection. None of which explained Father, his awful haircuts, stained undershirts, and suspicious oral hygiene. And yet, she attended to his every utterance. I know, because I was always watching. Planning.

It was the summer after Grandma died that everything went wrong. I was far too old for daycare, had given up on going to the pool, and we didn't own a television. So I wanted her cannoli? I had to amuse myself somehow.

Mother put me off. Ignored my requests outright. Until I knocked over Father's precious stereo cabinet. Of course it wasn't an accident, but how was Mother to know that? She wasn't paying attention. Made up her mind. Took away my paddleball and sent me to my room. Morning ticked by, and lunchtime came and went. I devised a plan.

IF YOU COULD ONLY SEE
> *What you mean to me*
> *But you don't even look*
> *In this poison that I took...*

. . .

THE MEMORY of my juvenile rhyme makes me giggle, which quickly morphs into a cough. I reach for the water jug, and what do I see? Another control box, one that's slipped between bed and the rail.

The television remote!

I click, and the old set sputters to life. A cartoon is coming into view.

"Oh the indignity," laments a cartoon train.

Children's cartoons are quoting Shakespeare? Or is that not the Bard? No matter. I must find the news.

The channels blur past—a soap opera, a game show—until I land on something title *FOX at Five.* The purported newscaster is nattering on about pumpkin carving, and I'm about to click when a graphic pops up, "Poisoned local critic released from ICU."

Finally, something about me. Briefly. Then, inexplicably, they're on to Jessica Greer?

They think *she* poisoned me? How does that even make sense?

I'm thinking about where to start on my list of grievances when someone I don't recognize enters the room. She's holding flowers. I suppose from here on out I'll have to resign myself to a life of fans and lookie-loos.

39

DINA

The television is blaring, a disjointed screech of newscasts starring, of course, Ted Harvey. Even if it weren't for the police clustered at his door, Dina would've had no trouble finding him. And they were only too happy to let his assistant drop off a bouquet.

He's propped up in the bed, an IV line snaking into his left arm as he casts a languid glance in my direction. His skin is fishier than normal—bright white with a blue tinge—his hair sweat styled.

"I'm very tired." His voice is hoarse. Scarcely a whisper.

Dina wonders if that's put on for her benefit. He's made no move to turn down the TV.

"Let me help you with that," she says with a cheery smile, prying the remote from his grip. Mutes the sound.

"Hey, I was watching—"

He's interrupted by his own dry cough. The man is repulsive.

"Have some water." She hands him a cup, waits for him to drink. "Very good." She counts to five in her head.

"You don't remember me, do you? We met at *City News*?" She extends a hand. "Dina Kowalski, fact checker."

He looks at her hand, back at her face. "Oh right, you got my details."

"I had your details. You gave me Ben Jones's information."

He closes his eyes. Bored? Perhaps it's better this way.

"Here." Dina digs into her bag. "I brought you a snack, too. You've gone too thin."

He smiles, eyes still shut. "Not possible," he rasps.

She sets the muffin on the rolling tray and nudges it toward him. He opens one eye. Looks at it. Looks at her.

"Blueberry," she says.

He closes his eye again. She could swear his nostrils flare, the instinct of a man who has eaten his feelings since childhood warring with the suspicion of a man who knows, better than most, what food can carry.

She laughs, low and easy. "Silly Ted! I'll leave it right here."

His expression doesn't change, but his shoulders drop a fraction.

She moves on. Lets the muffin sit.

"That's how I know you knew." She smiles. Keeps it conversational. Settles into the visitor's chair like she has nowhere to be. "About the symptoms. You recognized them immediately."

He says nothing.

"It's the only reason you're alive, really. Anyone else would have waited. Thought it was food poisoning, maybe. Gone to bed." She tilts her head. "Not you. You called nine-one-one. Told them you suspected ricin."

No reaction. Not even when his name appears onscreen with a photo, the one of him from his parents' funeral, cropped now so he's alone in the photo. She should've thought to supply something better. Never occurred to her that a photograph of him would be so difficult to pin down. The anchor on the television is saying his name again. He doesn't try to turn up the volume.

"My parents studied ricin for CMU," he squeaks out finally. "I was exposed to various compounds as a child." Each word clipped, careful. "I understand the immune response."

"Better than most, I dare say." She nods, as if she only now understands. As if she hasn't spent months in the university archives, reading his parents' correspondence, letters to doctors, insurance companies, each other. The careful clinical language they used to describe *Teddy's sickly constitution.* "That must have been frightening. As a child."

He makes a sound. He can do better.

"Though I will say"—she's almost speaking to herself—"your diary tells a slightly different story."

His head turns. Slowly.

"You know I've been helping Kris Novak with his book. I've spent months in the CMU archives." She smiles again. Her face is starting to strain with the unfamiliar effort. "You'd be amazed what gets donated." She watches his hands. "You may well have learnt a lot from your parents' work, but in your teen years? Someone was running their own experiments." She meets his eyes. "No?"

"I don't know what you're talking about."

His voice has a harsh edge now. That won't do at all. Angry people don't eat.

"Let's not quibble, Ted." She keeps her voice pleasant. "But I do know, Ted. I'm a fact-checker. That's the job."

Ted's heart rate monitor changes pitch. She can't have the nursing staff barging in.

She leans close, whispers in his ear, "You don't have to worry about me, Ted. I'll never say a word. It's your parents' fault."

Ted drops back in his pillow, drained. "My parents." Ted scoffs. Or chokes a little, Dina can't be sure which.

"They ignored you, did they?"

"I was a child left to my own devices in a house full of equipment, and my parents were—" He stops. Recalibrates. "They weren't paying attention."

"You're right. I can see that now. I've seen all the facts, and it's all there because of what *isn't* there. About you," Dina says. Gently.

Something moves across his face. She's given him the thing he wanted—recognition—and he doesn't quite know what to do with it.

"My mother kept a notebook beside the microscope," he says. "She wrote down everything. Every result. Every variable." He stares miserably at the ceiling. "Nothing about me."

Dina says nothing. She knows the notebooks. She's read every page.

"I started keeping my own record," he continues. "If she wouldn't—if no one was going to—" He exhales, a thin sound that catches in his damaged throat. "At first I wanted to understand what they were doing. But then, it worked. They would drop everything. Their guilt was... exquisite."

There it is. She'd known it was there. You could always find it, if you were patient—the thing a person most needed to say.

"Until I realized it wasn't *me* they were worried about. It was never about me. Always about them and their precious research. I'd gone to all that trouble, stealing from their supplies, just to dose myself with their stupid ricin."

"How old were you then? Fifteen? Sixteen?" Dina shakes her head. "It's so easy to go off the rails at that age. It's when you need your parents most." She knows from experience.

"That would have been enough if... if they hadn't been so small-minded."

Dina sits back. "What do you mean?"

"They didn't want me to study theater at Otterbein. They—" Another coughing fit slows him, which Dina considers a divine intervention. She refills his cup and hands it to him.

She needs to move this back in the direction of self-pity. *Indulgence.*

"You're saying they didn't know you were going to be famous?"

"They didn't appreciate my love of theater. Actually believed I cared about chemistry. But I was always cut out for bigger things, so... I had to take care of that problem."

"I always knew you were going to be famous, Ted."

He hands back his cup, sees Dina as being there for him. Ready to serve.

"I've been following your work for some time," she continues. "Even tried to get in at *Pittsburgh Voice*. Did you know that? They wouldn't take me, not even as a receptionist. Said it's because I don't have a college degree." She lifts a hand, drops it. "It's fine. I enjoy my career. Making other people's work better. Checking their facts. Correcting their errors."

She glances at the muffin on the tray, Ted's eyes returning to the television.

"Your work never has any. Errors, I mean."

Ted's gaze returns to Dina. What could he see but a woman in a hand-embroidered sweater and sensible shoes. She rides the bus. Checks facts for a living and has been reading his work for years. A woman who found something in the archives that could ruin him and has decided, for the benefit of all, to keep it to herself.

He reaches for the muffin, unwraps the paper towel around it. He's got it in his hand when the door opens. They both look up—Dina already composing her face—to find a woman in scrubs that don't quite fit and a surgical cap that's more than slightly askew.

It's Jessica Greer, and her arms appear to be smeared with coal dust.

Dina turns to Ted, puts her finger to her lips.

Ted speaks first.

"You look like a bargain basement Florence Nightingale."

40

———

JESSICA

For a second, I think Ted's joking.

Not because he's funny; he never is. But because he's not wrong. I *do* look like I've walked off a battle-field. The scrubs are too big, I know that. My arms are—I glance down at myself—

Jesus. Is it obvious I crawled out of a coal chute?

And why is the man I'm here to save... critiquing me?

"Budget cuts?" I say, a moment before recognizing Dina Kowalski in the visitor's chair.

"Dina?"

"Jessica."

"Oh my God, Dina. I'm so glad you're here. You're never going to believe what I found at Ted's."

She blinks. Is that jealousy? Little Miss Research is mad I found something she didn't know about?

Oh, who cares? This is too good to hold onto.

"A chemistry lab! There's a freaking chemistry lab in Ted's basement!"

Dina arches a single brow.

"You don't think that's weird?" I look at Ted, his pale face.

Bloodless lips. "Hello to you, too, Ted. You don't look so good yourself."

"No thanks to you," he croaks. His *voice*. He must've been intubated.

He reaches for the call button, and before I can say anything about Ben, Dina stops him.

"Hang on here. I think we can all agree the press has gotten this story wrong."

"Did you tell Ted?"

Ted's head jerks up. I can't tell if he's surprised or glaring. Dina is looking at me like I'm an alien.

"Tell him what?"

"About Ben and Ethan." What is with her?

"Oh, that." Dina exhales. "No."

"What about Ben and Ethan?" Ted's voice sounds stronger all of a sudden.

Dina shrugs. "Ted's just out of ICU. I came to bring him flowers from the office." She points to a bouquet from the hospital's floral shop that's under the TV set.

I look around the room, surprised to see hers aren't the only flowers Ted has gotten. None emits an odor. It's unnatural. The only thing I can detect, over the ever-present note of antiseptics, is whatever they boiled for lunch. He gets bouquets, I get public humiliation.

Not the point right now, I remind myself.

"Listen, Ted. I know this is hard, but... What happened between you and Ben? Why did you two part ways?"

Ted's eyes slide to Dina, a smirk forming on his bloodless lips. "You're trying to get out of this by blaming the ex-boyfriend? Jessica, darling, your lack of imagination is showing."

Dina giggles. What is going on between the two of them?

"Ted, listen to me. Ben has been in your house. He's had access to the lab. And he's not exactly playing the part of supportive former partner." I hadn't planned on mentioning specifics, but Ted has done it. Found my weak spot. The disappointment behind my family's catchphrase for me, *Oh, Jessica*. It's why I chose writing, so I could choose my words, a capability I too often lack in the moment. "He's sleeping with your new editor. I think he got what he needed from your house and now he's trying to frame me."

Ted's eyes glitter with what could be amusement or sedatives. "Ben?" Despite the sore throat, there's a smug quality to Ted's tone that makes my stomach clench. "Ben couldn't plot his way..." He pauses to catch his breath. "Out of a paper bag."

I want to protest. *You think everyone is a moron.* But I need to keep him sweet. "But it's easy to make ricin, no?"

"Easy enough to make, I suppose." He points at the water jug.

Dina fills the cup and hands it to him. Whose side is she on, anyway?

"But making a nonlethal dose? Much harder."

Dina makes a small sound. A laugh?

Something's off.

Not only the situation—that's been off for the last week—but this. The air in the room. The way they're looking at each other like I came in halfway through a conversation I wasn't invited to. He's on drugs, what's her excuse?

"Where's my mom? How'd it go with Agent Cole?"

"I dropped her off about an hour ago," she says, mild as milk. "I'm afraid, well... We told her everything, but I'm afraid Agent Cole is still rather interested in you as a suspect."

A shot of adrenaline courses through my body with nowhere to go. How can she be so casual?

"So you both decided not to do any more, whatever you said you were going to do? Research?" I might be sick.

"I needed to step back, Jessica. I'm no lawyer, but yours seems convinced."

Did she talk to the lawyer?

There's a muffin on Ted's tray table, untouched. Presumably from lunch. I haven't eaten all day. "Are you going to eat that?" I point, about to reach for it when Dina jumps up.

"I made that for Ted," she says, pushing the table closer to him.

In a bizarre twist, a chemistry lab is found in this Bloomfield home. Could this be the secret site of a bioterrorist's cell? Stay tuned—

Ted is pointing the remote at the screen, has turned the volume back up.

Then Agent Cole appears, badge already out, taking in the scene in one sweep. She fixes on me, and her gaze sharpens.

"Jessica Greer," she calls from the door, two officers trailing behind.

That's when I know what Dina's saying is true. No one is looking at Ben Jones. No one is looking at the door. No one is looking at anything except me.

I'm not sure who I came here to save, but it didn't work. Saliva fills my mouth, my knees buckle, my stomach quivers. A line of pure bile shoots out of my mouth.

41

LYDIA

Lydia Cole knows how this ends, Greer in custody, a clean line from motive to method. The kind of case that looks messy in the press but airtight in a courtroom.

She was not prepared for vomit.

"Oh for Pete's sake."

Her eyes sweep from Ted—propped up in his bed, pale but alert, eyes glued to the TV—to the visitor's chair, where Dina Kowalski has had a pile of sick dumped in her lap. Dina rushes into the bathroom, running water as she audibly yanks paper towels from the dispenser.

"Jessica Greer," Lydia repeats, stepping fully into the room to grab hold of the only normal she can find. Two officers fill the doorway behind her.

Greer tries to steady herself with the tray table, almost falls. "Oh God, sorry. I was just—"

"I'm sure you were." Lydia waves at the mess left behind. "Don't worry about that, we'll get it sorted out. Are you—"

Ted shifts, wincing, then pushes through it. "This is the

woman who tried to kill me. Now she's blaming Ben? You have a badge, of some sort. Help me. I—"

Lydia raises her palm to stop him. "I'll get to you, Mr. Harvey."

She faces Jessica. She doesn't have her warrant yet, but that doesn't mean she wants these witnesses contaminating each other's testimony.

"You know we saw his ex having sex with his new editor," Jessica blurts out, talking a mile a minute. Maybe she is having an episode. "There's a lab in the basement. How do you not think that merits more investigation? At the very least, Ted still needs to watch his back."

Ted lets out something like a laugh, cut short by his throat. "She's scrambling. You see that, right? Ben and I are friends. Whom he chooses to sleep with is his business."

"I came hoping to speak to you, Agent Cole," Dina is saying as she returns from the bathroom, dabbing uselessly at her skirt with a paper towel. "Kris Novak told me you might be coming."

Kris Novak? He should still be at the Harvey site. Shouldn't have access to a phone. What is Dina playing at?

"Didn't you two just see each other? Where *is* my mother anyway?"

"I'll ask the questions here. In fact..." She waves a uniform over, squints at his name tag. Alice is always on her about wearing her glasses. "Officer Patterson, would you take Ms. Greer out to the hallway and keep an eye on her?"

"Oh, she might want to hear this."

All eyes turn to Dina. She hesitates long enough to make it matter. "There was... an incident."

Jessica stiffens. "Dina—"

"A road rage situation," Dina continues. "We'd been stuck in the backup near Fort Pitt and got to talking. I guess the traffic started moving and Mrs. Greer didn't, and the next thing we know, the guy jumps out of his car, comes over, and starts screaming."

"At *my* mother?"

"That's not the worst part." Dina's voice quivers.

Either this explains how Kowalski's been acting or she's good at this. Too good.

"She, your mother, gets out of the car to give him a piece of her mind," Dina continues. "Tells him what she thinks of his driving. And he, well, he didn't like that very much."

"Then what happened?" Jessica's voice is frantic, and for a moment, Lydia feels the situation slipping from her grasp.

"He grabbed your mother's arm, shook her. When I tried to intervene, he shoved me back against the car," Dina says, fat tears magnifying her steely eyes. "Your mother tried to protect me, and he... he hit her on the head with a beer bottle. Then he left. Got back in his truck and drove off."

"A beer bottle? Oh my God." Jessica's eyes go wild. "Where is she?"

Lydia falls back on her FBI tutelage. "Did you get a license plate? A physical description?"

Dina shakes her head. "It happened so fast..."

"We need to call this in." Lydia reaches for the radio on her belt.

"No, wait." Dina crosses her arms across her chest. "Jeannine made me promise not to involve police. She said she was fine, just shaken up. Insisted I take her home instead of here. Said she'd rather rest in her own bed than deal with the paperwork. Honestly, now that I've had a chance to slow down, I could use a rest myself."

"I have to go to her." Jessica moves toward the door, but the police are blocking her exit.

"Lady," Ted cuts in, louder now, pushing through the

damage to his voice. "Why are you letting Jessica Greer control this situation?"

Cole shocks herself wishing Klavon was here. She needs to separate these people *and* hear what they have to say. But she is done with this configuration.

"Officers." Lydia takes Jessica by the wrist. "I'll be taking Ms. Greer—"

Jessica gasps. Dina looks at Ted.

Ted lets out a breath, triumphant. "Finally."

A strange voice cuts through the room. "That's enough out of you, young man."

Everyone freezes. Something shifts behind the curtain that splits the room in two. Lydia motions to an officer to push open the drape. Behind it lies a rail-thin gentleman atop another bed. His skin is as wrinkled as his hospital gown, but his eyes are sharp and alert.

"He's been yakking nonstop, and I've been stuck over here, listening to the whole goddamn racket." His voice is warbly but strong enough. "That fellow there is lying, and I'll say so in court. First he's yammering about his flowers, then he starts talking to the TV, saying he's gonna be famous. Then she comes in"—he points a long, elegant finger in Dina's direction—"she knows. He told her all about how he poisoned himself as a young'un to get back at his parents. Nattering on about how they ignored him. So he got their attention. Same thing he's doing now, looking for fame. All that boy needs is a good spanking. It's garbage, I tell you." He looks at Ted again. "You tried to kill yourself to be famous? Did you figure it out? Cause when you get to the end of it, fame is meaningless."

Jessica looks like she's about to say something, but Ted gets there first, pointing his index finger at his skull and twirling it around. "Taking notes from the peanut gallery now, are we?"

The old man looks directly at Agent Cole. "Lady, I fought in

Korea," he says. "I know what evil sounds like, and I heard it in that boy as soon as he opened his mouth."

The room falls silent except for the steady beep of monitors as Lydia scrambles for purchase in this new territory.

She looks from her elderly witness to Ted—still grimacing—to Jessica, standing straighter now. For the first time since they met, Jessica Greer doesn't look like she's hiding anything. But Ted Harvey? He looks downright abusive, like a predator toying with his prey.

But Ted poisoning himself? This isn't adding up either, but she needs to get to the bottom of it.

"Patterson, let the medical staff know that this patient is not to be discharged. You"—she can only point at the other officer, can't read his name—"you stay with Mr. Harvey. Monitor him."

"Monitor me?" The equipment beside Ted's bed begins beeping rapidly, his heart rate spiking. "But I'm the victim. That old codger is right about one thing, because it's not the first time. My parents used me—"

"Ted." Dina has stepped up to clutch the footboard. "You heard what Agent Cole said. I think the less you say right now the better."

Lydia puts an arm in front of Dina before she can throw herself onto the bed. "Thank you, Ms. Kowalski. I've got this."

Dina releases the bed, smooths her hair. "Well, then, I should let you work," Dina says, but makes no move to leave.

Lydia looks at Dina, registering her fully. Other than the damp spot on her skirt, she looks the same as always. Ready for another day of being the teacher's pet at her high school. It's a little odd the fact-checker didn't collect any information about her assailant, but surely the last twenty-four hours have been as much a trial for her as anyone. She hasn't had the benefit of FBI training.

"I'm going to need you to file an incident report, Ms. Kowalski. I don't care what Mrs. Greer said." Lydia steps aside to let her pass. "We'll talk more later, but in the meantime, don't go anywhere."

Dina inclines her head. "Of course not." She looks at her watch. "But right now I better go. The express bus is leaving soon."

The uniforms part, and she slips past them and into the hall.

Lydia turns her attention to Jessica. "Ms. Greer, will you step into the hall with me?"

Jessica hesitates.

"Now."

They move into the corridor. The door swings shut behind them, muting the room.

For a moment, Lydia stares at her. The scrubs. The grime. The fact that she came anyway.

The fact that Lydia still doesn't have her warrant.

"Your mother," Lydia says.

Jessica blinks. "What about her?"

"You should go to her."

"Really?"

"Yes, really. You might want to rinse out your mouth before you leave," she says. "Then get out of here, before I change my mind."

Jessica doesn't wait. Doesn't nip into the hall toilet. Simply turns and goes.

Lydia watches her disappear down the hall, along with her tidy win, before turning back toward the room.

Toward Ted Harvey.

"Nurse, would you be able send someone into 417? We need a biomedical cleanup."

WITNESS STATEMENTS —
FBI CASE NO. 95-PGH-0047

Concetta Marchetti, Bloomfield, Cedarville Street

My daughter says I should talk to you. So I'm talking.

The Harvey house I've been watching since before that boy was born. The parents, God rest them, they weren't bad people, but they weren't neighborhood people either. Always inside. In the basement. You'd knock with a plate, and the mother would come to the door like you woke her up from something, even in the middle of the afternoon. The boy answered the door himself from the time he could reach the handle. I used to send my Gino over with sfogliatelle on Sundays. He stopped going after a while. Said it made him sad. The boy was sick a lot.

Thursday night I'm in the sunroom with my knitting like always. You can see everything from there. So, I'm gabbing with Carole. We're both up all hours since the change. Anyways, it's getting close to midnight when I tells her—look. We seen the first boy go in, very handsome, good coat. Now mind you, Teddy's in the hospital. Everybody knows that. Now the first boy I at least recognize. Old friend of Ted's, so I figure he's watching the place for him while he's away or something. Twenty minutes later, along comes this other boy. Fancy boy, you know what I mean? Weird shoes and very ugly eyeglasses.

It's not fifteen minutes and I see the two of them, right there in the picture window. I'm not going to say what they was doing. You know what it was.

Then I sees a station wagon. Midnight blue, clean, right out front of the house. Do those boys stop?

Do they even notice?

Then these two women drive up. Sit there staring like it's the movies, then they leave fast. That's all I know.

Except… those two boys, they didn't do nothing to Teddy. Teddy was a weird little boy, and he's not much different as a man, and I'll tell you what kind. He's the kind who trips and calls it someone else's fault. His mother's fault.

That's all I got. You want coffee?

42

JESSICA

My chest tightens as the elevator descends. Dina's story has me rattled—the idea of some stranger grabbing my mother, threatening her. I should have been there.

Beyond the hospital's automatic doors I find an empty taxi stand. *Shit.*

Across the lot, the street's a jumble of three-story walkups with faded awnings, neon bar signs, a corner grocery. Yet there are no signs of life. It's weirdly empty. I rush back to the information desk, but the volunteer shrugs, cracking a piece of gum in her mouth. From its pepper smell I can tell it's Nicorette. "All the cabs are stuck in traffic," she says. "Rush hour delays."

I want to scream. I can't call Sofia for a ride. I have her car. Even if I *wanted* to drive it, that thing's a loaded gun. In all the hubbub I don't think Cole has called off the search on the plate. Maybe she can't. I did use the Nova in a hit-and-run.

There's no choice but to return to the entrance and wait for a cab.

I'm pitched against a concrete pole, staring helplessly into the parking lot, when I see it. Mom's station wagon. But Dina mentioned taking the bus. She must have left it thinking I could use it. She couldn't know I don't drive over bridges. This also means Mom has no car.

No one is coming to save me.

I clutch at my bag but know they're there, Mom's spare keys. Without giving myself time to think, I'm behind the wheel, starting the car, heading out. But I don't make it out of the lot before the feeling hits, my stomach bottoming out as my car tips over a bridge.

This is why I live in Dormont. There's no river between me and Mom, and for everything else I can take the T. Unless it's north of the Warhol. Then it might as well be another planet. Pittsburgh straddles three rivers, hence the nickname *City of Bridges*. Ask any Pittsburgher and they'll tell you their city has more bridges than any other in North America. None of us knows if that's true.

What it means for me, practically speaking, is that, since my father died and my bridge dreams began, I've had to organize my entire life around avoiding bridges.

No matter what car I take. Right now I don't have that luxury.

I close my eyes and force myself to breathe. Think about Mom. She needs me. She was there for me when... when...

I try to fend them off, but my thoughts rush past my mental barricades like a tidal wave over a sand castle. There he is, Dad. The man who let me ride his back while he swam laps, built me an intricate dollhouse with lights I could turn on and off, picked me up from prom after I barfed up Southern Comfort all over my dress, which we never told Mom. Now he's there, in front of me, limp off the end of a rope in the garage. My beloved father, and I couldn't breathe. Couldn't move. Couldn't save him.

That was when the dreams started, every night, always the same. My car tipping over the side, falling, then trapped as the

Mon waters—cold and foul-smelling—close in. I stopped sleeping.

They tried to get me to talk about it in the hospital. "Avoidance makes trauma larger than it needs to be, Jessica."

So did meds and time.

The dream was still there, ever-present in my lingering fear of driving over bridges, but the nightmares receded. Mostly they only came back in times of stress, like now. I've barely slept all week. Not since they announced Carson's promotion Monday.

I drop my forehead to the wheel, cold and hard beneath my skull. A burst of angry honks rouses me from this stupor, and I'm in the street, pointed toward Mom. I am sick to death of this phobia. Maybe if I occupy myself with something else, my body will keep moving. Charge the monster.

The radio crackles to life. Instead of Mom's oldies station, it's KDKA.

—traffic backing up at all major river crossings due to an accident on the Parkway East. Delays of thirty minutes or more on the Fort Pitt Bridge...

I snap it off. Tighten my hands around the steering wheel and pull out onto the Parkway with jerky movements, my heart drumming in my throat. I'm driving like I'm high, checking every which way.

As promised, the cars are backed up. Six lanes that must merge into two, brake lights stretching toward the bridge. For most people it's the tunnel on the other side. But for me? The idea of sitting on a bridge is absolute torture. I can't stop thinking about falling. My stomach lurches.

Look around.

Beside me a woman talks on her phone, gesturing with her free hand. The guy behind me is smoking through the crack in his mostly rolled-up window. Up ahead I see two kids fighting in the back seat while the woman leans back on the headrest. I'd bet her eyes are closed. People who cross bridges every day without thinking about it. Normal people doing normal things.

We inch forward together.

My mind wanders to Ted. *Freak.* But then, did he ever get the chance to be normal? If I'm this wrecked after one trauma, I can't imagine what it would be like to be your parents' test subject. Surprising as it was to see the depth of Ted's resentment over a three-year-old review, I'm not handling my life's trauma any better.

"You need to let yourself be angry, Jessica," the shrink had said. "Otherwise those feelings will get stuck. They won't just go away."

Another theory I'd rejected. What use was there in being angry with my father, a man already driven to such desperation? The person I was furious with was me. For failing.

Maybe part of me doesn't want to give up this obsession. This hang-up around bridges. Maybe part of me believes that if I let go of the nightmares, I'll forget my father.

Traffic opens, and with a sickening lurch, I see the bridge ahead. Suddenly it's obvious. My dream isn't about bridges. Or falling. Never was. It's about my powerlessness—the helplessness I'd felt seeing my father. That was the monster I'd been fighting all along.

I'd been losing.

I take in the bridge's tiered arch, connecting downtown Pittsburgh to the South Hills. My chest is tight and my palms are sweating, but I have to get to Murray Park. I squeeze left, joining the line for the bridge.

The monster isn't real.

Mom's injury is real.

The bridge is beneath me.

My stomach flips, but I keep going. I'm driving slower than the traffic demands, and soon I can't hear my thoughts over the honking. Then I'm across and into the tunnel. I'd held my breath the entire time. I'm drenched with sweat, and my head is pounding, fingers still clawed around the wheel. But I'm on the other side. Before I'm out of the Fort Pitt tunnel, traffic has picked up speed. Soon the South Hills stretch ahead of me, familiar neighborhoods leading home.

Murray Park is still fifteen minutes away through residential streets I know by heart. Streets where I learned to ride a bike, where Dad taught me to drive in empty parking lots on Sunday mornings. Everything looks the same, an average Saturday afternoon with kids playing in yards, people walking dogs, the ordinary rhythms of suburbia.

When I turn onto our street, I sense something's wrong. The house is dark, no lights in any windows. Is Mom even here?

I park in the driveway and run to the front door. "Mom!" I call out, fumbling with my keys. "Mom, are you okay?"

Silence.

The heavy, wrong kind of silence that means nobody's home.

I check every room, calling her name. Nothing. No signs of struggle, no signs she was ever here. Even Snookums is mysteriously absent.

The phone rings, and I lunge for it.

"Jess? Thank God." It's Seth. "I've been trying to reach you for hours."

"Seth, I can't find Mom. She was in some kind of road rage incident—"

"That's why I'm calling. I know where Mom is."

43

LYDIA

The PA flashes Lydia a thumbs-up signal. "All good to go in there," he says.

Lydia nods but doesn't leave the nurse's station. Klavon has filled her in on the details from the Harvey find—the canister on the counter does appear to contain castor beans, the kind used to make ricin, the only prints in the lab are Novak's, though not on any equipment. Everything squares up with the story he'd told, and he'd let Novak leave under caution.

Dina's story checked out too. The part about talking to Novak anyway. She doesn't mention Jessica Greer. Not yet.

"What does Chen have to say about the notebook?"

"Hasn't said anything yet, Lyd. She's only had it in her hands for maybe twenty minutes?"

He promises to call back if anything turns up.

She'd come here convinced Jessica Greer was, if not the serial bioterrorist the press had taken to calling the Mail Murderess, at least a *danger* to Ted Harvey. In less time than it takes her to brew a pot of coffee, Jessica looks wrong for this, Ted is absolutely guilty of something, and Ben Jones could be the psychopath at the center of the story. He had the means and opportunity, but could he have pulled this off from California? He claims to have mailed something *for* Ted. Why involve Jessica Greer? Unless he was *helping* Ted, or was aware she'd make an excellent patsy.

No matter how it turns out, that was no copycat package at Zimmerman. They hadn't released enough of the specifics. Still, she needs evidence that will actually hold up in court. More than the Ethan Silver intrigue—she needs physical proof.

Inside Ted's room, Lydia finds Ted and the two officers staring at the television. His roommate, the elderly man in the bed opposite, appears to have fallen asleep.

The officers nod, and Ted looks in her direction. She catches something in his expression—not fear, but anticipation. Like he's been waiting for her to come back.

"Took you long enough," he says, his voice rustling like sheets of paper.

Lydia freezes. A guilty man should be begging. Not taunting.

"...federal prosecutors say the second ricin package demonstrates a calculated campaign of terror. Legal experts tell us the person responsible could be facing consecutive life sentences under the federal bioterrorism statute. These charges carry the same penalties as murder..."

Lydia snatches the remote from Ted's hand, mutes it and rips the clicker from the cord, tossing it in the trash bin. Harvey's face reminds her of Justin's face at the Kmart studio, when the photographer took the toy away.

"Mr. Harvey," she says, scraping the visitor's chair closer to the bed. "Let's you and I have an honest conversation." She jerks her chin at the door, and the uniforms step out.

Once they're alone, she leans forward, sees the sweat beading on his forehead. Presumably he's lost weight, though he doesn't look like he spends time at the gym. To make anything stick she needs to crack him. He thrives on attention—performs for it—but not all attention is good.

"You want to spend the rest of your life in a federal prison, Ted? A gay man like you?" She scribbles onto her notepad, *leverage.* "You heard the news. Consecutive life sentences. Oklahoma City changed everything. That's what you're looking at under terrorism charges."

"Terr—" He coughs, winces. "But I'm the victim—"

"Listen to me, Ted. It's that second package. The feds see a campaign. But if you help me understand the real story, then maybe it's not bioterrorism."

"This is..." He takes a sip of water. "Persecution. First that filthy woman, my attacker, shows up. Then you. I—"

"Let's talk about Ben Jones."

His mouth twitches, but she cuts him off. "Ted, you need to think very carefully about Ben's role in this. He gave that list to Ethan Silver, but—"

"What list?" Ted's slackened face tells Lydia it's an honest question.

"Your enemies, Ted. He gave a list of them to Ethan Silver, which looks to me like a desperate man trying to cover his tracks."

Ted puckers as if she'd fed him a lemon slice.

Lydia sits back, folding her arms over her chest. Her jacket's gone tight through her shoulders. She needs to get back into her rollerblading routine.

"Listen, if Ben pressured you into this, that's a very different story than you masterminding it yourself."

"Please." He coughs again. "You believe a man who's sleeping with the enemy?"

"You're saying your brand-new boss is your enemy?"

Ted rolls his eyes. "Figure of speech—" He stops himself. "What did you say your name was?"

She shows her badge, giving him a nice long look.

"Lydia Cole," he says.

She corrects him. "Agent Cole." She shifts forward, fighting the suck of the visitor's seat. "So tell me, Ted, why is your ex-boyfriend staying with you? Were you reconciling?"

"No." His heart monitor jumps. "We were... celebrating our new jobs."

Lydia squeezes her thigh. Something's off. She pivots.

"Then give me something, Ted. The courts take mitigating circumstances into account." Another lie. If that were true, the Menendez brothers wouldn't be locked up for life. "Your parents had a lab in their basement. What did they do in there?"

Ted wipes his brow, his voice soft as a sigh. "Their work. Research."

"How much did you know about their research? About ricin?"

His eyes flail. "It was off limits. Too dangerous."

He's a terrible liar.

"So why does your roommate, the peanut gallery as you say, think you poisoned yourself as a child?"

Silence, but for the quickening beep of his heart monitor.

"What happened in that lab, Ted?"

A tear slides down his cheek. "I—"

"Agent Cole?"

The voice comes from the door, and Lydia whips around, fuming. "Not now, Patterson."

"But—"

"Did you hear me?"

"I did, ma'am, yes, but it's Ross. Ross Klavon? Your partner. Says it's urgent."

Lydia looks at the floor, summoning the strength not to bite Patterson's head off. "One minute. Now get out!" She tucks her hair behind her ears before turning back to Ted. "You were saying...?"

His tear has dried, or been wiped away. When he continues,

his words are still shaky but more resolute. "As a child..." He stops, swallows painfully. "My parents used me to test their compounding." His breathing is labored. "They said it was to build up my immunity, but..." He gestures weakly. "I think they just wanted to see what happened."

For a long moment, Lydia doesn't know how to react. His words are smooth. Are they practiced? Or is it true? Finally she says, "That must have been terrifying."

"It was. And no one cared." He crosses his arms, flinching and placing a hand over his IV line. "But I kept records." His voice fades to almost nothing. "Tracking everything. Hoping someday..." He catches his breath. "Someone would understand."

Written records? Lydia's pulse jumps. "Do you still have those notes?"

His eyelids flutter, a smile playing at his mouth. "It's somewhere safe. When they boxed everything up... I hid it somewhere it wouldn't disappear."

This is it. The thread she needs. If he's lying, it's a good lie. If it's true...

"Agent Cole—"

Jesus.

"Coming, Patterson." Lydia moves toward the door quickly this time. She has him now. And with any luck, Klavon's got something on Jones.

44

LYDIA

Lydia shuts 417 behind her and asks a nurse to transfer her call to a quiet room.

"Tell me."

"Chen has some intel on the notebook," Klavon says. "Preliminary, but she's already flagging pages. Formulas. Dosages. Timelines. A whole running record of compounds and symptom onsets going back years."

"How far back?"

"Mid-seventies through the early eighties, all handwritten. The earlier pages are from a child, but the later pages match what we have on file as his handwriting." He takes a beat. "Lydia, Chen thinks it could be consistent with self-harm. A dose calibrated not to kill."

"Consistent with."

"She's being careful. Always is. You know if she said that much, something's there. Here's the thing, though, the last entry is from November 1982. Chen won't swear to it yet, but that section looks like it was working out a lethal dose. Enough to do the job, you know? So nothing would be raised before any trace could be eliminated—"

He's still talking, but Lydia's mind is racing ahead. He's not only a bioterrorist, he's a serial killer who corralled his ex into participating in the scheme? This is a big score. Much bigger than anything she could've dreamed when she heard the scanner report Thursday morning.

Was it really only yesterday?

Klavon has stopped talking. "What about Jones?" she says, hoping that didn't come out while her mind was elsewhere.

"He's not here. No clothes that don't appear to be Harvey's, no suitcase out. Chen's phoning the airlines. Her read is he's on his way back to San Francisco."

A nurse pushes a med cart past her, and Lydia steps tighter into the corner. She should feel it now—the give, the release. Probable cause in black and white. Means, opportunity, the intent spelled out in the suspect's own hand. Everything Powell has been breathing down her neck for ever since he became her boss.

Instead there's a flatness behind her sternum. The facts add up. The notebook. The grudge. The thwarted desire for fame.

But the people involved aren't acting like they should.

What if Ted's parricide is one case, while whoever mailed the ricin is another case altogether?

Don't, Cole. Alice's voice, from this morning. *This isn't a crossword. You can't wait for the grid to fill in before you put down the pen.*

The case is the case.

"Ross, I need you to start on the warrant," she says. "Get it done tonight if you can. I don't want him transferred out of here on a medical discharge before we're locked."

"On it. What are you doing with him in the meantime?"

"Holding him. He's not walking out of 417. I've got two of Pittsburgh's finest on him now. Put a call in to Murphy and have him send over his A-team, please. And make sure he keeps 'em coming."

"You good, Cole?"

"Fine as frog hair, Klavon."

"Copy that."

"Let's regroup at 1800. I want everyone in the same room when we walk through this. Until then, keep it tight. Nothing moves without my sign-off before we regroup."

She ends the call, heads back for her confession.

Through the small window of 417, Ted is visible, propped against his pillows, pale under the television's glow. There's no sound—not after her stunt with the clicker—but his mouth is moving. Rehearsing something.

He looks satisfied. Comfortable. The look of a man who expects to be handled carefully. Who told a federal agent his parents experimented on him as a child and is now waiting for her to come back with softer edges.

Lydia straightens her jacket and pushes through the door.

Ted turns his head. Whatever he sees in her face puts a flicker into his, and for the first time since she's known him, he looks uncertain. She pulls the visitor's chair out of the way with her foot. The officer at the wall straightens. *Kyle* is his name, she sees.

"Stay," she tells him.

"Well," Ted says, voice rustier than before. "You look official."

"Ted, I need to ask you about the notebook."

He hesitates, not long enough to mean anything in a courtroom, but long enough for her to notice.

"What notebook?"

"The one my people took out of your house an hour ago. Composition book, marbled cover. Dates going back to when you were in middle school. Formulas, dosages, symptom progression, all in your handwriting, all written out like a script."

What little color there was drains from Ted's face.

"You worked out what to take yourself. Doses calibrated not to kill. That's what my analyst is going to tell me when she finishes at the lab tonight, isn't it?"

His fingers pluck at the hospital blanket.

"But that's not the half of it, is it, Ted?"

Ted's mouth opens, closes. For a moment she thinks he might actually confess, might give her the conspiracy she's been chasing. Instead, he turns his face toward the window, jaw set in stubborn lines.

"The last entries, from before your parents died. Worked out in advance. That was what you meant when you said you kept records, wasn't it, Ted? Friend, you planned this. All of it. And you are going away for a very long time."

His head snaps back. "You said if I had mitigating circumstances..."

"You didn't give me anything I didn't already have." She keeps her voice level.

"My parents! They—"

"Theodore Harvey, you are not free to leave this room. You are in federal custody pending arraignment. My partner is at the U.S. Attorney's office right now, getting your warrant. When it's signed you'll be transferred. Until then there will be an officer in your room and one in the hall outside your door. You will not be discharged, you will not use the phone, and you will not be left alone. Am I clear?"

"I want a lawyer."

"Absolutely," she says. "You're going to need one."

She holds his eyes a beat longer than she needs to. His mask is gone. Whatever is under it is raw and frightened and very,

very small. She should feel something about that but doesn't. The moment is over and she can't quite name what it was.

Out in the hall, she finds Patterson and tells him to stay on the door. No visitors. No press. Not even a chaplain without her say-so.

"Yes, ma'am."

She walks toward the elevator, feeling the weight of her tidy folder expanding. Powell will be thrilled. He'll have the arrest he wanted by Monday. And more. She should call him, tell him she's got Harvey, not only on ricin, but for a double homicide thirteen years in the making, all thanks to a notebook he himself kept.

And Kris Novak found?

That's the part that snags. She should be feeling satisfied. Instead she finds herself worrying over the gaps in the grid. The ex who happens to be in town. The former editor who happens to be writing a book about ricin. The fact-checker who happens to turn up with key evidence. The freelancer who happens to have a detailed plan for getting away with murder.

Too many people in the right place at exactly the right time. Too many to overlook.

She can't put the pen down. Not yet.

45

JESSICA

om is right where Seth said she'd be, behind Kuhns.

She's crumpled against the dumpster like discarded newspaper, hidden between the store's delivery ramp and a steep incline. There're no houses back here, no roads. She could've died and no one would've found her till Monday.

"Mom!" I'm out of the car without turning off the engine, my knees hitting the asphalt beside her. Blood has matted in her hair, dark against the silvery gray. A bruise is spreading across her forehead, already swelling and discolored.

"Jessica?" She blinks up at me, confused. "How did you get here?"

"You called Seth, remember? Thank God, he got a hold of me at the house. He told me where to find you."

"Did I?" She touches her head gingerly. "Good. That was sensible of me."

I help her sit up straighter, checking for other injuries. Her pupils look normal, thank God, but where is all this blood from? I begin probing through the matted hair.

"Ouch, Jesus, Jessica. Outside hands."

I pull back immediately. Even concussed, she's still my mother. Except—*outside hands*? She's not right. She must've been attacked after leaving the house. "Mom, what happened? How did you get here?"

She touches her head gingerly, wincing. "I don't... I'm not sure."

I need to get her to the ER. "Let's get you into the car. Can you stand?" She's shaky but steady enough to walk with a little help. It's maybe half a mile from her house to here. She could have made it here from her house on foot, but I take her purse, worried she might topple.

Her *purse*? Did she walk all that way with her giant bag, or was she assaulted a second time while she was already compromised?

As soon as she's in her seat, I start rifling through her tote. Her wallet's there with sixty-five bucks still in it. Nothing appears to be missing, but who could tell? The woman's ready for "Let's Make a Deal" with what-all's in that bag.

"Mom, why were you walking to Kuhns?"

"No, I... I don't think?" She flips down the visor. "Good God. Hand me that." She points at her bag.

I thrust it at her automatically, watching from the corner of my eye as her hand dives in and miraculously pulls out a tissue packet. My jaw unhinges—*now?*—but I force a steady voice. "What's the last thing you remember?"

"Ooh, ah... I was in the car. Near the tunnel. Yes, going to... Well, I'm not sure where I was headed... My, that's disturbing..."

Rage flares in my chest, white-hot and clean. If the tunnel is the last thing she remembers, then the asshole on the parkway left her in this condition. What in the fuck is wrong with Dina Kowalski to leave my mother like this?

"What happened!"

"I can hear you perfectly well." She puts down her tissue, dives back into the bag. "Here, dear. Have a mint."

"Mom, focus!" I force myself to take a breath, don't totally mind losing the dragon breath. I accept the Certs. "Do you have anything to eat in there? Preferably something coated in chocolate."

"Here." She hands over an oatmeal granola bar, resumes spitting into her Kleenex.

"So then what happened? You're at the tunnel..."

She leans against the headrest, closes her eyes. For a moment I worry she's fallen asleep, till her face crinkles.

"There was a man. Yes, a man by the tunnel entrance. He was mad, I tell you." She grins, eyes still shut. Suddenly she lifts her head, takes in the loading dock. The dumpster. Me.

"Shouldn't you be at work?"

"I'm taking you to the hospital."

"Hospital?" Mom protests weakly. "No, I'm fine. Take me home. I—"

"Going home is what landed you here in the first place. You have a head injury, Mom. We're not taking chances."

I shut her door and move to my side, heading for Bethel General. One bridge is plenty for the day.

Mom flips on the radio. It's still on KDKA, and they are still talking about Ted Harvey. I flick the dial off.

"What'd you do that for?"

"Mom." I want to tell her how unfair it is, what I've been through, how I may never get my job back. That I'm collateral damage. But then I see her, pale, disoriented and bloodied, and I know she's the one with real collateral damage. "My head hurts."

"Mine too," she says, like this is news. She hears it too, and soon we're giggling and it's almost like nothing is wrong.

FIVE HOURS LATER, we're back home. Mom has a mild concussion and seven stitches, but the doctor says she'll be fine. No permanent damage.

"Domestic?" the bleary-eyed intake nurse had asked before even taking our names, like that's the norm, *domestic abuse.* When I said it was road rage, she'd nodded. "Full moon 'n' 'at. Gonna be a long night."

Before sending us back to the waiting room, she advised we ask for the whole file. "If you're pressing charges." Then, "Next!"

How was she so calm? Even after the endless wait, my hands were still shaking as I jotted down the concussion protocols. Not that I needed to. The list in its entirety consisted of one item: check every couple of hours for slurring, worsening headache or memory.

Now we're propped on the couch with popcorn, *Murder, She Wrote* on channel two. Mom's memory is returning in fragments. She remembers why I'm not at work, being stuck in traffic, even calling Seth. But not much beyond that. Now we've agreed to let the story rest so we can sink into the comfort of Jessica Fletcher's case. Tonight it's a murder at a bed and breakfast, and Mom keeps trying to guide her.

"It's the innkeeper," she says confidently.

"It's never the innkeeper."

"This time it will be."

I nudge her when her eyes start to close during a commercial. "Stay awake at least till you go to bed, please."

In reply, she starts scrabbling in her leather tote—an unassuming thing that hardly looks big enough for everything she hides in there. She pulls out her wallet, her reading glasses case, the roll of Certs, some wadded receipts.

"I can't find my nail file." She's pawing through the bag with increasing frustration. "The metal one. I know it was in here."

"Maybe it fell out in the car?" The words are not out of my

mouth before I regret them. "I'll go check. I need to make myself some coffee."

"Oh, at least wait for the commercial."

She wants me to see her proven right about the innkeeper. "It's fine, I don't mind. You're right."

In the kitchen, I grab the car keys while the Mr. Coffee starts huffing and puffing.

"It's unlocked," she yells.

It's not. She might not lock her doors, but I do. And I was the last one in the car. As I approach the station wagon, I wonder where Snookums is. He picks and chooses his visits, and I can't help but wonder if he's lying in wait for me nearby, ready to pounce. But I make it to the car without incident, find the offending nail file under the passenger seat and am about to leave when I notice something else, a manila folder tucked under the driver's side. It's not like Mom to lose track of her papers, so I stretch for it.

The folder is slim, holding only a single memo. I shouldn't look, but I wonder how many employees Mom has reamed out for losing track of confidential documents. My fingers touch the page inside. It's textured. This isn't a photocopy. I scurry with it back to the house, quickly scanning under the porch light: Harvey Research - C. Kowalski.

Kowalski?

46

LYDIA

Lydia walks into the conference room to find Klavon mid-story, gesturing with his coffee cup while Campbell and Chen lean forward, hungry for it.

"—then he asks if I'm working for the CIA!" Klavon slaps the table. "Had to convince him I was not some assassin sent to silence the truth about ricin warfare."

"That Novak is in deep," says Chen, eyes wide as she absent-mindedly strokes her long dark ponytail.

Lydia shakes her head. Sandra is obviously straight.

"What'd you tell him?" she continues.

"For a hot minute I wished I *was* CIA." Klavon grins and, eyes landing on Cole, nods. "Unlike those Langley boys, we actually have to follow the Constitution."

"You gave him the old *I'm a government agent, not a spook, see?*" Campbell's Sam Spade impersonation is so bad, even Lydia erupts in laughter.

Nice as it is to hear banter in the office—the past few days have been like a death march—Lydia knows it's a cheap laugh when you aren't the one with everything on the line. And they're not wrapped quite yet.

"How did the cops catch Novak and not Jessica?"

"Beats me. Bloomfield's nonna network called the cops when they saw him walk into the house. They weren't even looking for her. Probably thought a strange man was more of a threat than a strange woman."

Lydia is tempted to comment on the sexist interpretation, but that would be unfair. He is, supposedly, guessing on their behalf. Besides, if they'd chased after Jessica, they wouldn't have the notebook.

"From the looks of him, Novak couldn't have been too hard to catch." From the looks around the room, she sees her miscalculation. She's put her foot in it. Taken away from her partner's accomplishment by suggesting his *gotcha* was easy.

Nothing for it but to move on. "Where is he now?"

"We sent him home," Klavon says, smile fading. "Guy cooperated with us fully, promised he wasn't going anywhere. Not that he could. He's living off his mother's social security."

The team jeers as one, and Lydia feels another twinge. Why would anyone ask that? And so what, besides? She decides it's better not to say anything. To keep it jovial.

"But we got the goods," Klavon continues, pointing at a grimy Moleskin sitting in front of Chen.

"This is really good," Chen says, gingerly lifting the notebook from the table. She's put on her latex, though whether that's to protect the evidence or her hands is unclear. "The notebook has entries that date back to the mid-1970s, when Ted would've been in high school."

"Right." Lydia settles into her chair. "Has the lab been able to corroborate your initial findings?"

Chen opens the small volume, its pages yellowed with age. "Not yet, and I'm no expert, but"—she snugs a pair of readers on the bridge of her nose—"it looks like these symptoms correspond to these formulas."

She moves her index finger between the left and right pages, pointing to a series of precise, if random-looking, set of numbers and letters lined up to various ailments—headache, vomiting, diarrhea. The handwriting is small and tight, pressed hard into the page with angular letters that lean in different directions, unable to decide which way to fall.

"From this it looks like he knew just what his parents were doing," Chen says. "Or he's got a photographic memory."

Chen turns to the back of the notebook, where the handwriting changes. "Looking here," she says. "These are his entries from the early eighties. They're a little different. Reads to me like it's not just about being dosed, but doing the dosing."

The room falls quiet. Campbell reads an entry beside a formula:

November 22, 1982. Final test complete. Symptom onset should peak midday.

"My God." Campbell lifts a hand to his mouth to cover a sharp intake of breath. "He killed his own parents."

"And this"—Chen flips forward a few pages—"is where he appears to develop his latest scheme, poisoning himself."

"When that comes back, I bet we find out he calculated a dose that wouldn't kill him."

The team is commenting on the strangeness of it all, but Lydia is still staring at the page. Something about it looks familiar.

She's about to chalk it up to lack of sleep and thinking about this case twenty-four/seven when she stops on a formula of some sort: 60-65 kDa.

This will turn out to be the molecular weight of ricin.

What catches her eye is the distinctive capital D, wide at the base, lassoed shut at the top with a looping oval. Her mind flashes back to the morning. Dina Kowalski sitting across from her desk, nervous, helpful. Her initials in red thread, stitched carefully into her cardigan: DK. That same unusual D.

"Lydia?" Chen's voice seems to come from far away. "You okay?"

Cole blinks, refocusing on the room. "Sorry, just—" She reaches for the notebook. "Can I see that for a second?"

Campbell hands it over. Lydia stares at the letters, at that telltale D. The same careful script she'd noticed on Dina's sweater, the same, slightly backward slant.

"This handwriting," Lydia says slowly. "In the adult sections. You're sure it's Ted's?"

"We're having it analyzed, but if it's a forgery, it's a good one." Chen wrinkles her nose. "Who else would it be?"

Klavon looks puzzled. "You think Jones could forge his handwriting?"

Lydia sets the notebook down carefully, her mind racing. "Maybe."

Or maybe it's the helpful research assistant who guided Kris Novak to these crucial notes. Had encyclopedic knowledge about the Harveys. Who'd been studying the CMU archives for months.

But why?

"I need to make a phone call," Lydia says, standing abruptly.

"What about—" Klavon starts.

"Give me five minutes," Lydia says, already heading for the door. "But when I come back, I think we'll be having a very different conversation about this case."

As she steps into the hallway, Lydia's mind is spinning.

47

JESSICA

The hair on my arms stands. I'm on the porch, still staring at the memo, when I get the distinct impression I'm being watched.

Dina's coming back for this memo.

She has to be. This document connects her directly to the Harveys. I burst through the front door, Chester Kowalski's memo in hand. "Mom! We need to—"

The words choke in my throat. The living room is dark. *Murder, She Wrote* plays to an empty couch, popcorn bowl abandoned.

"Mom?"

"Kitchen." Her voice is tight.

I find her standing by the wall phone, receiver in hand. Her face is pale in the dim light from the hallway. "I was trying to call Lydia back. I remembered. It was Dina. She's the one who attacked me." She puts the receiver on the hook. "But the line's dead."

Blood fills my ears, and my chest tightens. For a moment, I can't hear. I can't breathe. Then I remember about the doors I can slam shut. They may be slightly toxic, but they're also a tool, and right now I can use it. *Whack.*

Now I can think.

Dina must've been waiting for us to get back. I hold my index finger to my lips, mime holding a phone to my ear, then shrug my shoulders as in, where's your cell phone?

"Ran out of juice," she says. Zero whisper.

I bug out my eyes. "She's here," I mouth with the barest hint of volume. "Dina is here."

Before Mom can answer, the front door rattles. Hard. Like someone's testing if it's locked. Mom never locks her door. But I'd been the last one in.

We both freeze.

The rattling stops. Footsteps move across the porch and toward the window.

I always lock.

I grab Mom's arm and urge her toward the stairs. Behind us, glass shatters. The living room window.

We're halfway up the steps when I hear Dina curse. She must've climbed through.

Unfortunately this is suburbia. If any of the neighbors heard that over their televisions, they'll assume someone dropped a glass.

"Oh, Jessica." Dina's voice is strange, singsong and lower than usual. "I just need that piece of paper you got out of the car. Hand it over, and I'll be right out of your hair."

Mom and I reach the landing. Her bedroom or mine? Her room has a lock. We rush inside, and I shut the door, fumbling with the flimsy push-button lock.

"That won't hold," Mom whispers, finally.

She's right. The door is hollow-core, the lock probably older than I am. I look around frantically. Her window is open—if we survive the night, my mother's going to get a stern talking to about security—and below it, the roof over the porch spreads out. It would be feasible to drop to the ground from the eave, but not for Mom. Not with that concussion.

"I know you found that report," Dina calls out. It sounds like she's going from room to room downstairs. "That's all I want. Just give it back."

I clutch the memo tighter, stuff it into my pocket. Chester Kowalski is obviously related to Dina, and for some reason, the man filed a complaint about the Harveys. I'm not sure what it all means, but it's proof that her connection to this case is more than coincidental. How did she come to have it now? Had she taken it from the university's archives?

Footsteps on the stairs. She must've realized we aren't down there. Her movements are slow. Deliberate.

Mom grabs my arm, pulls me toward her closet. She opens it and points up—the attic access. A pull-down ladder I haven't seen since I was a kid.

"We'll be trapped up there," I whisper.

"Better than trapped in here." Mom's already reaching for the cord. "You go."

"And leave you? Nuh-uhn. No way."

The bedroom door handle jiggles. "I know you're in there."

Mom and I look at each other, fear flickering in her eyes. Too late.

Before either of us makes a move, the door bursts open, and Dina is in the room. She's dressed in all black, including a knit cap over her head. Not a whimsical embellishment in sight. In her right hand is Mom's kitchen knife—the big Wüsthof from the block.

"Don't make this harder than it has to be, Jessica," she says, eerily calm.

Her cat-eye glasses are gone too. Not dangling from a beaded necklace or perched on her head. *Absent.* I have a brief, irrational flash of them lying in the driveway. Or had she ever even needed glasses?

"I need that memo, Jessica."

I put my fists on my hips. "The one that proves you have ties to this case?"

"The letter proves nothing," she seethes. Her knuckles are white on the knife handle.

"Give it to me, and I'll leave. No one has to know I was here."

"You attacked my mother." The words come out hard. "Left her alone, bleeding."

"That was—" Dina's jaw tightens. "I didn't mean for it to go that far. She was going to—" She stops herself.

"I was going to what?" Mom asks. Her voice has that dangerous quiet she used when Seth and I were kids and she was done negotiating.

"I'm sorry about how everything turned out." Dina takes a step forward, and we back into the closet. "Truly. But Ted Harvey deserves whatever happens to him. Ben could just as easily have been the one to go down for this."

Ben Jones? She framed me? Thoughts ricochet in my head like a pinball machine till one finally spits out. "You poisoned Ted?"

"Oh please." Dina lobs an eye roll my way. "Ted Harvey *is* poison. Contaminates everything he touches, and he keeps getting away with it. It's right there in his journals. All the evidence points directly at Ted. If anyone would bother to look. The man killed his own parents, and everyone just... let it go. Accident, they said. I couldn't let him—not after what I—" She stops. Her jaw tightens. "Give me that piece of paper."

My mind is reeling. Ted killed his parents? What did *she* do? But neither of those questions is the next right move. "You know what, Dina? You're right," I say, trying to keep her talking. "You're right. Ted's a total dick. But, wow, how did you figure out—"

"Give me the goddamn paper." Gone is the girlish trill. Dina's voice is a growl.

She lunges.

But Mom moves first, faster than I would have thought possible. She steps inside Dina's knife arm, her hand snapping up to grab a wrist as she drives into our assailant's center. It's beautiful, economical—some kind of move I didn't know my mother was capable of.

Dina flies over Mom's hip and crashes into Mom's dressing table. Wood splinters. The knife skitters across the floor.

"How the—"

"Self-defense classes," Mom pants, keeping her grip on Dina's wrist.

But Dina is young and wiry and desperate. She twists, driving her elbow into Mom's freshly stitched head wound. Mom gasps, and her grip loosens, sending her backward.

That's when Snookums explodes into the room through the open window.

He must've sensed Mom was in danger because he launches himself at the scene with a demonic yowl. But Dina is quick. She pushes my mother between herself and the cat. Instead of taking out Dina, Snookums smacks into Mom's abdomen. Fifteen pounds of fury latch on like a Tasmanian devil between her legs.

Mom lands on the floor as Dina breaks free, scrambling for the knife.

"No!" I throw myself forward, knocking the knife away. It slides under the bed. Dina pops to her feet, wild-eyed, looking between me and Mom and the knife's hiding place.

Outside, tires screech. Car doors slam.

"FBI! We're coming in!"

A battering ram connects with the front door, sending a thundercrack clap of wood splintering, hinges tearing loose, and the door slamming against the wall hard enough to rattle the window. Boots flood the threshold before the echo dies.

Dina's face goes white. She looks desperately around the room, stopping on the window. She's over the sill in one leap. I watch as she drops over the edge.

I'm on the floor with Mom as Agent Cole enters, gun drawn, Agent Klavon right behind her.

"Out there!" I'm pointing at the window, breathless. "Dina Kowalski—she ran out the window."

Lydia's already moving, barking into her radio as she heads downstairs. I hear more agents flooding around the sides of the house.

Mom sinks against the bed, holding her head. Snookums, proud of his heroics, winds between her shins, purring.

Klavon stays behind a moment longer, gentle and professional as he checks Mom's stitches. "Stay still now, we've got this under control. The EMTs are on their way." Then he's out the door too.

Through the window, I watch flashlight beams cut through the darkness of the yard. The light grows more distant. The voices thin.

The oscillating wail of an ambulance is growing louder as Lydia returns. Her face is grim. "She's gone."

Gone? Nerdy, overprepared Dina. Researched everything. Cautious in the extreme. Forging documents and manipulating evidence for years. Now she's a ninja too? That snake in the grass.

"She'll run," I say, my heart still pounding. "She'll have been planning for this. She'll have money, papers—"

The keening sirens close in.

"I don't need an ambulance," my mother says, palming the bed for leverage to rise, taking the bedspread with her as she crashes.

"Mom!" I yell as the blanket takes out the family photo that lives on her nightstand.

"That's it!"

The way Dina looked at our picture wall, asked about my father and Seth, talked about her own family. I bet I know who she can't leave without saying goodbye.

48

———

LYDIA

Lydia is halfway down the porch steps when Klavon's voice crackles over her radio. *Perimeter's clean. No vehicle. She's in the wind.*

Talk about worst case scenario. The night is dark, and there are a hundred ways to disappear in these hills. If Lydia doesn't come up with a plan quickly, they'll lose Dina. She'll lose her case.

A wailing siren nears outside, reaching a crescendo before it cuts out. Scenes come crashing back to Lydia. Over the past two days the woman's behavior has been erratic, but her instincts have been eerily solid. She'd researched the Harveys first. Sent Novak to the basement lab. Even her words the first time they met—*too bad you can't ask Ted*—seem oddly prescient now. They'd all been fooled by the helpful researcher.

Footsteps race down the stairs behind her. She turns to find Jessica Greer, panting.

"She went to see her mother! Agent Cole"—she pauses, gulps for air—"I'm so glad I caught you."

"You think she'd do what now?" Lydia does not have time for this.

"Look, it's a hunch. But Dina was very weird about family." Jessica reaches into her pocket and thrusts a sheet of paper into Lydia's hands, a proposed termination of the Harveys' research, citing Ted's suspicious childhood illnesses as cause.

"She told us she worked out that Ted killed his parents. It's why Ted deserved to die. Look at the date."

Lydia's eyes fly to the page. October 1982. "That's right before the Harveys died. But—"

"And the name."

Kowalski.

"I'm sure she went to see her mother!"

"My God, Jess."

"Mom! You weren't supposed to move."

She reaches for her daughter but falters. Lydia extends a steady arm. "That's when Dina clocked me in the car. I was telling her how proud I was of you two."

Jessica reaches for her mother's hand. Lydia feels a pang of jealousy. Her mama's been gone too long.

"But I have no idea where Dina's mother lives," Jessica says, looking at Lydia.

"Not a problem. We ran a background on Kowalski."

They hear Klavon outside, directing the EMTs to the house.

"I know right where her mother is," Lydia continues.

Heavy footsteps hit the porch.

"What are we waiting for?" Mrs. Greer asks, but her voice is weak.

"Jesus, Mom," Jessica says. "You're not going anywhere. I'll go."

"Neither one of you is going." Lydia's hand shoots out, grabbing Jessica's arm. "You stay here with your mother. This is FBI business."

"Would you mind?" A man from the ambulance squeezes through the door, headed for Mrs. Greer.

Lydia doesn't wait for a second opportunity. Without a word, Lydia spins on her heel and heads for the door.

"Go," she hears Mrs. Greer say.

Good Christ. A tagalong is the last thing she needs.

"Agent Cole," Jessica calls from behind.

Lydia keeps moving.

"I know Dina," she says. "She doesn't like you."

Lydia has scarcely cleared the porch when the words land. This is Jessica's real talent, an unnerving ability to read people. But Lydia hadn't survived her childhood to get played like that. "I am aware." She resumes toward the driveway.

"I'll follow you," Jessica says. "And you know what a great driver I am."

Lydia stops. "Are you threatening me?"

The hint of a grin spreads across Jessica's face as she grabs a coat from the rack by the door. "Not at all."

Lydia is unlocking her car, one hand on the roof. She wants this promotion, but Alice is right. It's deeper than protocol. Lydia wants to be nearer to Justin. Now that dream is in sight, she feels a pang of guilt.

She'd pushed him to pick Virginia Tech. Wanted him there when she arrived, triumphant, as a profiler for Quantico. She'd almost fooled herself thinking she was doing it for him. Almost.

Family is what this whole case has been about. Everything twisted up in what parents do to their children, and what children do to survive it.

Greer is the perfect case study. Her decision-making has suffered, but she's shown excellent instincts. Best to keep her close.

"Come on then, we don't have time to stand here arguing."

"Where's her mom?" Jessica asks as they pull onto the road.

"McKeesburg. Mount Calvary Cemetery."

49

DINA

The grass is damp beneath Dina's knees, soaking through her black jeans. She doesn't care. The cold wet feels right, appropriate. Penitent.

She traces the letters carved into the modest headstone with one finger. Margaret Ruth Atkins, 1947-1985. Beloved Mother. No "beloved wife" for her. As if Chester Kowalski had never existed for Dina and her mother.

"I tried, Mum," she whispers.

The cemetery is silent except for distant traffic on Route 51. She chose this spot deliberately when her mother died—the newer section, away from the old-money plots with their angels and obelisks. Margaret didn't belong among those families. She'd scrubbed their toilets, pressed their shirts, raised their children while her daughter fended for herself. Learned to become invisible.

Dina had thought killing Chester would fix things. Her mother hadn't been happy since his infrequent visits had stopped altogether. At seventeen she was still naive enough to believe that removing the source of pain would heal the wound.

Mummy wouldn't long for him once he was gone for good. She didn't know about the cancer then. Didn't know how people can live with you long after they leave your life.

Her father's hunting cabin was a rickety old shack, possibly less attended to than she was. She'd followed him there as soon as she got her driver's license, certain he was meeting yet another mistress. But no, the only date he had was with his guns. If he wanted nothing to do with her, she would be as unlike him as possible. She stopped eating meat. Refused to handle guns. But never could resist going through the briefcase he always left in his car. He did himself in, really.

Chester Kowalski had failed her, failed her mother, all while enjoying his real family and investigating other people's suffering. But when he began his investigation of child abuse? On someone else's behalf? Mummy wasn't going to do anything about it. It was up to Dina to make sure he'd never file another report.

The cabin's heater was old, temperamental. Easy to jimmy. It was cold enough that fall she knew he'd turn it on sooner or later. That he'd need a warmth that would last all night. But to make sure, she'd burned the pages, all his kindling. Left nothing for him to start a fire with when he returned that night.

Dina was in the kitchen when it happened, her mother gasping. No mere cry but a soul-deep wrenching. She'd raced into the room to find her standing at the counter, still in her nightgown, the *Post-Gazette* on the floor, open to the obituaries.

"Mummy?" Dina's voice was tentative. She already knew.

Her mother answered by sinking to the floor, tracing a finger down the page, her lips moving silently as she tapped the notice of Chester Kowalski's death. When she finally looked up, her eyes were glassy.

"Your father," she said, her voice quavering. "He's dead."

The words didn't land at first. Dead was too small a word for the man whose absence had filled every corner of their lives. Dina dropped beside her mother, staring at the pages, the bland print—survived by his wife, Rina, and his beloved son and daughter, Chet and Gracey. No Dina. No Marge. Dina's first tragic mistake—she would never be recognized as his daughter.

It was only years later, going through the university's archives, that she understood. What his report would have uncovered. What she had buried with her father. Not only had Ted Harvey dosed himself for attention, he'd turned around and poisoned his parents. That was when she'd changed her last name from Atkins to Kowalski.

In the three years that passed before her life ended, Marge Atkins rarely spoke. The end brought relief. Then guilt about the relief. Then something darker she couldn't name. Her second tragic mistake.

A car door slams in the distance. Dina's spine stiffens, but she doesn't turn. It's her turn to be tired. Tired of being helpful. Tired of being invisible. Tired of carrying sadness like a weight around her neck.

Footsteps on grass. Deliberate. Approaching.

"Dina Kowalski." Agent Cole's voice cuts through the October air. "FBI. Put your hands where I can see them."

Dina turns slowly. Without her glasses—she left them in the Greers' driveway, somewhere in the chaos—Cole's face is blurry. But she can make out Jessica Greer standing behind the agent, wrapped in her coat, watching.

She's hardly surprised to see her, that Jessica knew where to find her. Despite her many flaws, the woman had a talent for seeing through people's performances.

How had she beaten the FBI to the Harveys'? Dina had gone to such trouble returning the notebook for the FBI. Had Kris handed it over, or had they spoken? Send a man to do one thing, and the next thing you know he's enlisting a woman for the job.

Dina lifts her hands, letting them hover in the air like an offering. Or a surrender.

"I just wanted to tell her that all I ever wanted was to fix everything," she says, gesturing to the headstone. "She deserved more. So did I."

"Stand up. Slowly."

Dina rises, her legs stiff from kneeling. She's been here longer than she realized. The sky has gone full dark, stars pricking through the clouds. For a moment she thinks about running. She'd planned for this—cash hidden, papers ready, a whole escape route mapped in her mind.

But what's the point? Mummy's gone. And Ted Harvey is still alive. She's already a ghost. Running merely delays the inevitable.

Agent Cole approaches with handcuffs, professional, careful. Dina doesn't resist. The metal is cold against her wrists, the click of the mechanism final.

She looks past Cole to Jessica, who's watching with those sharp, observant eyes. The eyes that saw through Dina's helpful routine from the start, probably. Jessica, who'd had every reason to trust her and hadn't. Smart girl. But Dina's smarter. There's no third mistake here. As far as anyone knew, Dina had been at the office all morning. Couldn't possibly have dropped off a package for Ben Jones to mail, complete with a handwritten note from Ted Harvey. Or her version of Ted Harvey's handwriting.

"You'll never prove anything," Dina says. The words come out soft, deliberate. She lifts her chin toward the headstone, toward the dark Pittsburgh sky, toward whatever's coming next. "I kept my promise."

She means it. Every detail has been accounted for—the journal, the evidence, the story itself. Years of practice at moving through life unseen has taught her how to rewrite truth without leaving a trace.

The relief Dina feels, walking toward that car, is the same relief she felt when her mother finally stopped breathing.

It all pales when the radio in Agent Cole's car crackles to life.

50

JESSICA

Mom and I have settled into position—Mom on the couch, me on the floor between her knees—when the doorbell rings. I flinch before I can stop myself, my body's way of remembering something my mind has mostly let go.

"I'll get it," Mom offers.

The anchor is telling viewers to stay tuned for the one o'clock briefing that will be coming live from the FBI's headquarters in Pittsburgh.

"Hurry, that's in one minute," Mom announces as she swoops back in with Sofia. "Look who's here."

I'm looking, a little in awe. Sofia could be at this press conference too, under the guise of representing the Chamber. The whole affair certainly would've affected tourism had it not ended before the national news cycle could get a proper hold of it.

"I had to be here with you," Sofia says, dropping a box of Better-Maids on the coffee table, shrugging out of her coat.

I knew she wasn't mad about her car. I think she liked that it had emerged from battle unscathed.

We both know how wrong this presser could go for me.

She positions herself beside us on the sofa, leaning forward to nab a glazed twist—my favorite—but I can't even think about food.

What are they going to say about me now?

Next thing I know, I'm holding an old-fashioned, a donut I don't even like. It was there, and my hands need something to do, so fine.

The anchor is doing that thing where they recap everything we already know—ricin, U.S. mail, *City News*, suspected bioterrorism—in the flattest possible voice, trying to drag out the moment. I check my watch. 1:02. I hope they're only starting late. That there hasn't been some dread new development. Mom's fingers find my shoulder and stay there.

Then the FBI seal fills the screen.

Powell steps up to the podium, looking much the same as he did last week—same set to his jaw, same FBI-issue gravity, better suit. Cole, too. Same sharp eyes, same defiance, same mismatched jacket and pants. Another Monday for them.

Powell taps the microphone. "Good afternoon. I'm Special Agent in Charge Edward Powell of the Pittsburgh Field Office. Today I'm pleased to announce that the Bureau has charged Dina Marie Kowalski, age thirty, of McKeesport, Pennsylvania, with using a biological agent—*ricin*—delivered via the U.S. Postal Service in order to carry out a personal vendetta against Theodore Harvey. Ms. Kowalski is in federal custody and is expected to be arraigned—"

A sigh of relief escapes me. Mom's hands tighten on my shoulders.

Over the past few day, Dina's voice has haunted me more than I'd care to admit—*You'll never prove anything!* Not to the point of keeping me up at night, thank God, and the bridge dream hasn't been back, still. Cole and Klavon aren't taking my calls. Knowing she's in custody is a win. I'll take it.

Powell is still talking.

"—will be available to the public through the U.S. District Court for the Western District of Pennsylvania. Now I'll turn the podium over to the Pittsburgh Police Department to address related matters under their jurisdiction."

Murphy steps up, looking like a man who did not volunteer for this. I tense again, praying he says nothing about the car. He can't, can he?

"Thank you, Special Agent Powell. Pittsburgh PD is currently reviewing the 1982 death of Chester Kowalski, who died of carbon monoxide poisoning at his hunting cabin in Westmoreland County. The circumstances of Mr. Kowalski's death, originally ruled accidental, are being reexamined—"

"What?" I say, through a mouthful of donut. *When did I start eating?*

I feel Jeannine's fingernails now. "That woman, my God. She killed her own father?"

"Shh!" says Sofia, shutting us both down.

"...still looking into the possibility that Theodore Harvey may have been involved in the deaths of his parents, Drs. Michael and Patricia Juergen-Harvey, in 1982. Ted Harvey remains in critical condition at Allegheny General. We have no further details at this time. Agent Powell?"

I look up at my mother in shock. Powell is blathering on about interagency cooperation and the Bureau's commitment to the safety, and I am not processing a single word because Ted Harvey killed his own parents and somewhere in the back of my head a door is opening into a room I did not know was there.

"Why aren't they giving Agent Cole a chance to speak?" Mom asks, bringing me back to the room.

Sofia and I hush her in unison.

Powell opens the floor for questions. Once again, I brace myself. The media pool is smaller than at the initial briefing—Gene Collins, for one, is conspicuously absent—but my name could come up at any moment.

A woman from the AP starts things.

"Agent Powell, how did the Bureau identify Ms. Kowalski as a suspect?"

"A handwriting analyst confirmed Ms. Kowalski forged portions of a notebook that included formulas specific to ricin poisoning. That a notebook was removed from the university's archives," Powell says. "And while I can't relay the specifics of our methodology, I can assure you that the Bureau uses sophisticated profiling tools to hold criminals accountable."

I snort. Sophisticated profiling tools. Agent Cole told me she'd noticed the "D" on Dina's sweater matched the notebook that Kris found at Ted Harvey's house.

Pete Zelinski from the *Trib* doesn't even stand all the way up. "What can you tell us about Chester Kowalski? Specifically his connection to the Harveys."

Powell moves aside for Detective Murphy.

The police chief clears his throat. "Prior to his death, Mr. Kowalski—acting in his capacity as a compliance officer with the state's workplace safety bureau—was looking into the Harveys' research, following allegations that they'd used their child as a test subject. That connection is part of a broader investigation."

The room goes quiet.

Mom pulls me back against her knees, hard. I melt into the hug.

"¿Quién haría eso?" Sofia says quietly, to no one.

Then Candy Watson stands.

I should've known she'd be there.

"Is it true that Dina Kowalski, née Atkins, lived with her mother's corpse for several days after she'd passed away?"

I was not expecting that. From the looks at the podium, no one was.

The camera focuses back on Powell, who's working his jaw furiously. "May I remind the press that we are in the business of solving federal crimes, not speculating on open investigations. I would also remind you, this office takes a dim view of trial by newspaper. Reporting that is inaccurate, irresponsible, or damaging to the reputations of innocent citizens has consequences. I'll leave it at that."

He scans the room. "If there's nothing further—" He doesn't wait. "This press conference is concluded."

He files out, Murphy, Klavon, and Cole trailing behind. The podium stays put.

Sofia clicks off the TV.

No one speaks. I look down. At some point I've eaten most of the old-fashioned. My hands are still. I hadn't noticed either of those things happening. Candy Watson, of all people, has offered up a little nugget effectively wiping me from the story. Then the head of Pittsburgh's FBI defended me. Spoke to cameras. In front of everyone. Whatever I am, I am no longer the story.

Mom's hand is still on my shoulder. She presses it tight. I reach up and put mine over hers. She is the first to speak.

"Well, I guess that's settled," she says. "Let's go get Vincent's."

I'm flabbergasted. How can she think about pizza at a time like—

I stop. I'm staring at a half-eaten old-fashioned on the table in front of me. It's the only thing I've had all day. What could be more life affirming than food?

"Perfect," I agree. "Except we're going to Fiori's."

Together we look at Sofia, the natural tie-breaker.

"I don't care," she says. "Whichever one is harder to poison."

"Fiori's, it is," I say. "You'd never taste anything under all Vincent's cheese."

"Vincent's," Mom insists. "You'd never know the difference with Fiori's."

Sofia groans and reaches for her coat. "Fine, then," she says. "We'll get both."

51

LYDIA

Powell doesn't slow until his office door shuts behind them.

Lydia had watched the back of his head the whole way from the briefing room—down the corridor, past the evidence room, past Klavon peeling off toward his desk with a look she couldn't read. Murphy and his contingent had vanished somewhere around the elevator bank. Now it's her and Powell and the hum of the fluorescents.

She's already composing the call to Alice. Went well. Home by six. The weekend had been a blur of paperwork, coordinating with Murphy's people, getting the charges filed so Powell could have his Monday headline. But they'd done it. Kowalski was arraigned. Harvey was on lockdown at the hospital. The notebook evidence was airtight. Even the Candy Watson question hadn't landed—Powell shut it down cold.

He'd defended her. Defended the whole office. *Trial by newspaper has consequences.*

Powell moves behind his desk. Doesn't sit. Doesn't invite her to sit.

"You may have noticed I kept your name out of that," he says. "You're welcome."

"Sir?"

Powell plants his knuckles on his desk, leaning forward. "Don't play coy now. Not after that shitshow of an investigation. Three days of treating an innocent woman like a terrorist. That fucking 'Mail Murderess' nickname? You fed them that narrative. Now I've got Jeannine Greer's lawyer up my ass."

He keeps talking, but Lydia is frozen. Powell had *insisted* she wrap the case. "Monday, or I find someone else and you better hope like hell that doesn't mean D.C. sends in a team," he'd said.

Greer was their only suspect. Had she misread that?

She zooms back in as Powell's face is going red. "You made the Bureau look incompetent. Worse, you made me look incompetent."

There it is. The real crime. "I caught the actual susp—"

"Consider yourself off fieldwork," he barks. "Administrative duties until further notice. No more investigations until you learn some judgment." Powell waves his hand dismissively. "That's all."

Lydia should argue. Should defend herself. Point out that she did solve the case, by Monday, as demanded. After Dina Kowalski had fooled everyone. When even Jessica Greer's own mother wondered if her daughter might be guilty.

But standing there, looking at Powell's jowly face, his expensive suit, his corner office, Lydia realizes something.

She doesn't care.

She should. This is her career. Her advancement. Everything she's worked for since the day she put on the badge. The path to Quantico, to profiling, to proving she belongs in rooms where men like Powell make the decisions. All gone now.

But all she can think about is the growing silence between her and Alice. The burgeoning stack of crosswords that they used to fill in together. The way Alice's smile doesn't reach her eyes when Lydia promises to be home for dinner.

"Is that all, sir?" Lydia asks.

Powell looks surprised she's not fighting. "Yes. Dismissed."

Lydia walks out, past Klavon, who gives her a sympathetic look she doesn't need, past the evidence room where the notebook still sits in its plastic bag, past all of it. What she does think about are crosswords. How the grid never fully fills in. How sometimes you have to put down your pen and call it done.

She's in her car before she realizes she's smiling.

THE HOUSE IS LIT when she pulls up on Monterey Street. Early-afternoon sun catches the brick facade they spent six months repointing, the new black shutters gleaming against the red brick. Alice was right about that, too.

Through the kitchen window she sees her moving around, pulling something from the oven. Lydia sits in the car for a moment, watching. Her partner of ten years, wearing the ratty U of I sweatshirt she refuses to throw out, standing in the kitchen they gutted together four summers ago. She's made this house a home, and Lydia almost blew it.

Years of pushing her away for the sake of her career. Proving herself time and again and getting nowhere. Chasing something she's not sure she wants anymore. Sitting here now, watching Alice through the window, she realizes what she almost lost.

Alice looks up when she walks in, flour on her cheek. "You're home early." Not a question, not even surprise. She sets down her wooden spoon. Waits.

"I couldn't wait to see you," Lydia says. And means it.

Alice crosses to her, wraps floury arms around her waist. "Yeah?"

"Yeah." Lydia breathes in the smell of chocolate and vanilla and home. She wants to talk about the crosswords, her failures, her adoration. "I've been an idiot."

"Little bit," Alice agrees, smiling against her shoulder.

On the counter, a cake is cooling. Next to it, a wrapped box with a card that reads *Next step up the ladder, 8 letters.*

Lydia's stomach flips. Q-U-A-N-T-I-C-O.

But right now, all she needs to say is, "I love you."

"I know," Alice whispers back. "I know."

52

JESSICA

After lunch—we'd settled on Il Pizzaiolo—I practically have to force Mom to drop me off at my house. I haven't been back since last Thursday. The place is a wreck, and I need to decompress. *Alone.* I'm stuffing the last of the police tape into a garbage bag when the doorbell rings. Through the keyhole I spy Mrs. McMunn on my porch, clutching what looks like a plate of cookies covered in plastic wrap. She's rugged up for the arctic, but it's a fairly warm October day, mid 50s. *Maybe there's a bulletproof vest under there.* Her gift announces *concerned neighbor*, but her eyes have that hungry glint I recognize from her Six on Your Side stint.

"Jessica, dear!" she gushes when I crack the door, her voice dripping false sympathy. "I brought you some cookies. Chocolate chip—I made them myself this morning."

Curious choice, all things considered.

I open a little wider so I can peer through the plastic wrap at her perfectly uniform rounds. Those are Chips Ahoy! if I've ever seen them, the chocolate worn to a lighter shade of brown where it's rubbed against the package. She couldn't have poisoned them. I think.

"How thoughtful," I say, not moving to take the plate. "Though I gotta tell you, Mrs. McMunn, I'm not eating many sweets these days. As you pointed out, with your keen eye for detail, I have a steady roster of gentleman callers to think about. Gosh, we're all so fortunate to have someone so thorough keeping watch over the neighborhood."

Her smile stays bright, but a cloud crosses over her face. I almost want to tell her she's right to think she's been insulted, but she recovers quickly. "Well, safety first, that's what I always say. Speaking of which"—Mrs. McMunn leans closer—"I saw they arrested that newspaper woman. Such a relief for everyone, I'm sure."

"Mmm." I lean against the doorframe, arms crossed. "Though I imagine it must be disappointing for some folks. You know, people who were hoping for a more dramatic conclusion to the story."

This garners a look from Mrs. McMunn I'd have to describe as *coquettish*. "Do you think?" she asks, clutching the cookies tighter. "Well, we're all just so grateful you're safe. Though some people are still asking questions, of course. The whole thing has left the neighborhood quite unsettled."

Mrs. McMunn goes quiet, waiting for a reply. Jessica relaxes her shoulders. Let her nosy neighbor fill in her own blanks.

"People are wondering," she begins, "if there might be more to the story?"

And there it is. How can she think I'd spill something juicy, or even something dull as a cake of soap, for her to take back to Candy Watson? Or her weekly euchre game, which would be longer lasting.

But I was expecting something like this once I spied her discount bribe. I don't let on. "What kind of questions, Mrs. McMunn?"

"Well, you know how people talk. They're wondering about

your... involvement in the investigation. Will you be part of the trial? I'm sure you will be. I heard you were quite the detective yourself, finding all those old research papers. I bet that information could be valuable..."

And that's that. I've let this go on long enough. Besides the fact that it was Dina who found the documents, my involvement in uncovering evidence has not been made public. Where does this woman come up with her information?

"Mrs. McMunn, I'm going to have to interrupt you. I'm on deadline right now. Thanks for stopping by." With that, I step back and shut the door in her face, fantasizing about flinging her damn plate into her pristine front yard so I can watch it shatter against her concrete garden gnome while the store-bought evidence of her deception scatters to the winds. The satisfying crash, the look of shock on her calculating face. I'm tempted to open the door and ask for the plate after all.

But then I remember Chelsea and all the other assorted neighborhood cats and dogs and squirrels who shouldn't be eating whatever artificial preservatives and corn syrup Nabisco pumps into their products.

Another knock makes me jump.

Assuming it's Round Two of Cookie-gate, I yank the door open with a considerable fury.

"Listen, I told you—oh!"

Carson Miller is on my stoop, looking genuinely startled by my aggressive greeting. His hair is slightly disheveled, like he's been running his hands through it, and he's wearing the gray wool coat I always liked on him.

"Sorry," I say, grabbing his sleeve to rush him inside. "I thought you were someone else." But it's too late. Once Carson is out of the door frame, I see her, gaping. "Oh look, Mrs. McMunn! My diet regimen is working already!"

I hear her huff of indignation followed by the satisfying slam of her front door.

Carson raises an eyebrow. "Should I ask?"

"The less said, the better." I guide him past the garbage bag full of crime scene tape, the upended cushions, the open drawers, deposit him in my eat-in kitchen. He smells better than I remember, annoyingly. Neither of us sits.

"What brings you here, Carson? I assume this isn't a social call."

He shifts uncomfortably, about to deliver news he doesn't particularly want to share. "How are you holding up? Really?"

I know him well enough to know he means this. It's only been a few days since I hit a car in front of his house. He deserves more than this frosty attitude from me.

"Really? I've been better. But I'm not dead or in federal prison, so I'm calling it a win." I lean against my counter, studying his face, keeping my distance.

He might deserve better, but I know me, and despite everything that's happened, I still feel it. I am still attracted to this tool. "Now that's out of the way, what can I help you with? I know you didn't come here to chat."

"No," he says, looking down.

I know it shouldn't, but his easy agreement stings my heart.

He reaches into his coat and pulls out a manila envelope. "This is from Zimmerman. A severance package."

My stomach drops. I don't know what I was expecting, but not this. "You came to fire me?"

"Jess... Look at this more as a... a mutual parting of ways. Very generous terms, actually. Six months' salary, continued health benefits, a positive reference letter." He sets the envelope on my counter. "All you have to do is sign a standard nondisclosure agreement."

I cup my elbows, staring at the envelope like it might bite

me. "What am I not supposed to disclose, Carson?" At this point I'm proud to sound like such a bitch, but my heart is pounding.

Carson's jaw tightens. "Nothing specific. It's standard-issue confidentiality. Internal company matters, client relationships, that sort of thing."

"Like the fact that Kelley Knight's car was parked outside your apartment in the middle of the workday?"

"Jess, c'mon. We were discussing the potential crisis situation we had on our hands." His voice is unchanged, shows zero reaction to my accusation. I have to admit, idea-thief that he is, Carson is damn good at his job. "We had to talk damage control strategy."

Anger flares in my chest. The damage on client relationships? What about the damage to my reputation? I didn't do anything. Meanwhile, I saw him in the copy room. And his window. *Jagoff.*

He looks into my eyes. "Kelley isn't pressing charges, as you know."

And this is when I do know. Carson defended me, but only because it was in Zimmerman's best interests. Not because he believed me.

Something in me settles. The anger drains out, and with it, all things Carson. The years I've spent carrying a torch for this guy—through the excuses, the stolen ideas, all of it. Turns out it only took one sentence to kill.

I look down at the envelope he's handed me. Six months' salary would solve a lot of problems, not the least of which is paying to repair Kelley's car. The money would mean I could take some time to figure out what comes next, maybe write something that really matters. Maybe do some work on my duplex.

"I'll think about it," I say finally.

"There's one more thing." Carson shifts again.

What now?

"The holiday party next month. It would be... beneficial if you attended. Show of unity. No hard feelings and all that. For the optics."

I lift my eyebrows.

"People will be watching to see how we handle this. How *you* handle this."

I almost laugh. After everything—the investigation, the media circus, the neighbors treating me like a pariah—now they want me to put on a happy face for their convenience? Show up in my best dress and smile while they congratulate themselves on their magnanimity.

"I'll think about that, too," I say, knowing that if it's a contingency in this paperwork, I will damn sure be there with clean hair. Unlike right now. If it's not written in? He can fuck right off.

"Take your time with the paperwork. No rush." Carson nods and rises for the door. "And Jess? I'm glad you're okay. Really."

After he leaves, I sit at my kitchen table and stare at the envelope. Six months of freedom, bought and paid for. All I have to do is promise not to talk about what I saw in that copy room, not to mention where Kelley's car was parked, not to embarrass Zimmerman Public Relations.

Outside, I hear Mrs. McMunn's front door slam again. Probably heading off to spread the news about Jessica Greer's latest male visitor.

I tear open the envelope and start reading.

Gene Collins, *Pittsburgh Post-Gazette*

I've been covering this city for twenty-two years. The day we ran "Mail Murderess" on A1, I asked my editor if we had it cold. He said we had enough. I said that's not the same thing. He said run it. I ran it.

I think about that conversation a lot more than I'd like to.

Stu Johnson, KDKA NewsRadio

We report what law enforcement tells us. The Bureau issued the armed-and-dangerous bulletin—we broadcast it. The hit-and-run on Shady Avenue? Jessica Greer's vehicle, witnessed, not disputed. That charge didn't go away because she didn't do it. It went away because she cooperated. There's a distinction. People want to treat this like we made things up. We didn't make things up.

Rita Holt, *City News*, Arts Editor

We've moved to a rotating critic model for the time being. It's —look, it seemed like the right call given everything. We're still figuring out the permanent arrangement. I think I speak for everyone at the paper when I say we're glad Jessica is okay. That's the important thing.

Pete Zelinski, *Pittsburgh Tribune-Review*

Everybody's very sorry now that the story's over. The same people who called me for quotes when she was the suspect aren't returning my calls today, and I find that interesting. You know what sold papers when she was the Mail Murderess? The same people buying them now. I don't think I'm the only one in this room with something to answer for. I'd put that question to anyone who picked up a copy.

"Pittsburgh Voice" (Editor, name withheld by request)

I genuinely try not to read the news. It gets into your head, affects your editorial judgment. I was aware of the broad strokes, obviously, but I made a conscious decision not to follow it closely. So I don't have a lot to add.

Candy Watson, Channel 6 "Six On Your Side"

I reported what was there. A woman with a documented psychiatric history, a professional grudge, and access to information about ricin—add the attempted poisoning. That's a story. The fact that someone else turned out to be responsible doesn't change what I was looking at. If I had it to do over, I'd report the same story. Maybe I'd add a line about presumption of innocence. Maybe.

Now this Kowalski character? With the dead mom in her apartment? That's going to be huge.

53

JESSICA

"Here in this section, about the media coverage." Ethan is sitting back in his office chair, pointing at one of the eight pages I just handed him. "It's a little... self-indulgent. Readers don't need the whole Marcia Clark comparison—"

"Ethan." My voice cuts through his editorializing. "I'm not here for notes."

"You—" He blinks. "Then what—"

"I just wanted you to see it before it hits newsstands." I stand up. "*Pittsburgh Monthly* is running it as their cover story next month. They're calling it 'Pittsburgh's Poison Pen: An Inside Account.'"

He squints at me, color rising in his cheeks. "You sold this to *Pittsburgh Monthly*?"

"For five times what you would've paid me." I reach across and pluck the pages from his hands. "Plus they're not asking me to change a word."

"Jessica, wait." He stands too, his chair rolling backward. "We could match that. And I could give you the crime beat permanently. Full-time."

I almost laugh. Almost. "The crime beat? Covering car accidents and purse snatchings?"

"Real crime stories. Investigative pieces. Like this one." He gestures at the envelope. "You've obviously got a talent for it."

The way he says it, you'd think this is a clean start. A promotion, even.

But I know what he's after, can feel the shape of it—take what happened, sand it down, make it compulsively readable. Give it a spine, a villain, a version people can repeat over coffee.

I could do that. That's the problem.

But then I remember sitting down to lunch with him mere weeks ago, waiting while he answered his phone in the middle of our meeting, chasing him through the streets of Pittsburgh. His casual dismissal. All based on the assumption I'd be grateful for whatever scraps he threw my way.

"I'm sure that's your best offer, Ethan. But I know what it's worth." I slide my story back into its envelope.

"This isn't charity, it would be a regular column. You—"

"I'd what, Ethan?" I sling my purse over my shoulder. "Two weeks ago you replaced me without a conversation. What makes you think I'd want to come back?"

He has the grace to look uncomfortable. "I never said... I specifically said we weren't... I hear what you're saying, but... Can I at least read the rest of it?"

"You know..." I look at the envelope in my bag. "I don't know what I was even thinking. You can read it along with everyone else."

"You know, Jess, this is harder than it looks."

I turn at his door, a grin playing at my lips. "Do enlighten me."

"We're all a hair's breadth away from extinction. The internet is cannibalizing alt-newsweeklies. At this rate, they'll all be gone in five years. And once the conglomerates own what's left—like they already do over at *Pittsburgh Monthly*—forget about a free press."

For once, I actually agree with him. He even sounds a little like Kris Novak. But sympathy is a luxury I can't afford.

"Well then," I say, "do better."

In the hallway, I check my watch. I'm going to be late to meet with my new therapist.

54

JESSICA

"Oh my word, Jessica Lane, you're not going to believe this."

I look over my desk at my mother, trying to hold her head at the perfect angle to avoid using her readers. Probably because she's sitting in front of the wall of windows that drew me to buy this place—a brick row house in Lawrenceville that was already kitted out with a storefront, zoned business and residential.

"Believe what?"

"Remember when Ted Harvey took a turn after he'd been released from ICU?"

"Is he dead?"

"No, but apparently, it's another charge for Dina Kowalski."

I think back to seeing her in Ted's room. That muffin. I shudder. I almost ate that thing.

"You're going to need filing cabinets," she announces, moving on already.

The new office smells like fresh paint, and she's worried about storage? I've furnished with what I think is the perfect combination of IKEA and vintage. Dad would've liked this room. My living space upstairs is another story, but it's all mine: Jessica Greer Crisis Communications.

She's seated at the conference table I found at an estate sale, surrounded by legal pads covered in her meticulous handwriting. "And a proper phone system. That answering machine is from 1987."

"It's fine. It works." I can see she's still looking around. "I thought you were absolutely not getting involved."

"I'm not." She returns to her paper. "I'm just... consulting."

I bite back a smile. She's been "just consulting" every day since I signed the paperwork. Helping me write my business plan, reviewing my pricing structure, even negotiating with the seller on closing costs.

The irony isn't lost on me—opening a crisis communications firm after being the subject of a national manhunt. But as my lawyer pointed out, there's no such thing as bad publicity. Especially when you're proven innocent.

"What about this for a tagline?" Mom taps her pen against the pad. "'When your story needs telling, we make sure it's heard.'"

"Too vague."

"'Crisis management with a human touch'?"

"Too touchy-feely." I turn from the window. "How about we just start with getting clients?"

"You'll get them." Mom's voice is firm. "You're good at this, Jess. Better than you know."

The compliment catches me off guard. We've been dancing around each other since everything happened—both of us trying to figure out this new dynamic where I'm not the broken daughter she needs to fix.

"I'm going to get us coffee," I say, grabbing my jacket. "Crazy Mocha or that new place on Penn?"

"Surprise me." Mom's already back to her notes.

Outside, Lawrenceville is alive with spring. Even in the short time since I bought in, the neighborhood has changed—more galleries, more restaurants, younger crowds. It feels possible here. New.

I'm halfway to the coffee shop when I spot him.

He's leaning against a patrol car parked at the curb, talking into his radio. He's in uniform, that same chiseled jawline I remember from the hospital stairwell. When he sees me, his face lights up.

"Hey! Nurse Greer, right?" He grins. "Or should I say, Not-Actually-A-Nurse Greer?"

I laugh despite myself. "Just Jessica is fine."

"Michael." He extends his hand, and I shake it. His grip is warm, confident. "Good to see you out and about. Off the hook for breaking and entering and terrorism."

"Cleared of all charges, thanks." I gesture toward my building. "Actually just opened a business. Crisis communications."

"Really?" His smile widens. "This is my neighborhood. I live right over there." He points. "And you've certainly got the experience."

"Not sure that's the best endorsement."

"Hey, you survived the FBI and the evening news. That's impressive." He shifts his weight, suddenly a little less confident. "Listen, I know this is random, but... would you want to grab coffee sometime? When I'm not on duty?"

My heart does a little skip. He's cute. Really cute. And there's something disarming about his directness.

Then I notice the pack of Marlboros tucked into his shirt pocket.

Charmed as I am, I hold back. He didn't insult me exactly, but telling me I'm *off the hook?* He was joking, and he could be another dude who wants me to prove myself.

"I appreciate that," I say carefully. "But I don't date smokers."

"I'm trying to quit."

"Good for you. Come find me when you have." I smile, not to soften the blow but because for once, I've managed to turn the tables. Put him in a position of deserving *me*.

His face falls a little, but he nods. "Fair enough. Can't blame a guy for trying."

I head for Crazy Mocha with a stupid grin on my face. Nancy, my new therapist, would be proud I'd set a boundary. Me? I'm happy I didn't catastrophize the moment into a dozen different disasters. I simply existed in it. Maybe he'll even call someday.

Progress.

By the time I get back to the office, juggling two lattes and a bag of biscotti, I find Sofia standing in the doorway.

"Sofia!"

Mom rushes over and grabs my load so we can have a proper hug. She's a little stiff.

"What brings you here in the middle of the day?"

She glances past me, out the door. "She's parking right now."

"Who?"

Before she can answer, the door swings wide, pushing me into Sofia. Behind me stands Beverly Jo, aka The Beev.

She's not exactly as I remember. The bangs are piled high as ever, but she looks almost normal in jeans and a Steelers Super Bowl XXX shirt. We're all still feeling the loss.

"Jessica?" She extends a hand, nails bitten to the quick. "I hope you don't mind me dropping by unannounced. I looked up your address after your article came out. Nice piece, by the way."

She is a good publicist. "Thank you. That was the whole point of the byline." I smile. Beverly Jo might not realize it, but I'm a good publicist too, but I'm wearing a hat that suits me better. One that makes considerably more money too. If it succeeds at all. I direct Beverly over to the table. Mom pushes aside the paper, and we sit across from Sofia and Beverly Jo.

"What can I do for you?"

Beverly Jo is looking around the room, taking in the decor. She says nothing about it, which I consider a testament to its sophistication.

"We have a situation we need help on. I can't go into details unless you're willing to sign an NDA."

I feel Mom tense beside me. Feel Sofia watching. Feel the weight of this moment—my first real client, my first real case that isn't about me.

"I can do that," I say. "Did you bring one? If not, I can print ours."

But Beverly Jo is already fishing her copy from her bag, thank God. I was bluffing.

After Mom and I sign, the four of us talk for about twenty minutes. Beverly Jo is sharp, no-nonsense, and by the time she and Sofia leave, I have my first contract in hand—crisis communications for a museum.

Mom stares at the last page. "That's... that's real money."

"That's rent and payroll," I correct. I look at her pointedly. "You know you work here now, right?"

"What?"

"I can't do this alone. I need a good researcher. Someone who knows Pittsburgh. Someone who won't let me spiral when things get weird." I cross my arms. "That's you. If you want it."

"Sweetheart, I'll do all those things anyway." She taps the table. "I think the person you need to hire just walked out that door."

"Why do you think I didn't sign the retainer yet?"

Mom is giving me that satisfied smile she gets when her plans come together. "You work here now too, Mom," I say. "As a consultant, of course."

Outside the window, Butler Street hums with life. Somewhere out there Dina's in jail, and Ted, last I heard, had hired a very expensive lawyer. He can't be happy about Ben Jones' book deal.

I walk back to my desk, slide open the drawer and pull out the kitty cat Beanie Baby I've been carrying around for months. It's missing an eye now. I could've returned it to its owner, but I didn't want to deal with her questions. I doubt Nancy would approve.

I don't need her to.

In here, in my new paint-fume-infested office with its questionable furniture and uncertain future, I'm building something that's mine. And for the first time since Dad died, that feels like enough.

THE END

Want to read the article Jessica wrote? Get your copy of this bonus epilogue, free.

COMING NEXT IN THE STEEL CITY MYSTERIES
***The Heist** Pittsburgh, 1996*

A new standalone. New trouble. Same Pittsburgh.

Nicolette has spent her career protecting priceless art. When her son gets sick, she's going to steal some.

A psychological suspense novel about motherhood, survival, and what an honest woman will do when the rules stop working.

Get a front row seat: llkirchner.flodesk.com/heist

ABOUT THE AUTHOR

L.L. Kirchner is an award-winning screenwriter and Pushcart-nominated author whose life and work as an expat in Asia became the basis of two memoirs that combine humor with "her discerning eye" (Foreword Reviews). As an NPR interviewer said, her memoir is "like *Eat, Pray, Love,* but funny." Her writing has appeared in the *Washington Post, Salon,* and *The Rumpus,* among numerous other outlets.

Drawing on her eclectic journalism background as a religion editor, dating columnist, and bridal editor, her work explores feminist narratives. Read more at her blog, IllBehaved-Women.com or LLKirchner.com.

She lives in Florida with her favorite husband and their best boy, Pepper. RIP Hartley.

On socials everywhere @llkirchnerauthor.

ALSO BY L.L. KIRCHNER
THE QUEENPIN CHRONICLES:

The Queenpin Chronicles:

Florida Girls — Book 1

When the mob hits Florida's Gulf Coast,

wartime showgirls hit back.

Vegas Girls — Book 2

What happens in Vegas... doesn't always stay there. Especially when the girls run the game.

Havana Girls — Book 3

The series culmination, a dual timeline set between pre-Revolutionary Havana and 1978 Miami, where revenge is had and so are happy endings.

* * *

Nonfiction Memoirs:

Blissful Thinking — The decade I spent searching for spirituality in gurus, ashrams, and other people.

American Lady Creature — I hoped moving to Qatar would change everything. Until it did. A true story.

Full catalog at llkirchner.com/books

FOR BOOK CLUBS

I bet you love your book club as much as I love mine. In honor of that mutual adoration, I've put together a discussion guide. Find it on my website, **LLKirchner.com/FOR BOOK CLUBS.**

WANNA TALK ABOUT THIS BOOK?

Tap the "let's connect" button on the page above. Happy to Zoom in whenever possible!

AUTHOR'S NOTE

The mid- to late-1990s marked a turning point in the American psyche—the first real awareness that terrorism could be homegrown. Between the 1993 bombing of New York's World Trade Center, the 1995 tragedy at the Oklahoma City Federal Building, and the looming shadows of the Minnesota Patriots Council and the Unabomber, the FBI faced unprecedented pressure to identify and prosecute domestic threats.

While these events were unfolding at home, the 1995 sarin gas attack on the Tokyo subway system added a terrifying new dimension to the global landscape: the realization that even the air we breathe could be weaponized. For those of us working in news at the time, tracking these incidents wasn't just a job; it became an obsession.

Writing this book allowed me to explore how trauma ripples through our lives, impacting our memories and everyday experiences. For Jessica, hyper-vigilance is a survival mechanism—a way to navigate a world that feels increasingly precarious. This state of high alert is mirrored in Lydia, who must navigate the entrenched discrimination of the FBI, and in Gail, for whom poverty and neglect made life a literal, daily fight for survival.

I lived in Pittsburgh during this time, working in alternative news while recovering from trauma. Given the fractured state of our current media landscape, I wanted to explore the desperation that takes hold when your past and present feel equally unstable. And how different people's experiences of the same events can be diametrically opposed. There's never been a better time to examine how and why we try to prove our own versions of reality.

Most importantly, I wrote this for anyone who has ever felt their voice was being written over by a narrative they didn't choose.

ACKNOWLEDGMENTS

Writing is often viewed as a solitary act, but this book would not exist without a sprawling community of support.

First and foremost I want to thank you, the reader. A story only truly comes to life when you're holding it in your hands, and your support and encouragement are why I keep showing up to my keyboard. We all need the entertainment right now.

I owe a debt of gratitude to Elise Hart Kipness, for her meaningful encouragement and critique early on. Many thanks also to Beverly Katz Rosenbaum, for challenging me to make this story the best version of itself. To my editors at Red Adept: thank you for your eagle eyes. To the talented team at 100Covers: thank you for a cover design that so perfectly captures the mood and tension of 1990s Pittsburgh.

A huge and heartfelt thanks to my dear friend, author Tamara Lush, who helps me stay in the game every single day with her wisdom, wit, and strategic insight. Huge thanks to my critique partner of the last decade, Betsy Farber. To my friends and colleagues at the Women's Fiction Writers Association: your camaraderie and shared passion for the craft are invaluable. I cannot overstate the importance of this community; I doubt I'd be here without you.

Thank you to my many dear friends in Pittsburgh—and Pittsburgh itself—for inspiring this series. Of all the places I've lived, this is where I've made the most enduring friendships and I couldn't be more grateful.

To my husband and my family—thank you for cheering me on, listening to my incoherent rambling about staging and plot points and 1990s trivia. Your belief in my work means more than I can say.